SPIDER-MAN

CONCRETE JUNGLE

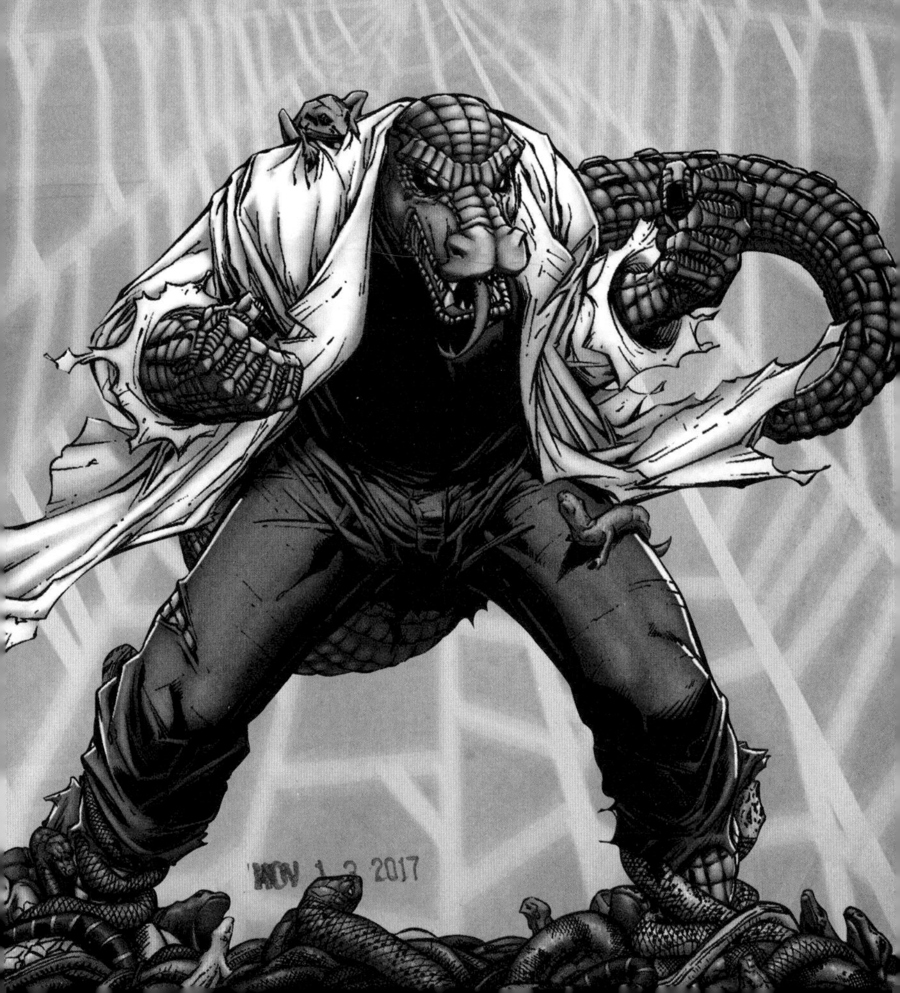

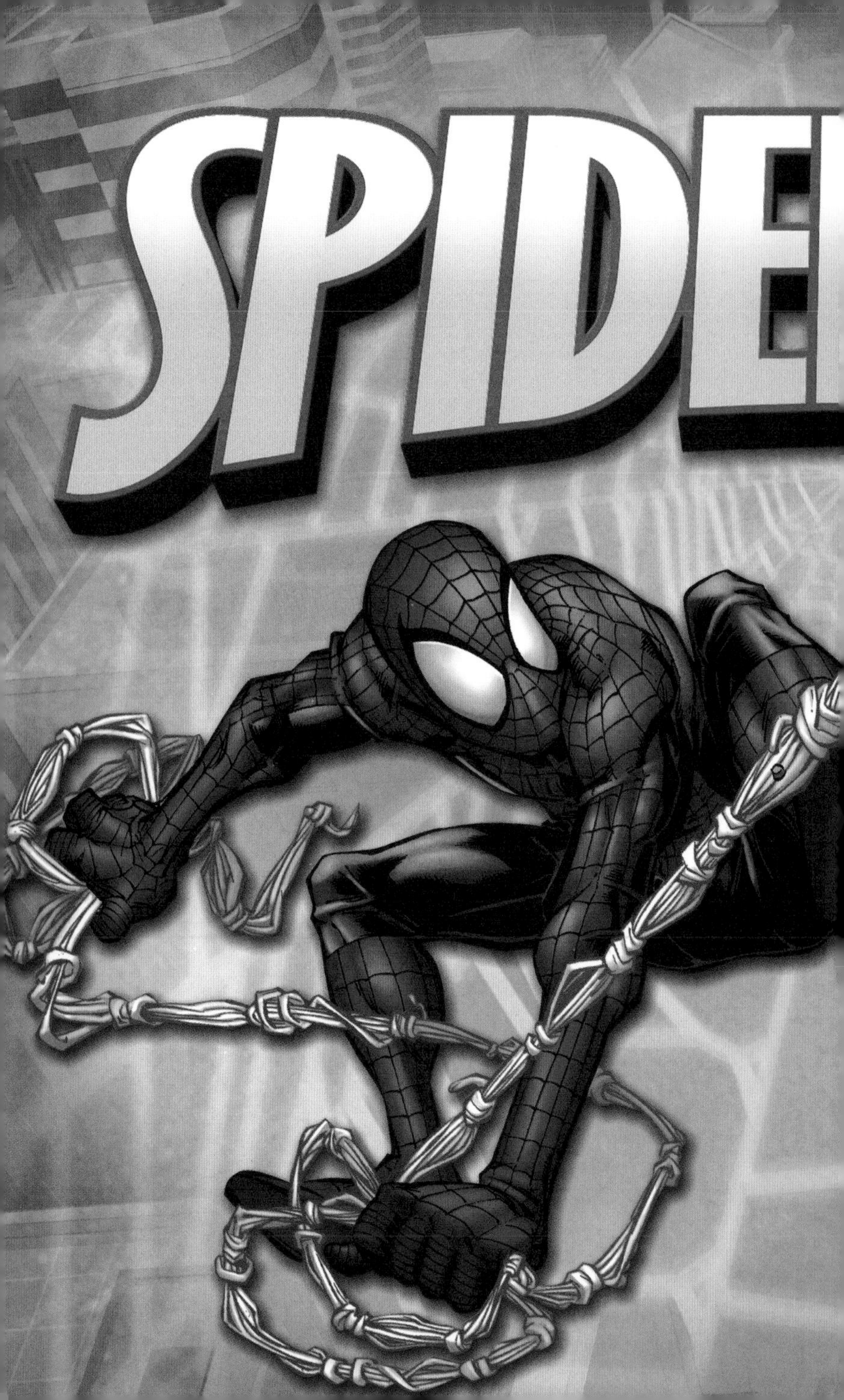
SPIDE

:-MAN

CONCRETE JUNGLE

Writer
Zeb Wells
Pencils
Patrick Scherberger

Inks: **Norman Lee**
Colors: **Guru eFX**
Letters: **Dave Sharpe**
Cover Art: **Amanda Conner with Jimmy Palmiotti,
Chris Sotomayor & Christina Strain**
Assistant Editor: **Nathan Cosby**
Editors: **MacKenzie Cadenhead with Mark Paniccia**

Collection Editor: **Jennifer Grünwald**
Assistant Editor: **Michael Short**
Senior Editor, Special Projects: **Jeff Youngquist**
Vice President of Sales: **David Gabriel**
Production: **Jerron Quality Color**
Vice President of Creative: **Tom Marvelli**

Editor in Chief: **Joe Quesada**
Publisher: **Dan Buckley**

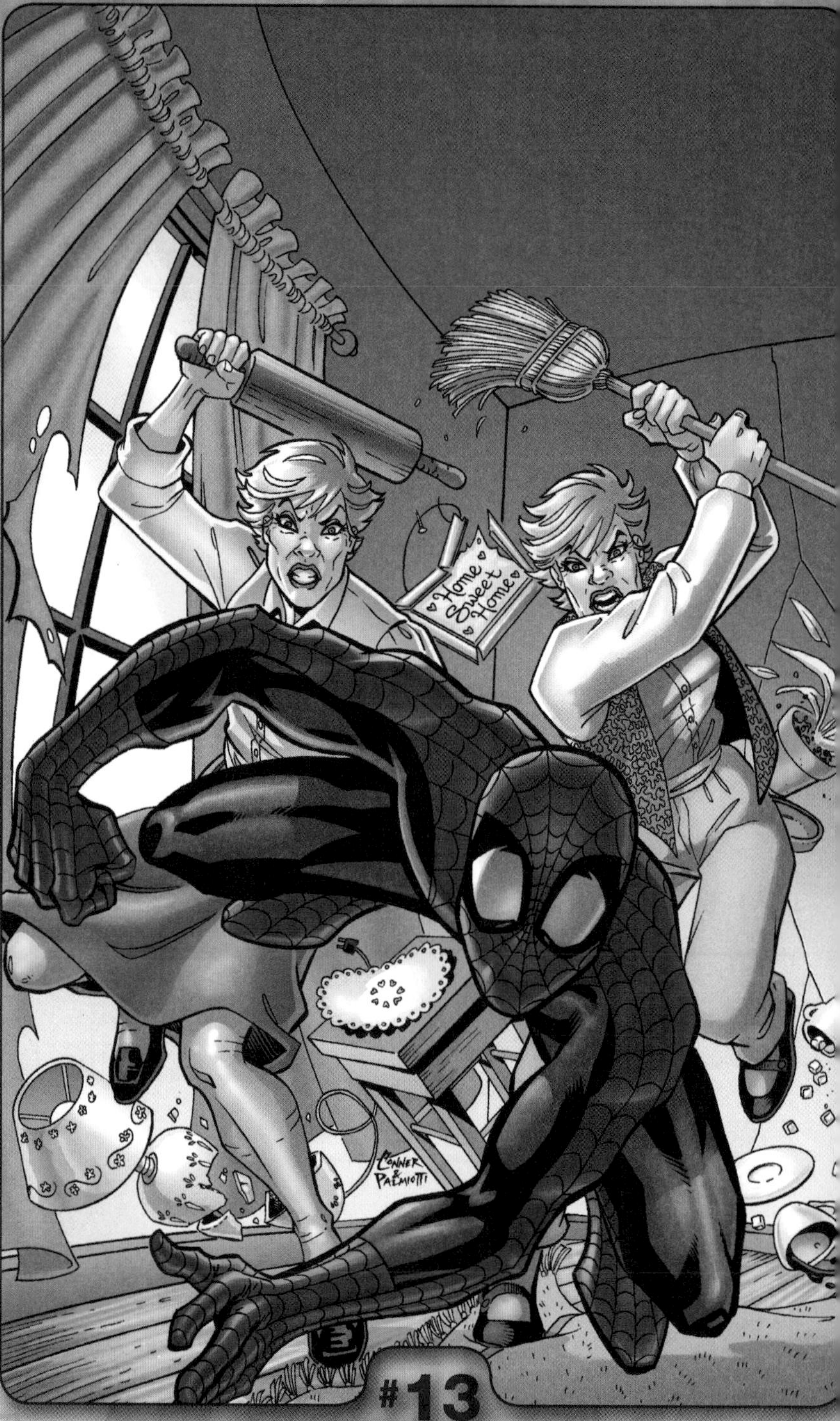
Home
Sweet
Home
CONNER
&
PALMIOTTI

#13

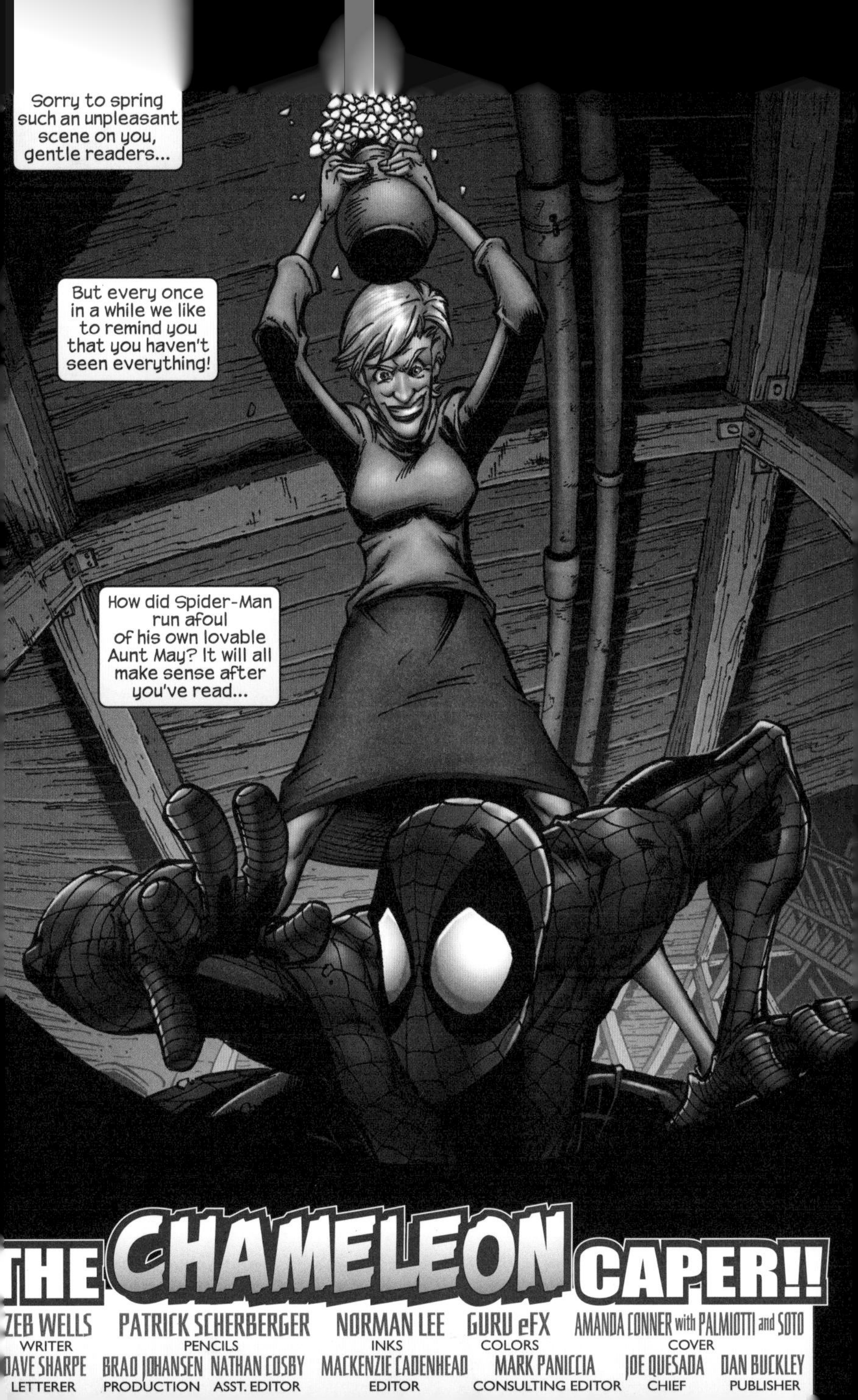
Sorry to spring such an unpleasant scene on you, gentle readers...
But every once in a while we like to remind you that you haven't seen everything!
How did Spider-Man run afoul of his own lovable Aunt May? It will all make sense after you've read...
THE CHAMELEON CAPER!!
ZEB WELLS WRITER
PATRICK SCHERBERGER PENCILS
NORMAN LEE INKS
GURU eFX COLORS
AMANDA CONNER with PALMIOTTI and SOTO COVER
DAVE SHARPE LETTERER
BRAD JOHANSEN PRODUCTION
NATHAN COSBY ASST. EDITOR
MACKENZIE CADENHEAD EDITOR
MARK PANICCIA CONSULTING EDITOR
JOE QUESADA CHIEF
DAN BUCKLEY PUBLISHER

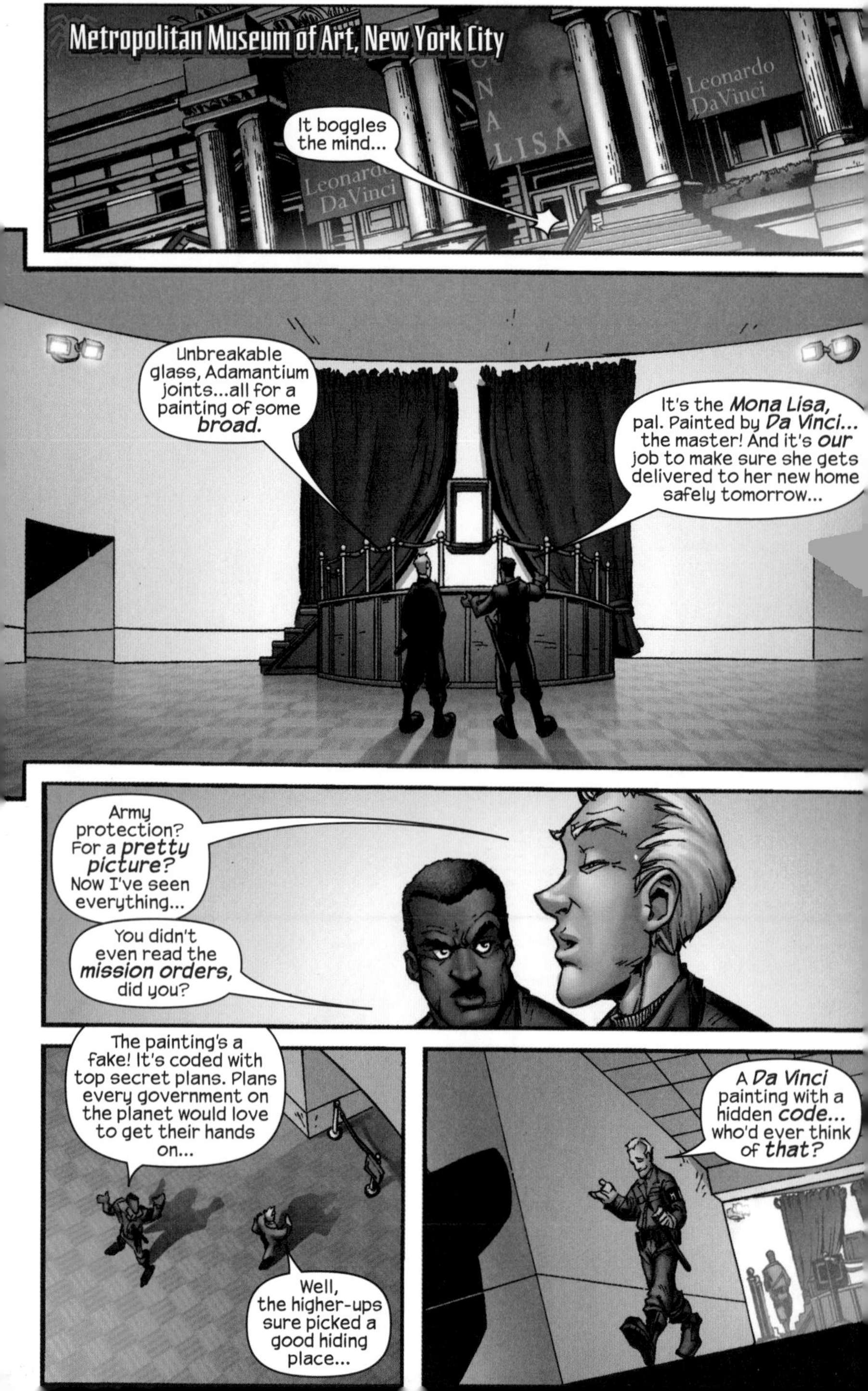
Metropolitan Museum of Art, New York City
Leonardo DaVinci
MONA LISA
Leonardo DaVinci
It boggles the mind...
Unbreakable glass, Adamantium joints...all for a painting of some broad.
It's the Mona Lisa, pal. Painted by Da Vinci... the master! And it's our job to make sure she gets delivered to her new home safely tomorrow...
Army protection? For a pretty picture? Now I've seen everything...
You didn't even read the mission orders, did you?
The painting's a fake! It's coded with top secret plans. Plans every government on the planet would love to get their hands on...
Well, the higher-ups sure picked a good hiding place...
A Da Vinci painting with a hidden code... who'd ever think of that?

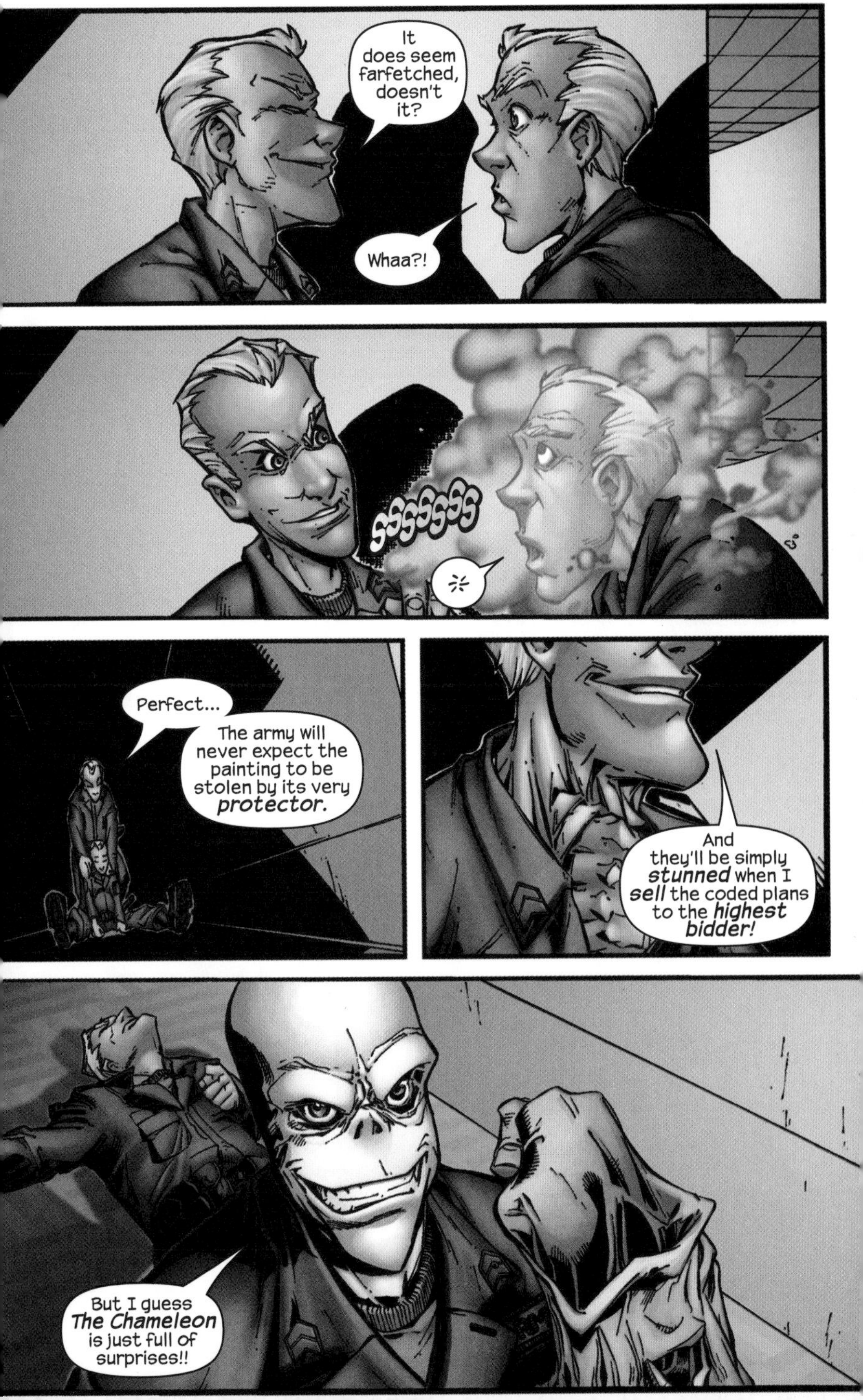

It does seem farfetched, doesn't it?
Whaa?!
SSSSSSS
Perfect...
The army will never expect the painting to be stolen by its very *protector*.
And they'll be simply *stunned* when I *sell* the coded plans to the *highest bidder!*
But I guess *The Chameleon* is just full of surprises!!

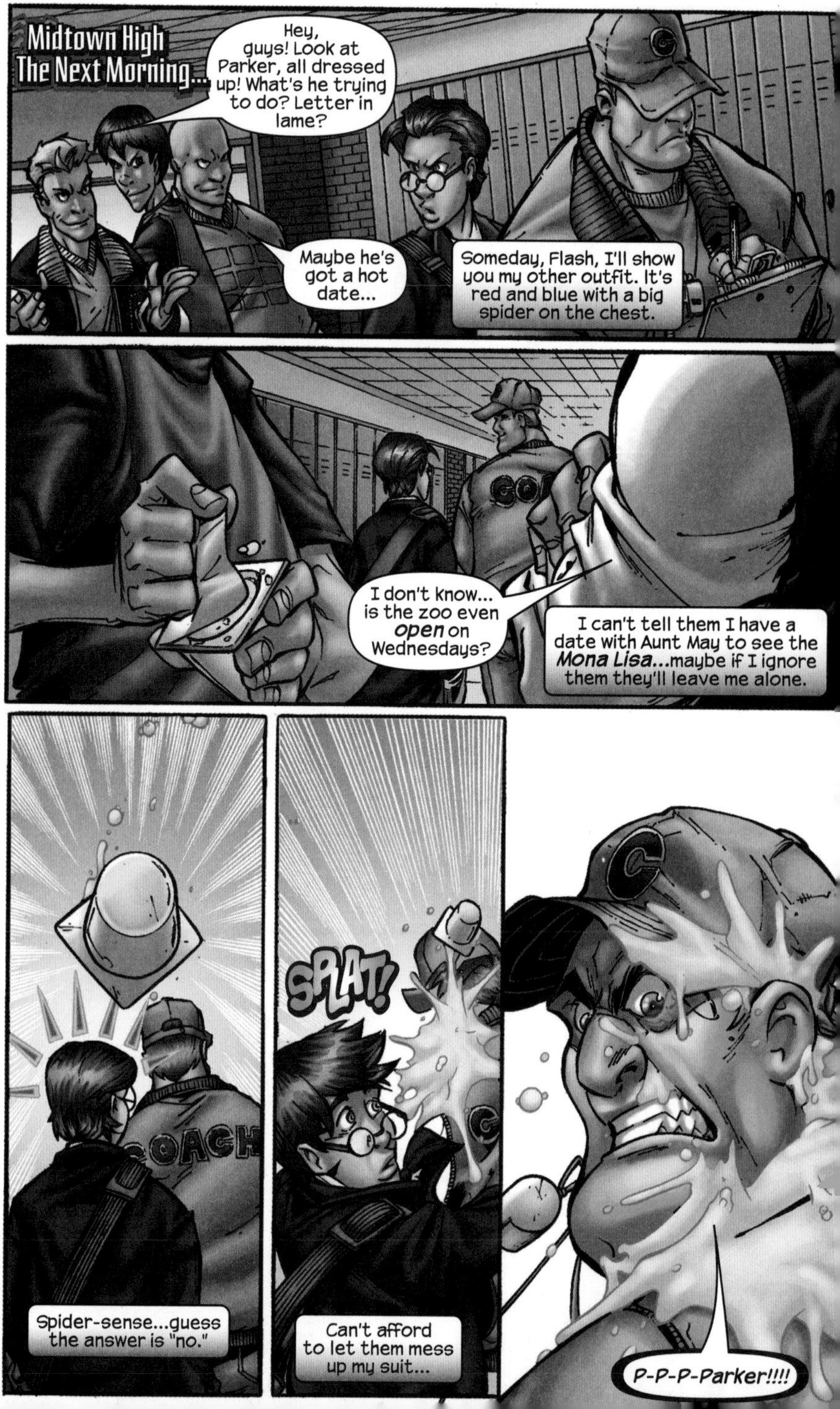
Midtown High The Next Morning...
Hey, guys! Look at Parker, all dressed up! What's he trying to do? Letter in lame?
Maybe he's got a hot date...
Someday, Flash, I'll show you my other outfit. It's red and blue with a big spider on the chest.
I don't know... is the zoo even *open* on Wednesdays?
I can't tell them I have a date with Aunt May to see the *Mona Lisa*...maybe if I ignore them they'll leave me alone.
Spider-sense...guess the answer is "no."
SPLAT!
Can't afford to let them mess up my suit...
P-P-P-Parker!!!!

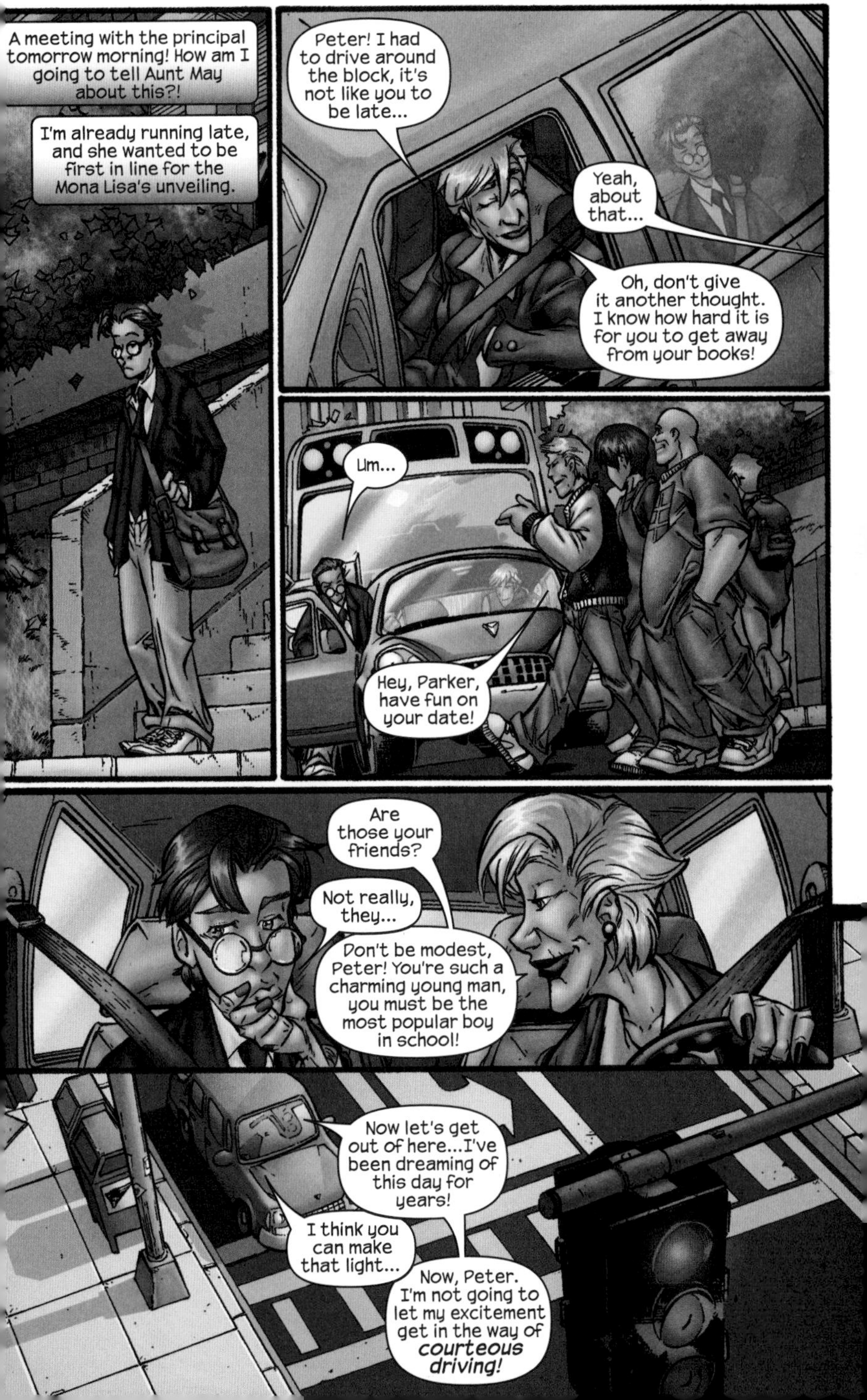
A meeting with the principal tomorrow morning! How am I going to tell Aunt May about this?!
I'm already running late, and she wanted to be first in line for the Mona Lisa's unveiling.
Peter! I had to drive around the block, it's not like you to be late...
Yeah, about that...
Oh, don't give it another thought. I know how hard it is for you to get away from your books!
Um...
Hey, Parker, have fun on your date!
Are those your friends?
Not really, they...
Don't be modest, Peter! You're such a charming young man, you must be the most popular boy in school!
Now let's get out of here...I've been dreaming of this day for years!
I think you can make that light...
Now, Peter. I'm not going to let my excitement get in the way of *courteous driving!*

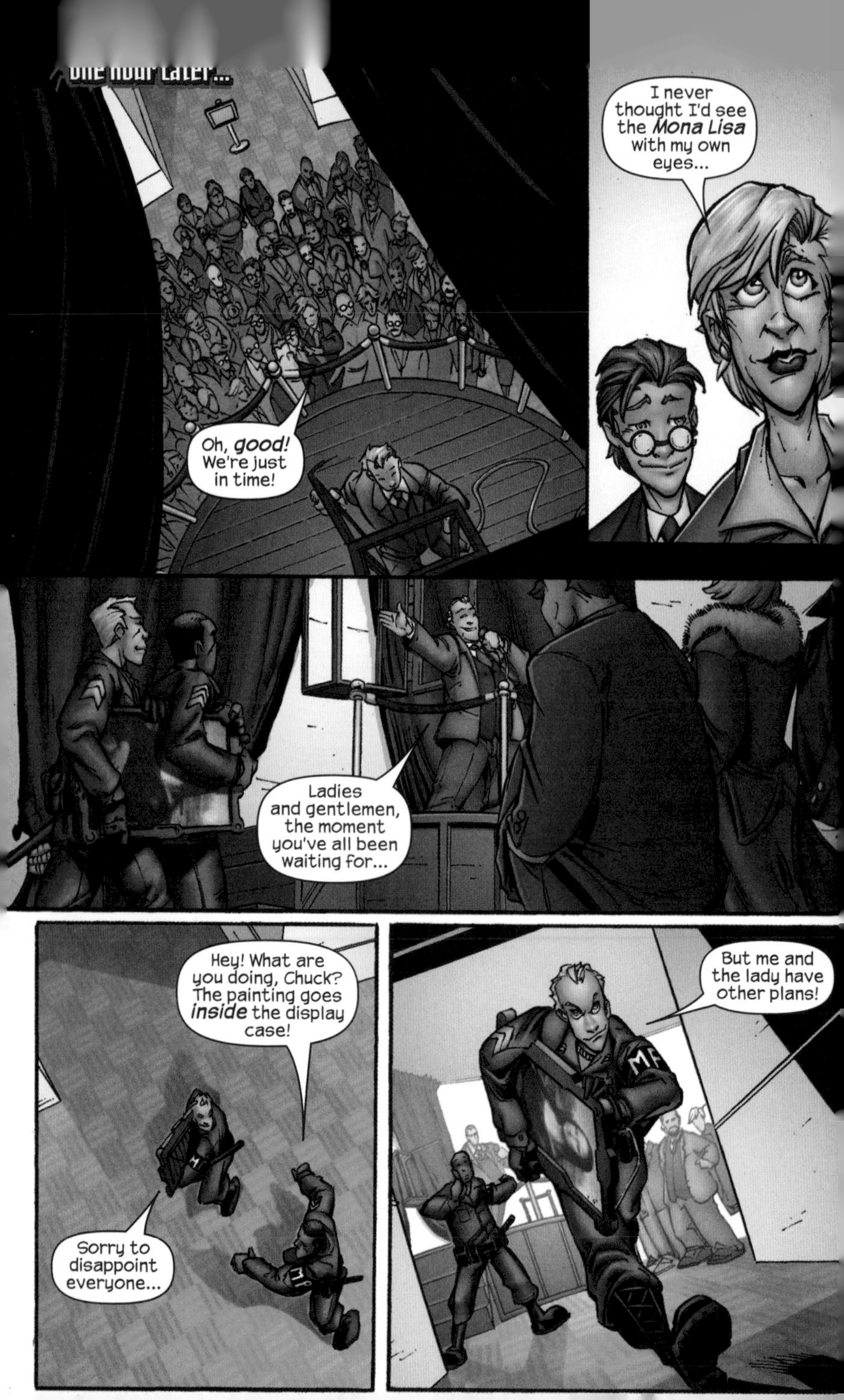
Oh, good! We're just in time!
I never thought I'd see the Mona Lisa with my own eyes...
Ladies and gentlemen, the moment you've all been waiting for...
Hey! What are you doing, Chuck? The painting goes inside the display case!
Sorry to disappoint everyone...
But me and the lady have other plans!
MP

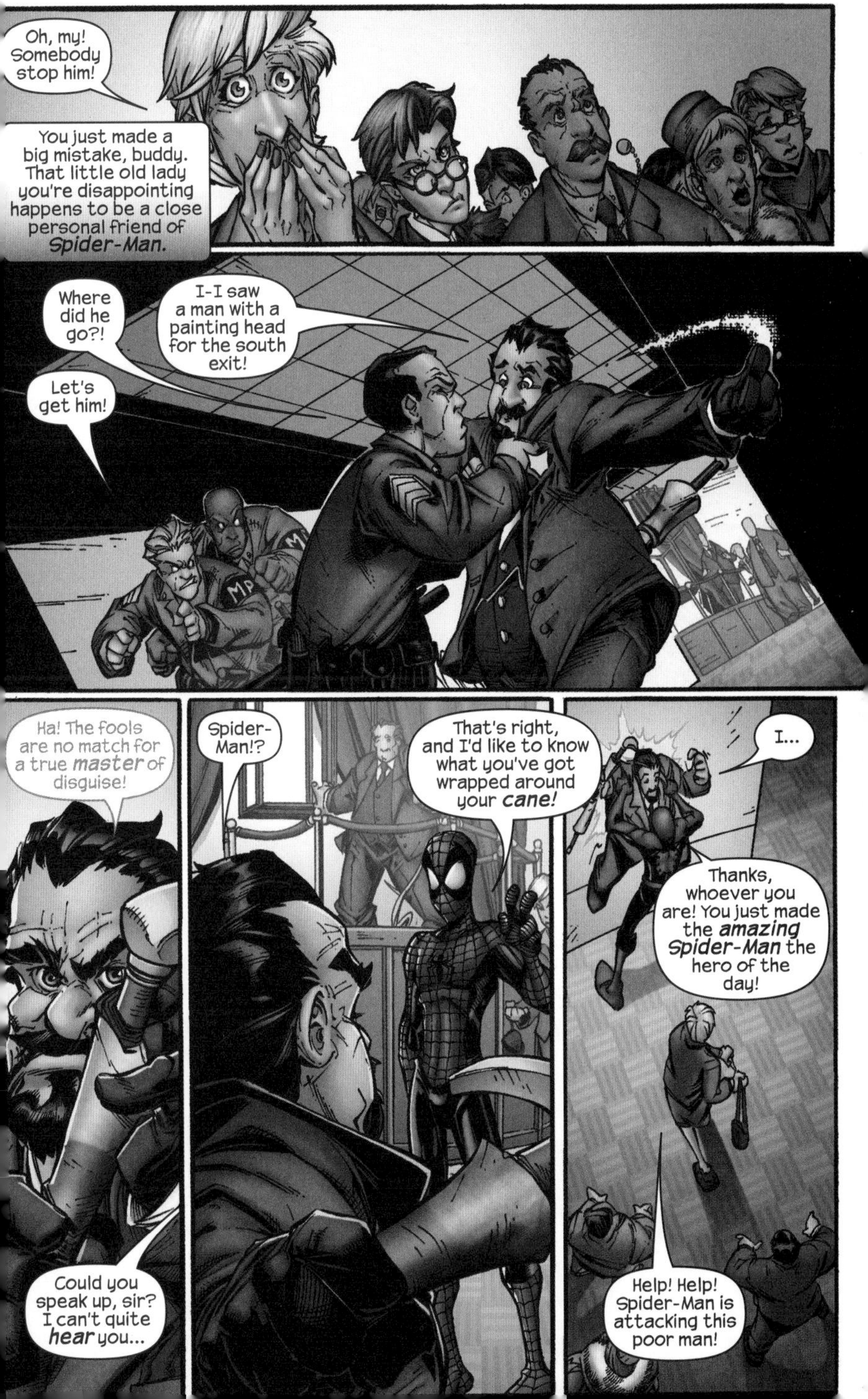

Oh, my! Somebody stop him!
You just made a big mistake, buddy. That little old lady you're disappointing happens to be a close personal friend of Spider-Man.
Where did he go?!
I-I saw a man with a painting head for the south exit!
Let's get him!
Ha! The fools are no match for a true master of disguise!
Could you speak up, sir? I can't quite hear you...
Spider-Man!?
That's right, and I'd like to know what you've got wrapped around your cane!
I...
Thanks, whoever you are! You just made the amazing Spider-Man the hero of the day!
Help! Help! Spider-Man is attacking this poor man!

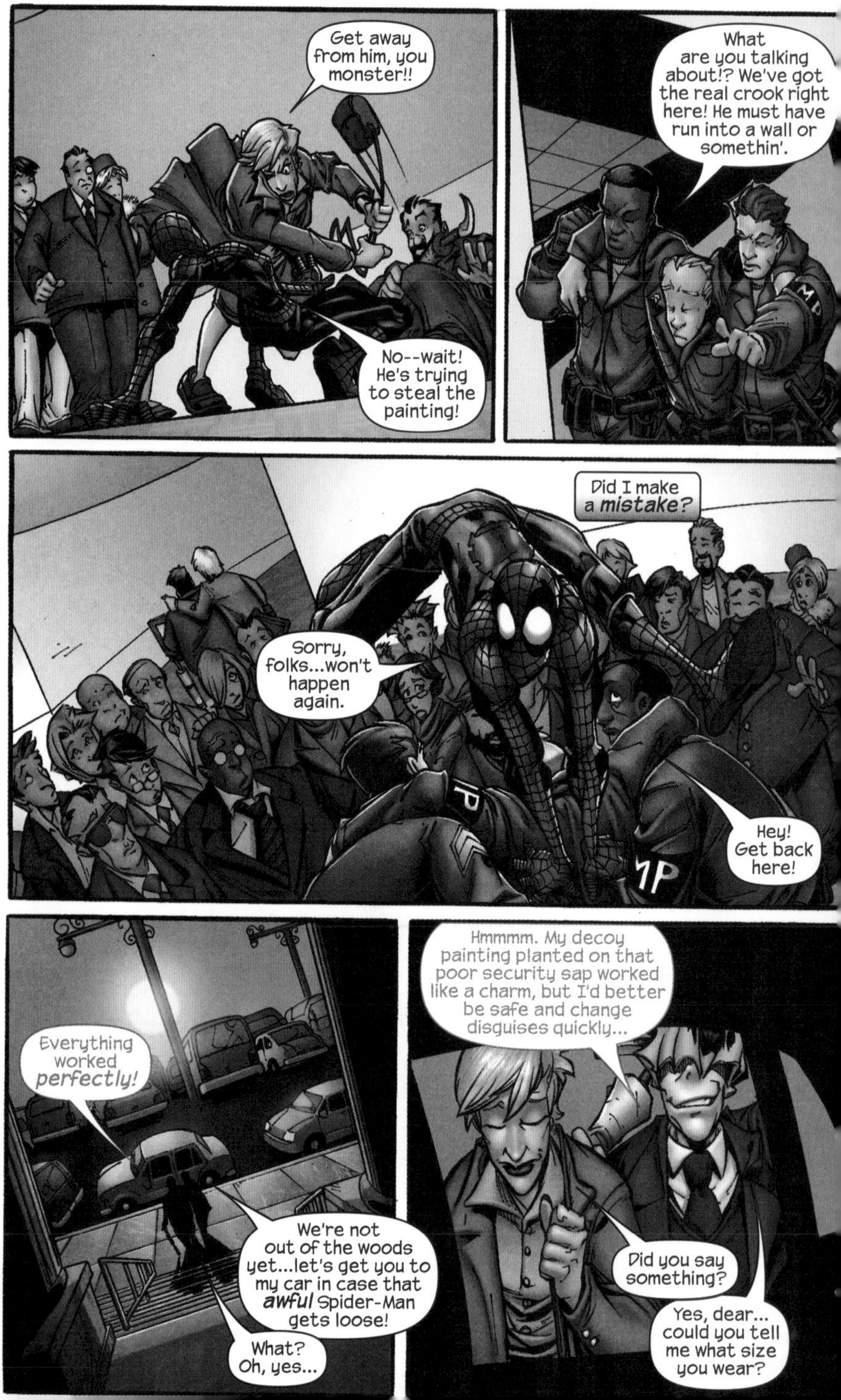
Get away from him, you monster!!
No--wait! He's trying to steal the painting!
What are you talking about!? We've got the real crook right here! He must have run into a wall or somethin'.
Did I make a *mistake?*
Sorry, folks...won't happen again.
Hey! Get back here!
Everything worked *perfectly!*
We're not out of the woods yet...let's get you to my car in case that *awful* Spider-Man gets loose!
What? Oh, yes...
Hmmmm. My decoy painting planted on that poor security sap worked like a charm, but I'd better be safe and change disguises quickly...
Did you say something?
Yes, dear... could you tell me what size you wear?

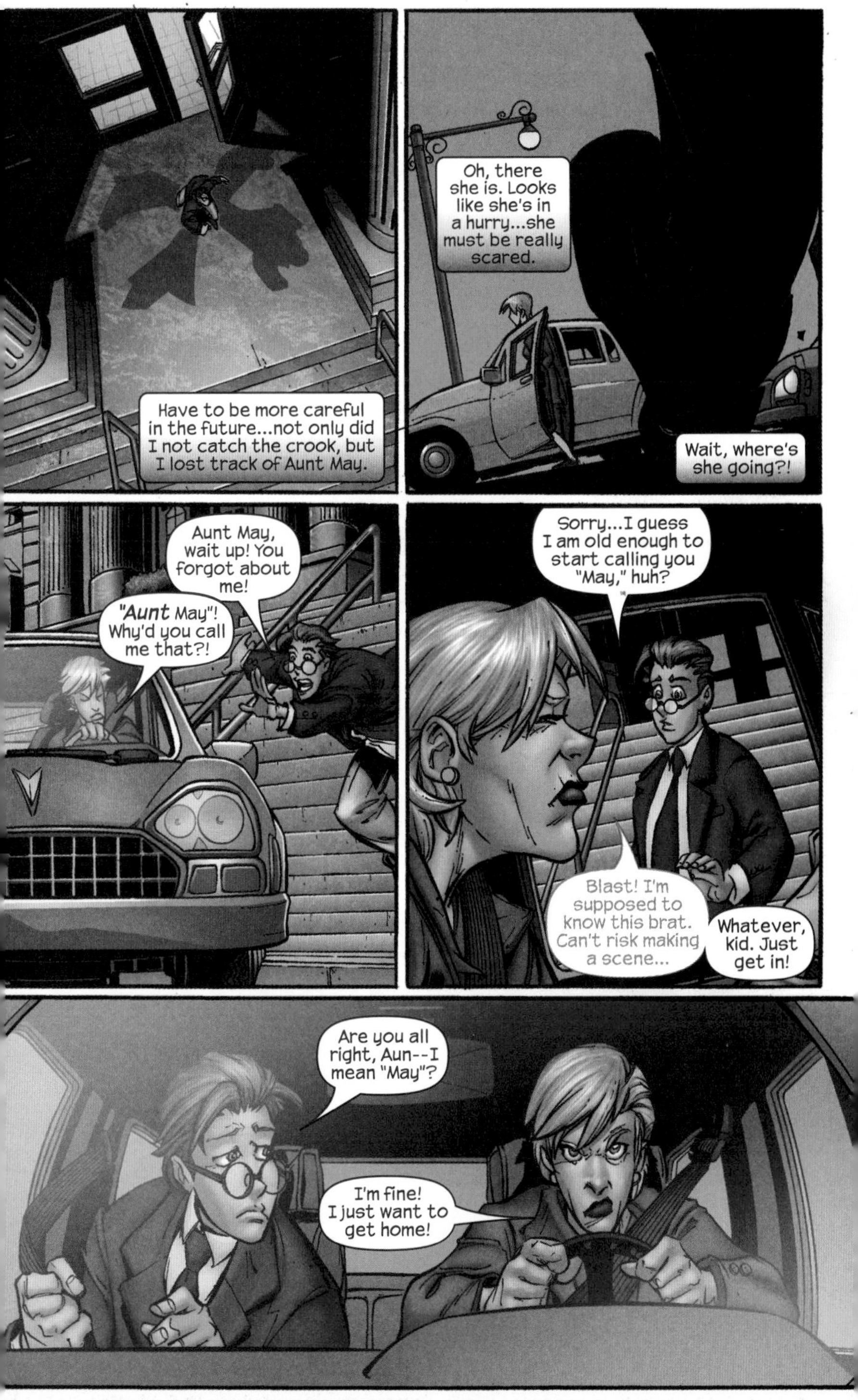
Have to be more careful in the future...not only did I not catch the crook, but I lost track of Aunt May.
Oh, there she is. Looks like she's in a hurry...she must be really scared.
Wait, where's she going?!
Aunt May, wait up! You forgot about me!
"Aunt May"! Why'd you call me that?!
Sorry...I guess I am old enough to start calling you "May," huh?
Blast! I'm supposed to know this brat. Can't risk making a scene...
Whatever, kid. Just get in!
Are you all right, Aun--I mean "May"?
I'm fine! I just want to get home!

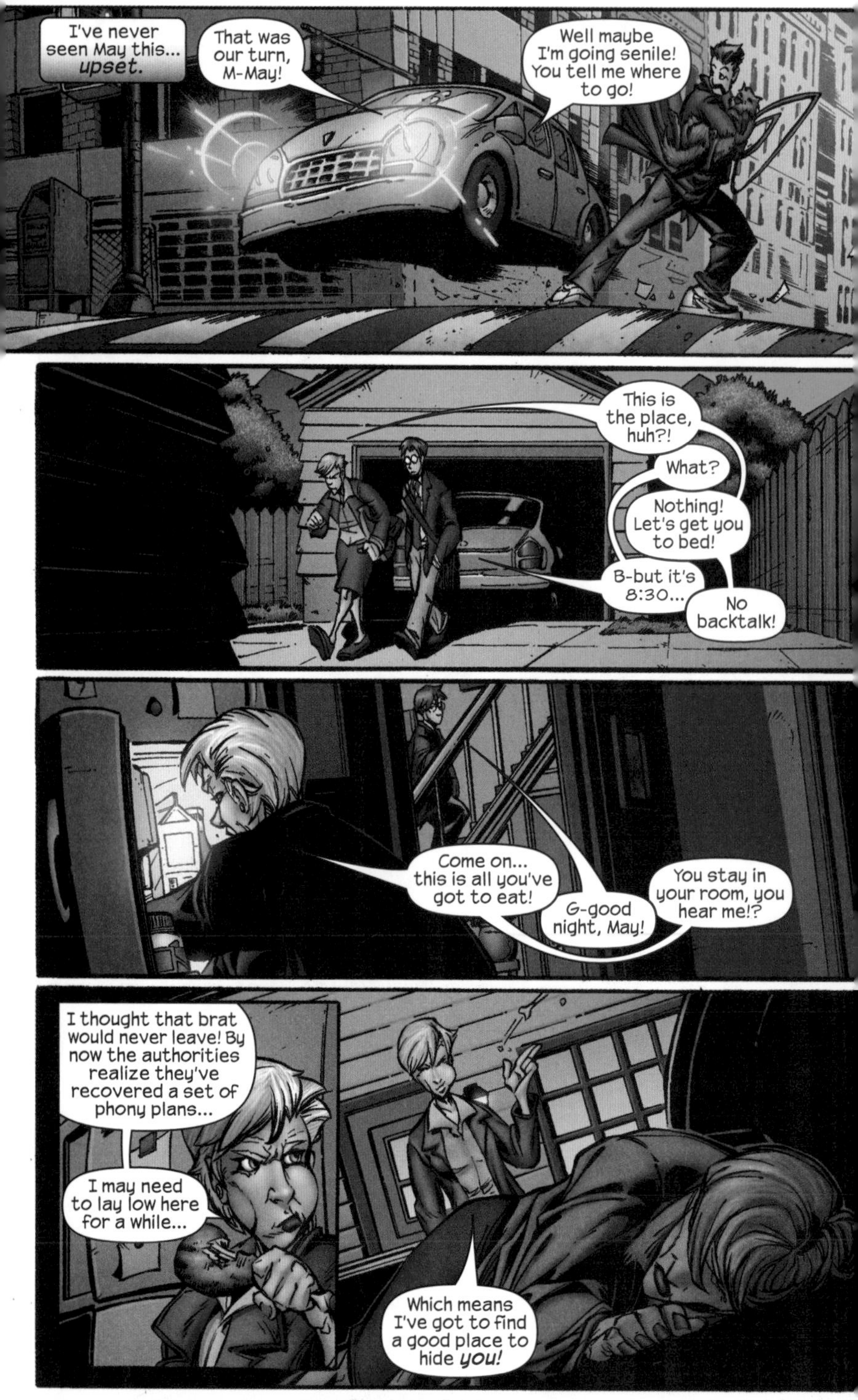

I've never seen May this... *upset.*
That was our turn, M-May!
Well maybe I'm going senile! You tell me where to go!
This is the place, huh?!
What?
Nothing! Let's get you to bed!
B-but it's 8:30...
No backtalk!
Come on... this is all you've got to eat!
G-good night, May!
You stay in your room, you hear me!?
I thought that brat would never leave! By now the authorities realize they've recovered a set of phony plans...
I may need to lay low here for a while...
Which means I've got to find a good place to hide *you!*

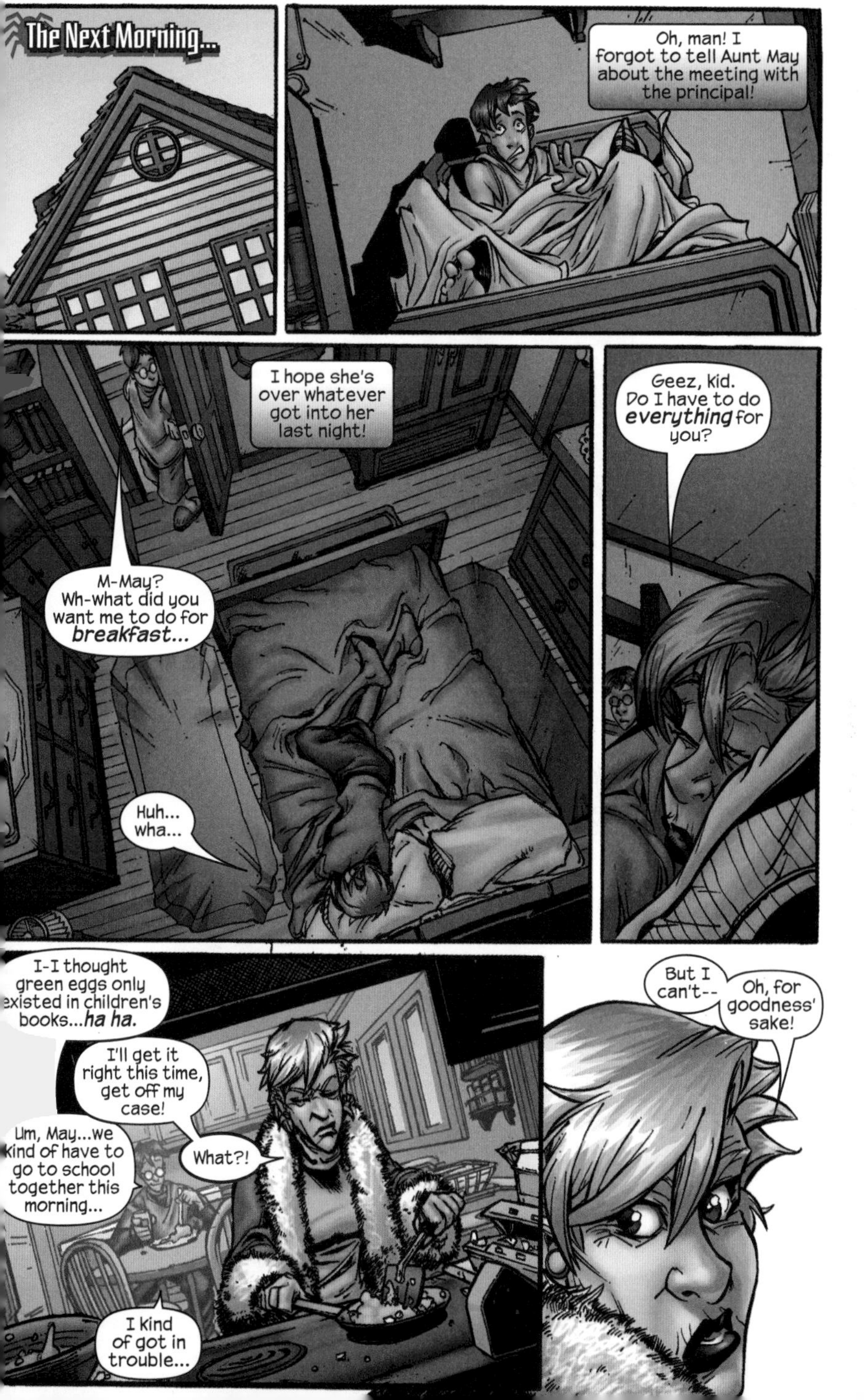
The Next Morning...
Oh, man! I forgot to tell Aunt May about the meeting with the principal!
I hope she's over whatever got into her last night!
M-May? Wh-what did you want me to do for breakfast...
Huh... wha...
Geez, kid. Do I have to do everything for you?
I-I thought green eggs only existed in children's books...ha ha.
I'll get it right this time, get off my case!
Um, May...we kind of have to go to school together this morning...
What?!
I kind of got in trouble...
But I can't--
Oh, for goodness' sake!

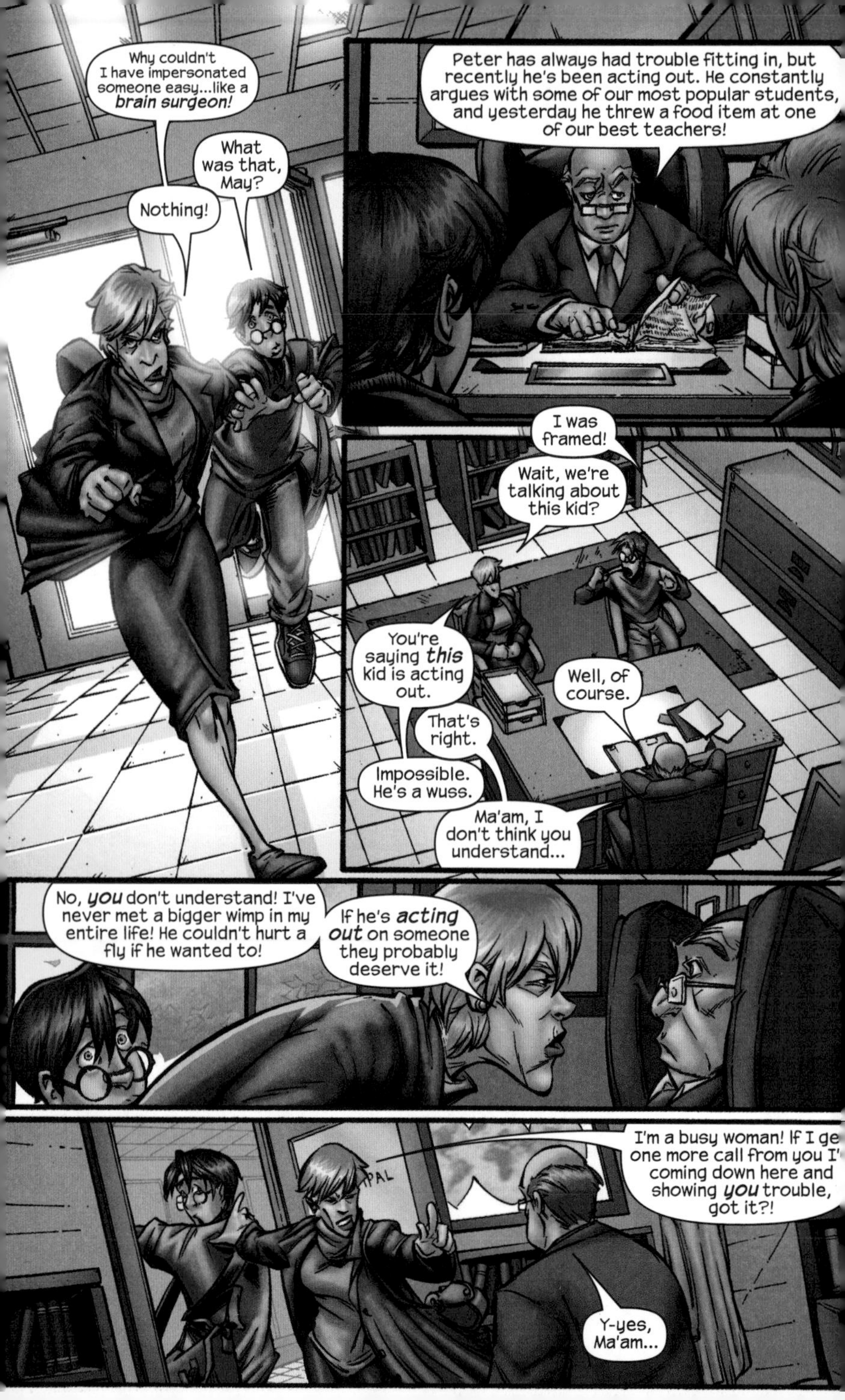

Why couldn't I have impersonated someone easy...like a brain surgeon!
What was that, May?
Nothing!
Peter has always had trouble fitting in, but recently he's been acting out. He constantly argues with some of our most popular students, and yesterday he threw a food item at one of our best teachers!
I was framed!
Wait, we're talking about this kid?
You're saying this kid is acting out.
Well, of course.
That's right.
Impossible. He's a wuss.
Ma'am, I don't think you understand...
No, you don't understand! I've never met a bigger wimp in my entire life! He couldn't hurt a fly if he wanted to!
If he's acting out on someone they probably deserve it!
I'm a busy woman! If I ge one more call from you I' coming down here and showing you trouble, got it?!
Y-yes, Ma'am...

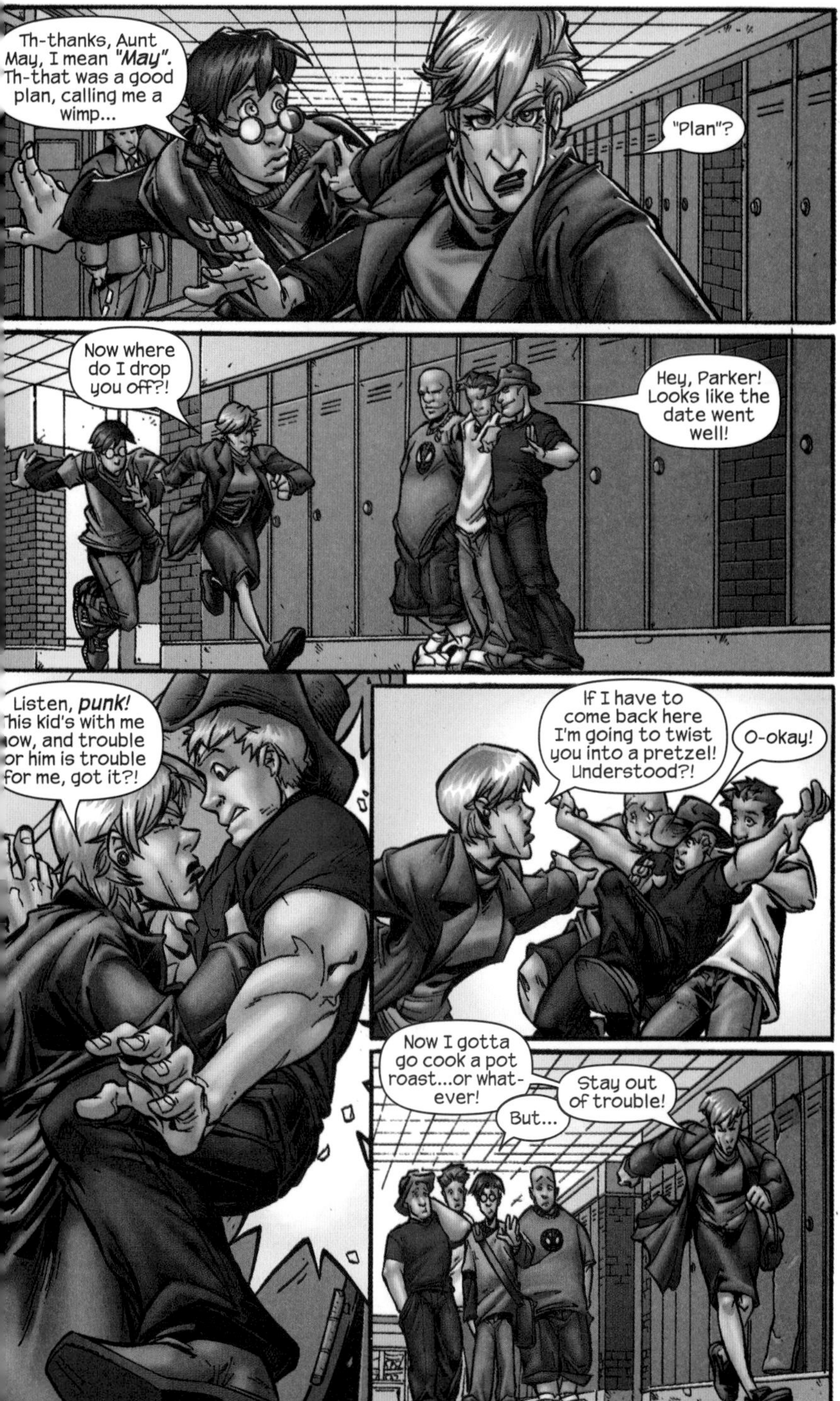

Th-thanks, Aunt May, I mean "May". Th-that was a good plan, calling me a wimp...
"Plan"?
Now where do I drop you off?!
Hey, Parker! Looks like the date went well!
Listen, punk! This kid's with me now, and trouble for him is trouble for me, got it?!
If I have to come back here I'm going to twist you into a pretzel! Understood?!
O-okay!
Now I gotta go cook a pot roast...or whatever!
Stay out of trouble!
But...

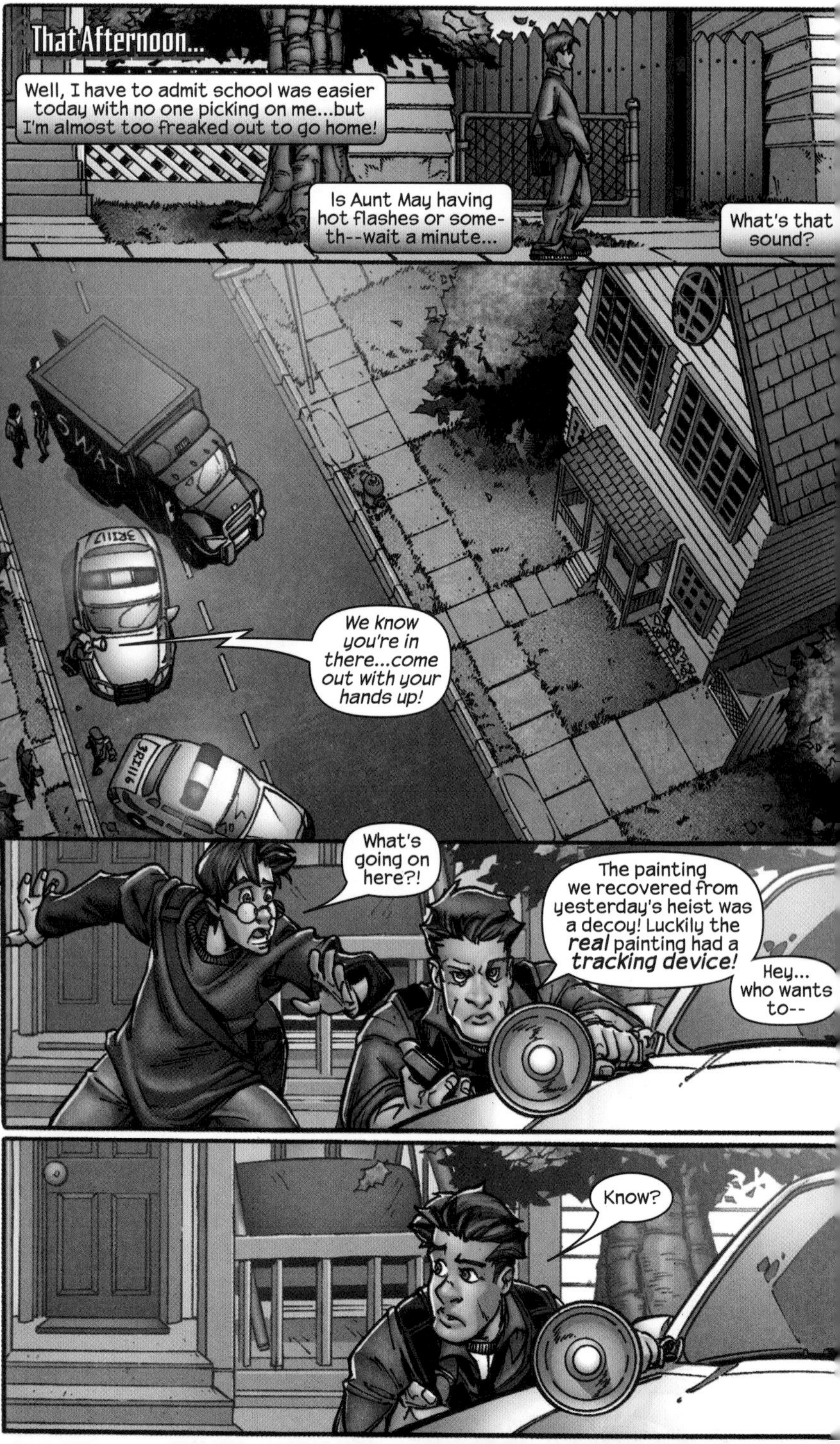
That Afternoon...
Well, I have to admit school was easier today with no one picking on me...but I'm almost too freaked out to go home!
Is Aunt May having hot flashes or someth--wait a minute...
What's that sound?
SWAT
We know you're in there...come out with your hands up!
What's going on here?!
The painting we recovered from yesterday's heist was a decoy! Luckily the *real* painting had a *tracking device!*
Hey... who wants to--
Know?

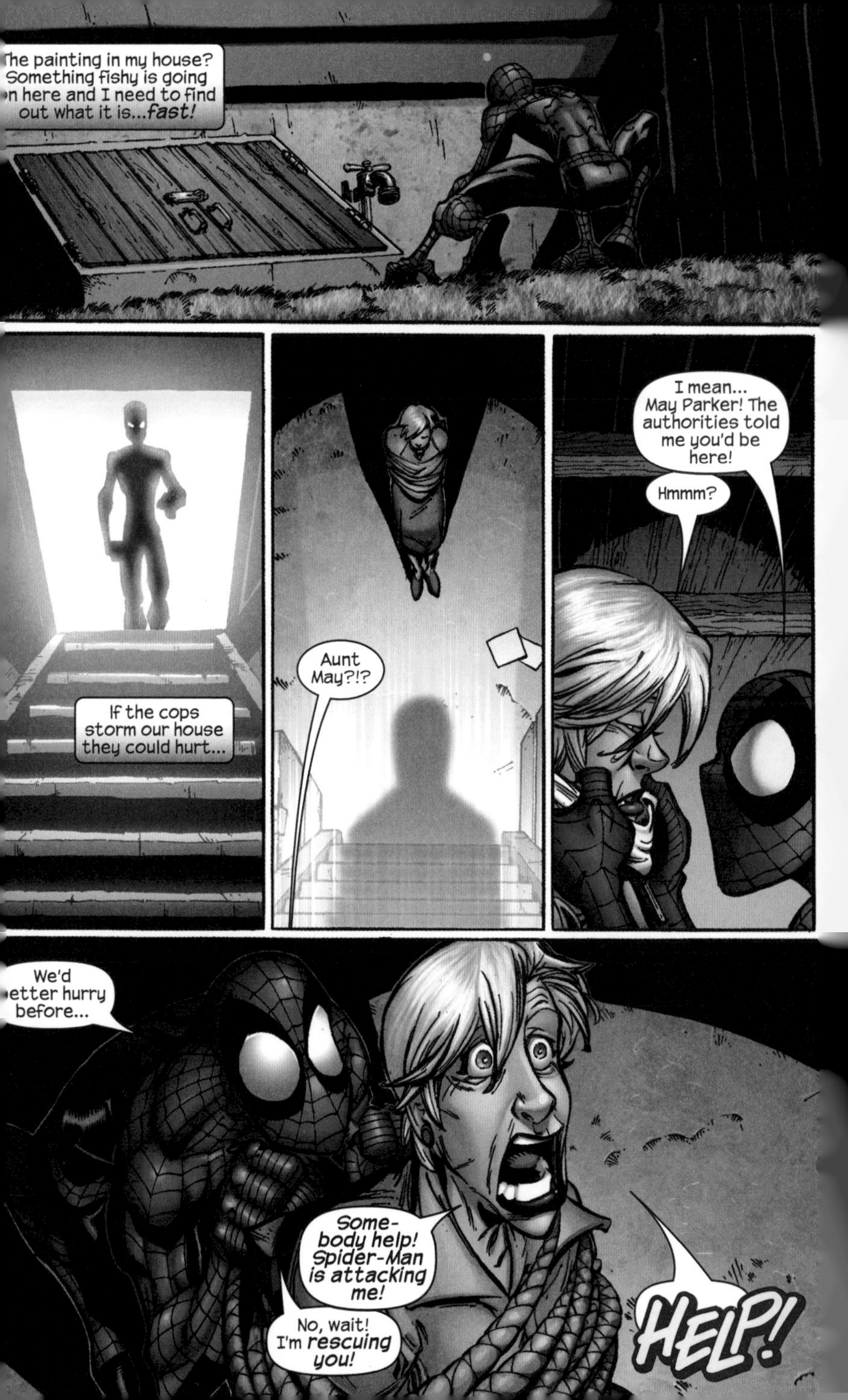

The painting in my house? Something fishy is going on here and I need to find out what it is...fast!
If the cops storm our house they could hurt...
Aunt May?!?
I mean... May Parker! The authorities told me you'd be here!
Hmmm?
We'd better hurry before...
Some-body help! Spider-Man is attacking me!
No, wait! I'm rescuing you!
HELP!

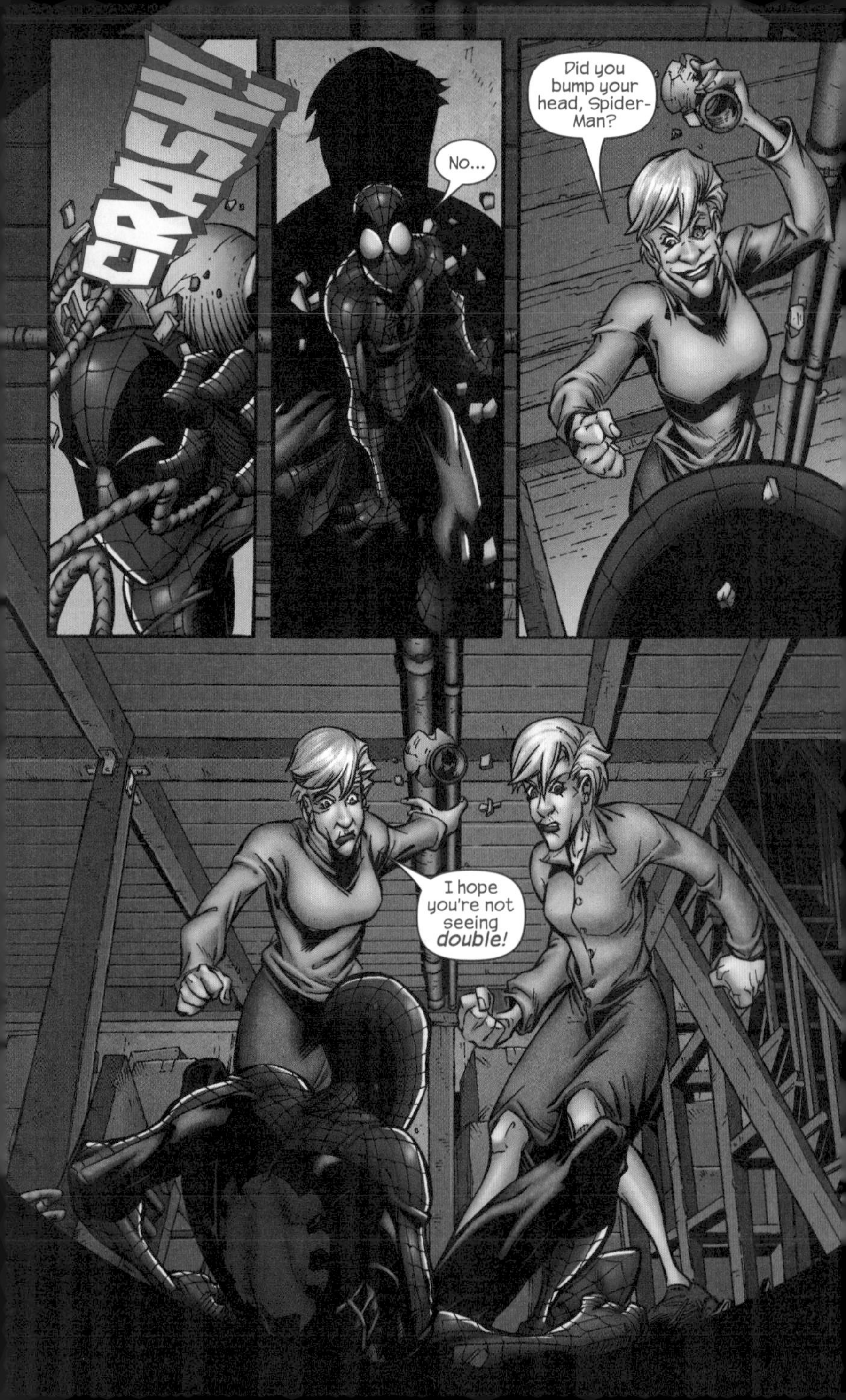
CRASH!
No...
Did you bump your head, Spider-Man?
I hope you're not seeing *double!*

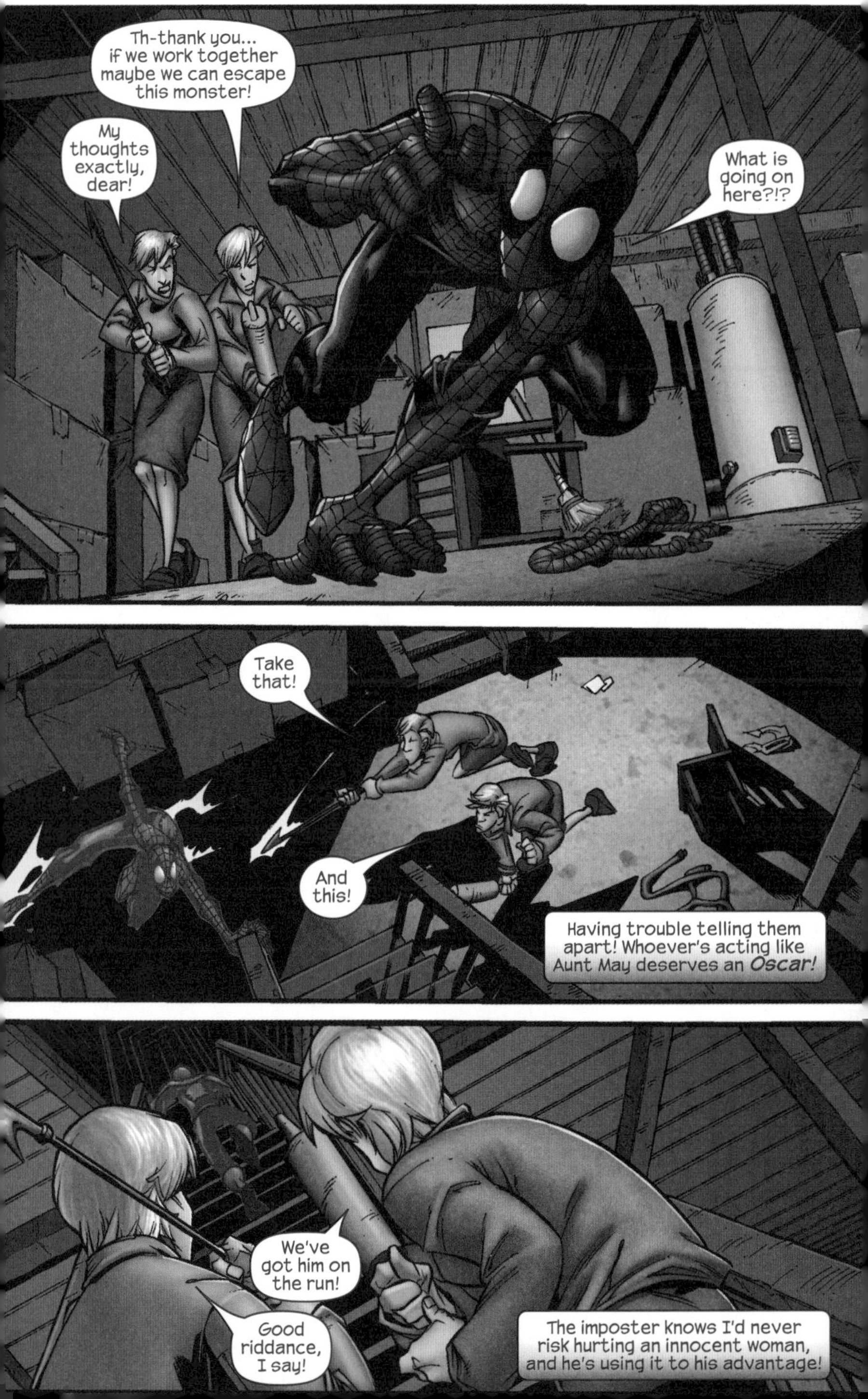
Th-thank you... if we work together maybe we can escape this monster!
My thoughts exactly, dear!
What is going on here?!?
Take that!
And this!
Having trouble telling them apart! Whoever's acting like Aunt May deserves an *Oscar!*
We've got him on the run!
Good riddance, I say!
The imposter knows I'd never risk hurting an innocent woman, and he's using it to his advantage!

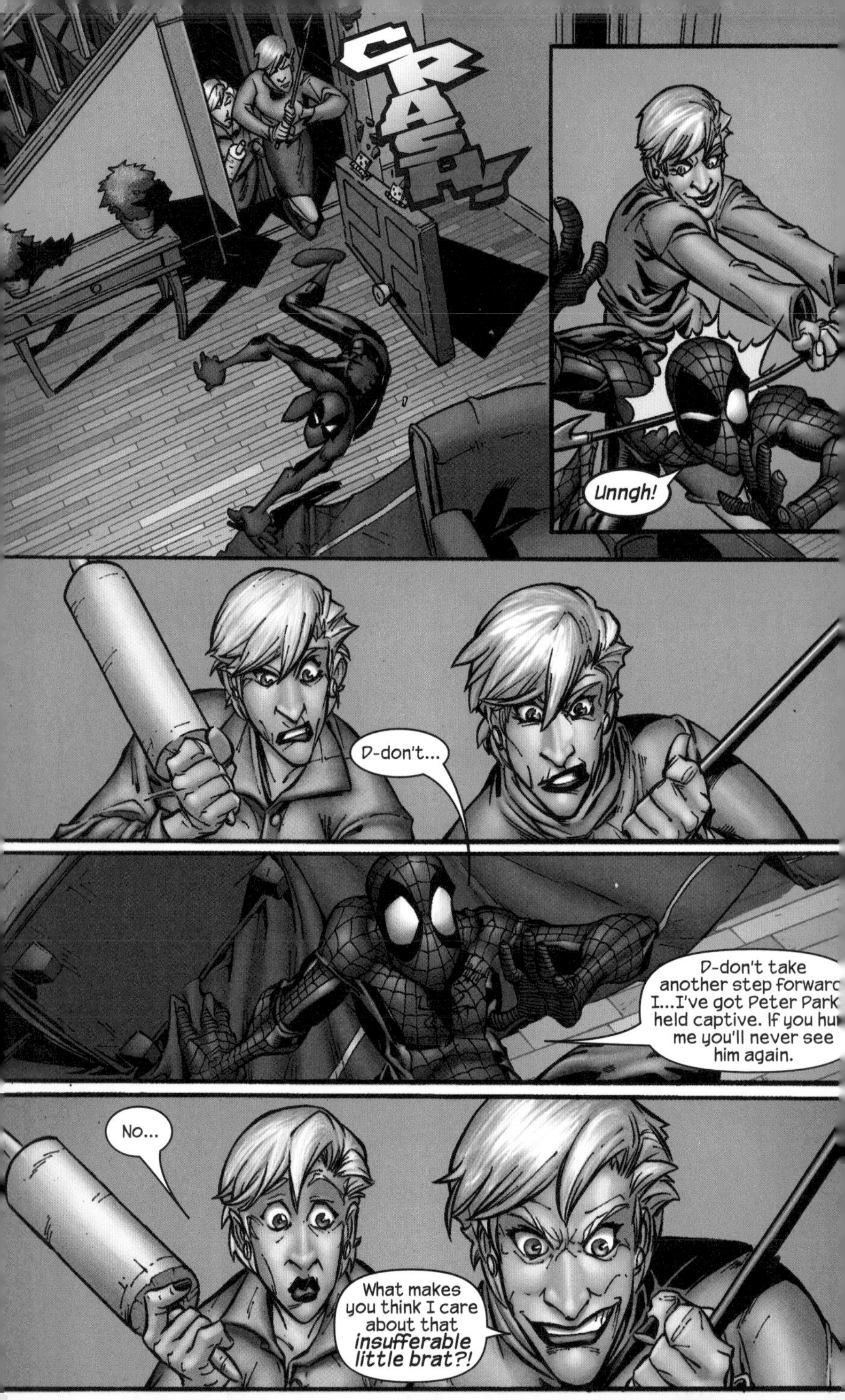
CRASH!
Unngh!
D-don't...
D-don't take another step forward I...I've got Peter Park held captive. If you hu me you'll never see him again.
No...
What makes you think I care about that *insufferable little brat?!*

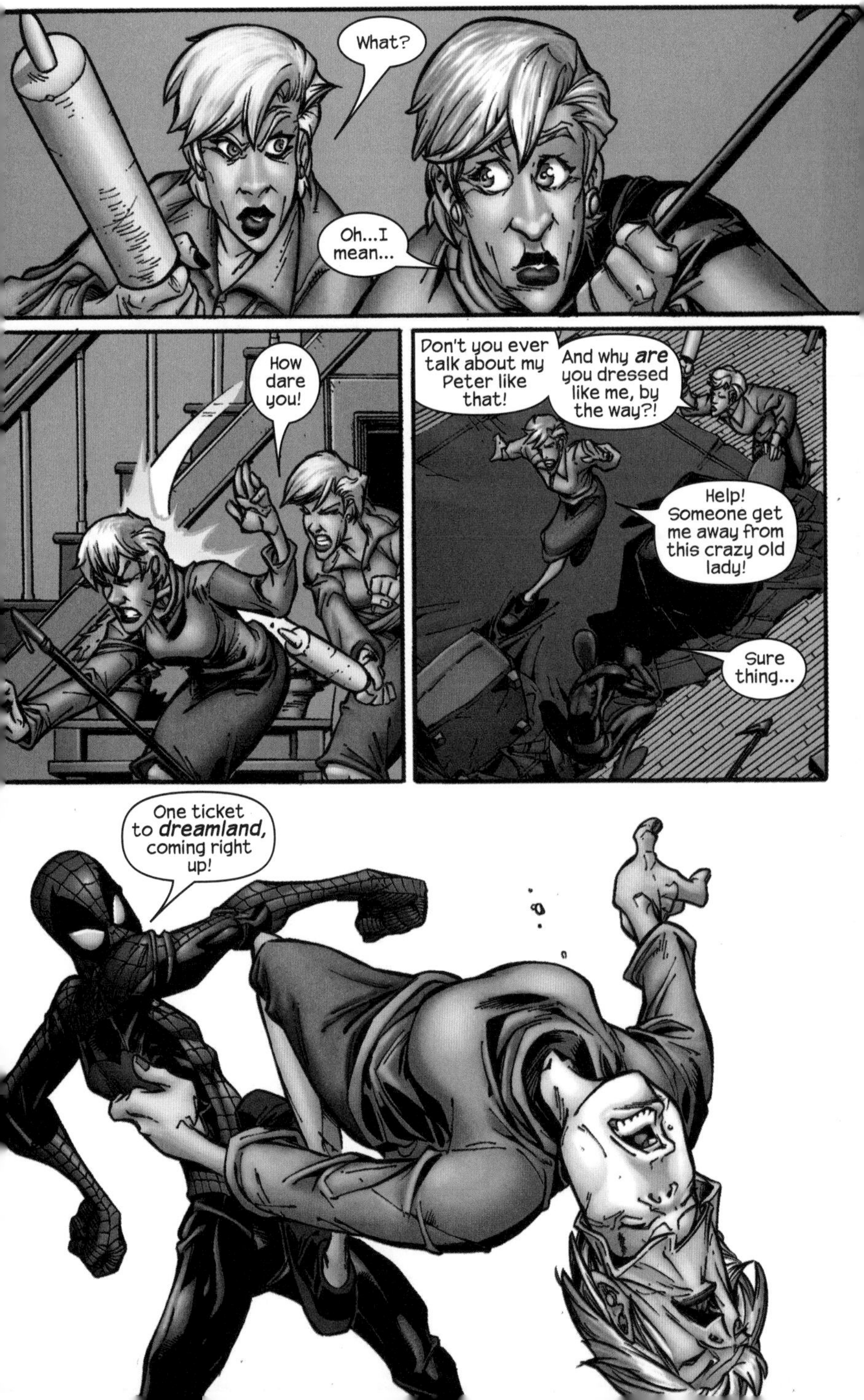
What?
Oh...I mean...
How dare you!
Don't you ever talk about my Peter like that!
And why *are* you dressed like me, by the way?!
Help! Someone get me away from this crazy old lady!
Sure thing...
One ticket to *dreamland,* coming right up!

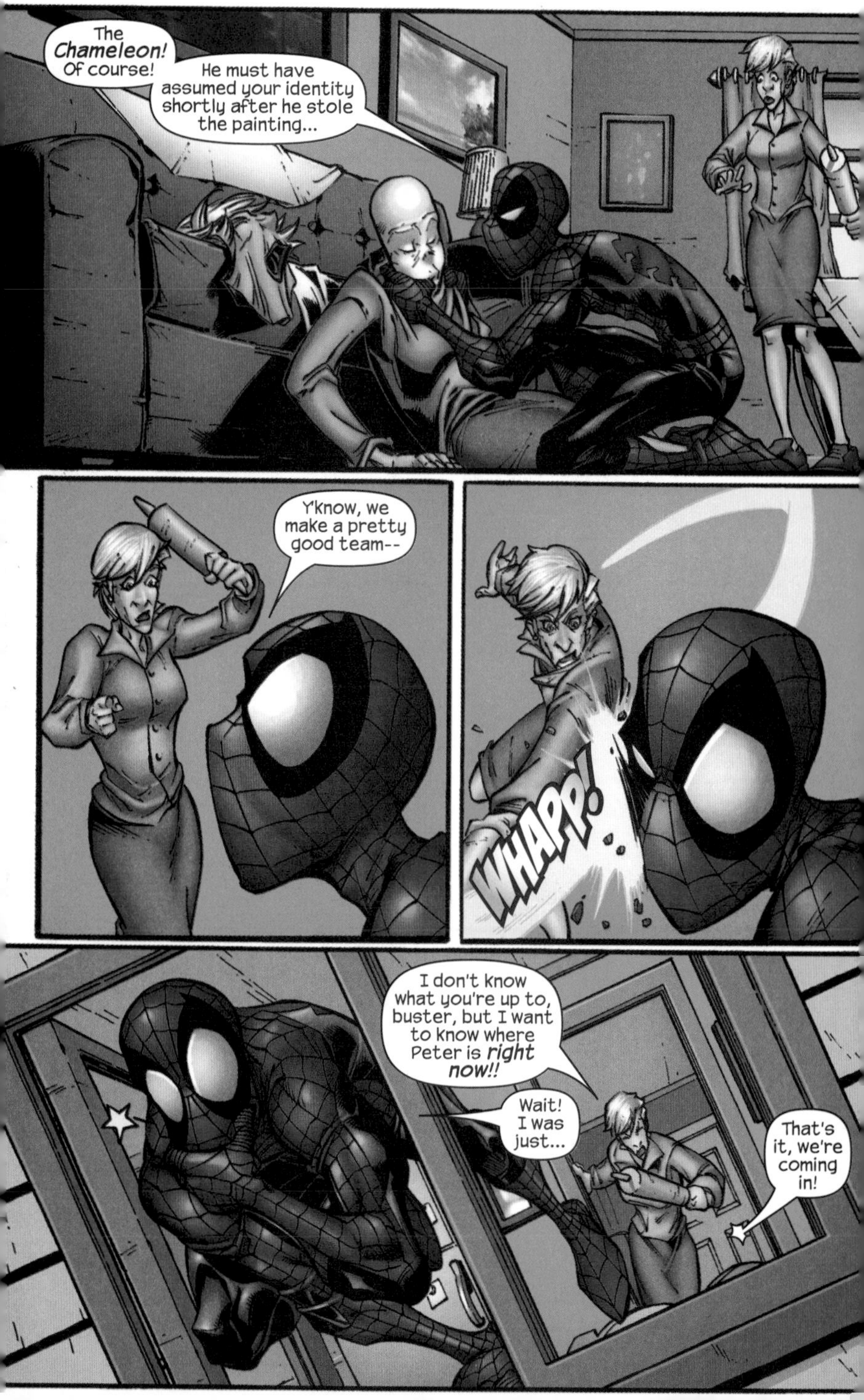
The *Chameleon!* Of course!
He must have assumed your identity shortly after he stole the painting...
Y'know, we make a pretty good team--
WHAPP!
I don't know what you're up to, buster, but I want to know where Peter is *right now!!*
Wait! I was just...
That's it, we're coming in!

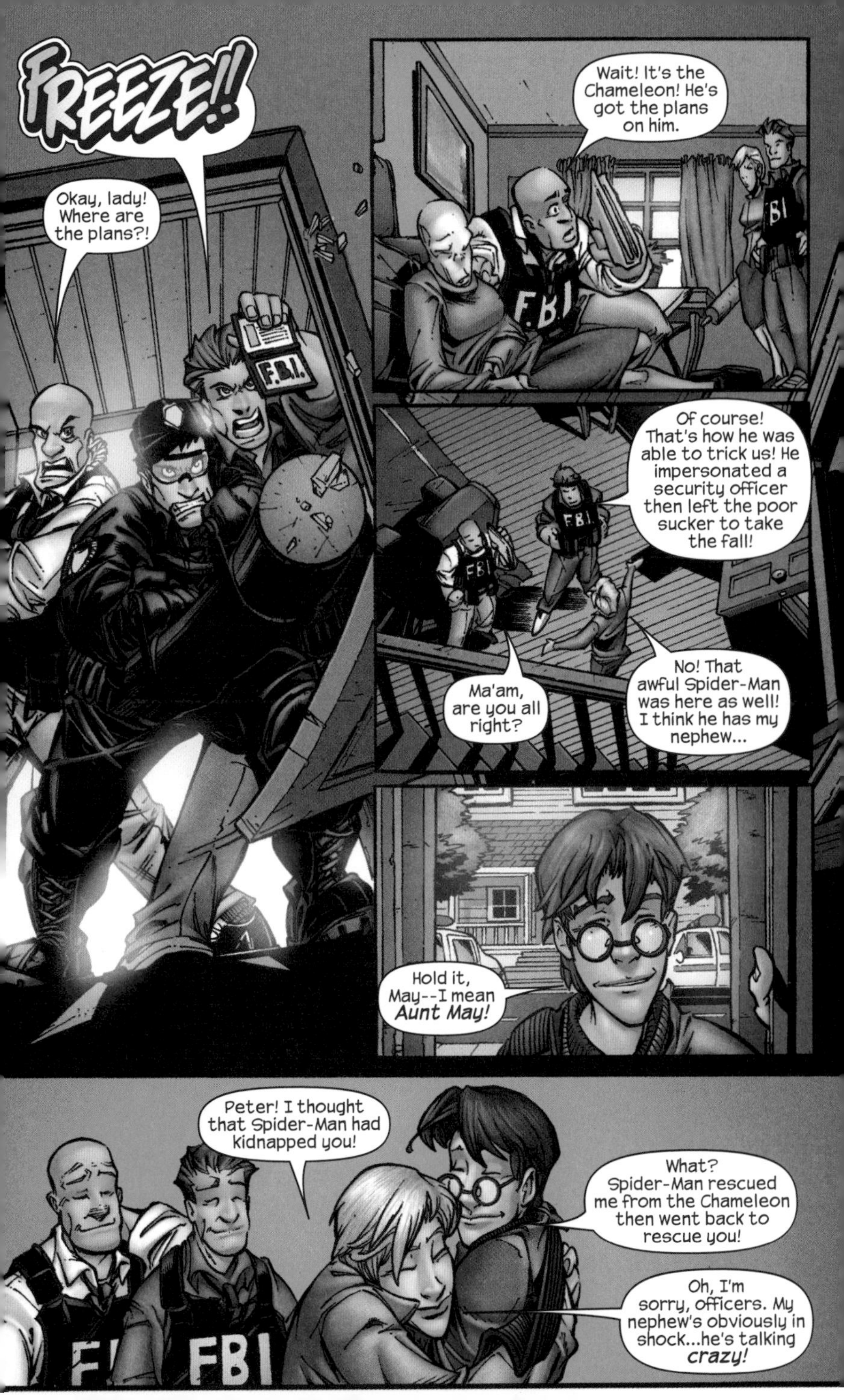
FREEZE!!
Okay, lady! Where are the plans?!
Wait! It's the Chameleon! He's got the plans on him.
Of course! That's how he was able to trick us! He impersonated a security officer then left the poor sucker to take the fall!
Ma'am, are you all right?
No! That awful Spider-Man was here as well! I think he has my nephew...
Hold it, May--I mean Aunt May!
Peter! I thought that Spider-Man had kidnapped you!
What? Spider-Man rescued me from the Chameleon then went back to rescue you!
Oh, I'm sorry, officers. My nephew's obviously in shock...he's talking crazy!
FBI

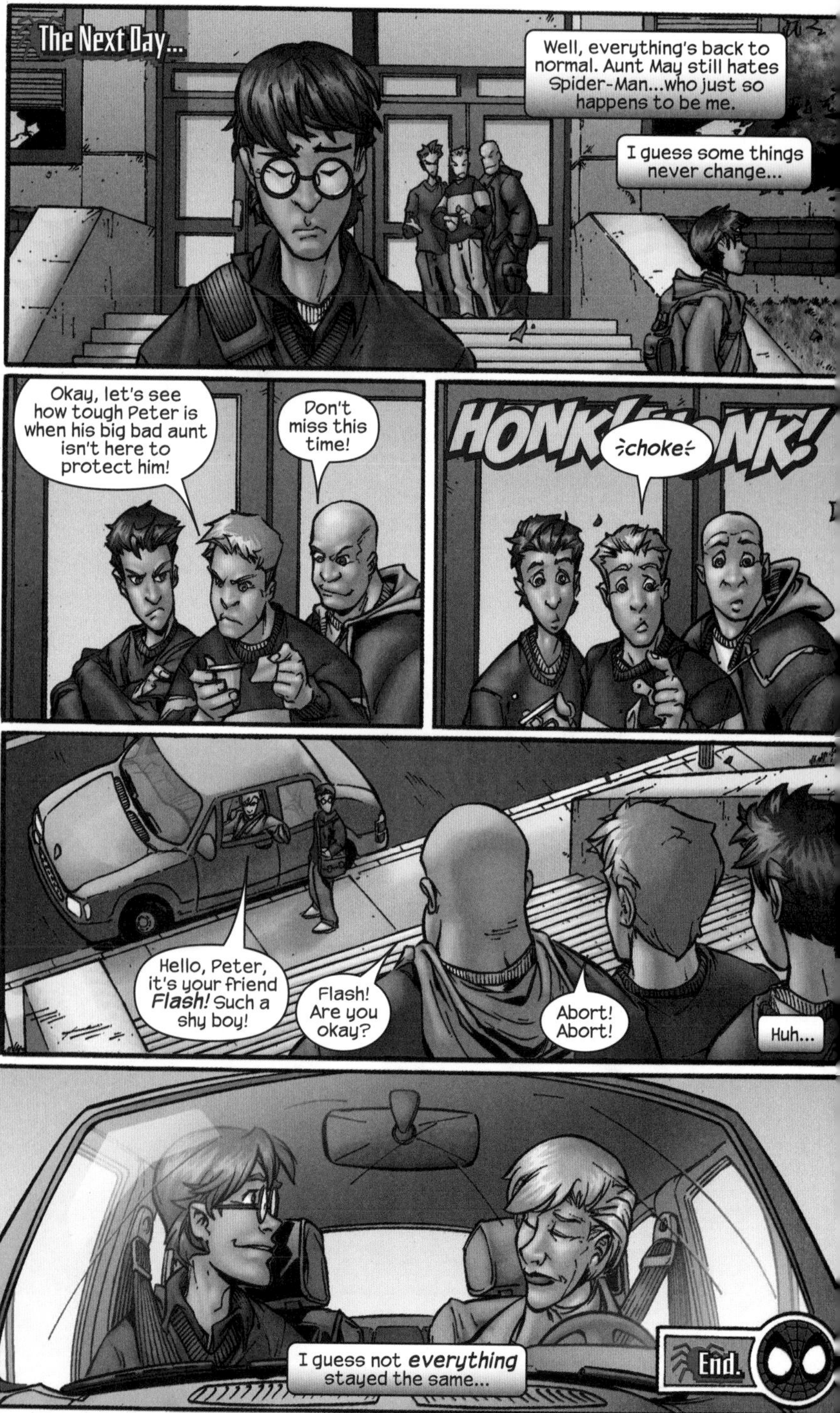
The Next Day...
Well, everything's back to normal. Aunt May still hates Spider-Man...who just so happens to be me.
I guess some things never change...
Okay, let's see how tough Peter is when his big bad aunt isn't here to protect him!
Don't miss this time!
HONK! HONK!
choke
Hello, Peter, it's your friend Flash! Such a shy boy!
Flash! Are you okay?
Abort! Abort!
Huh...
I guess not everything stayed the same...
End.

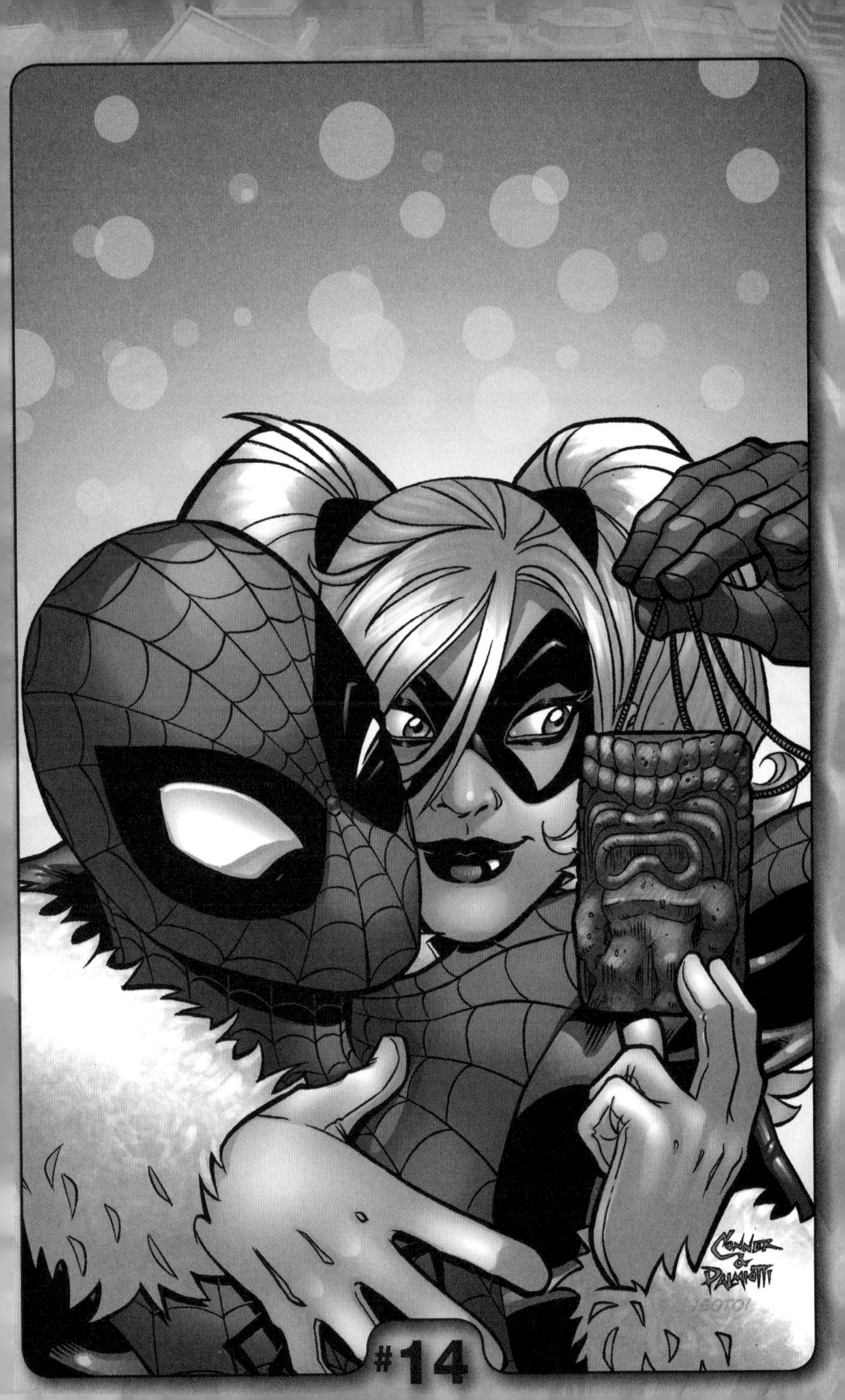
CONNER & PALMIOTTI
#14

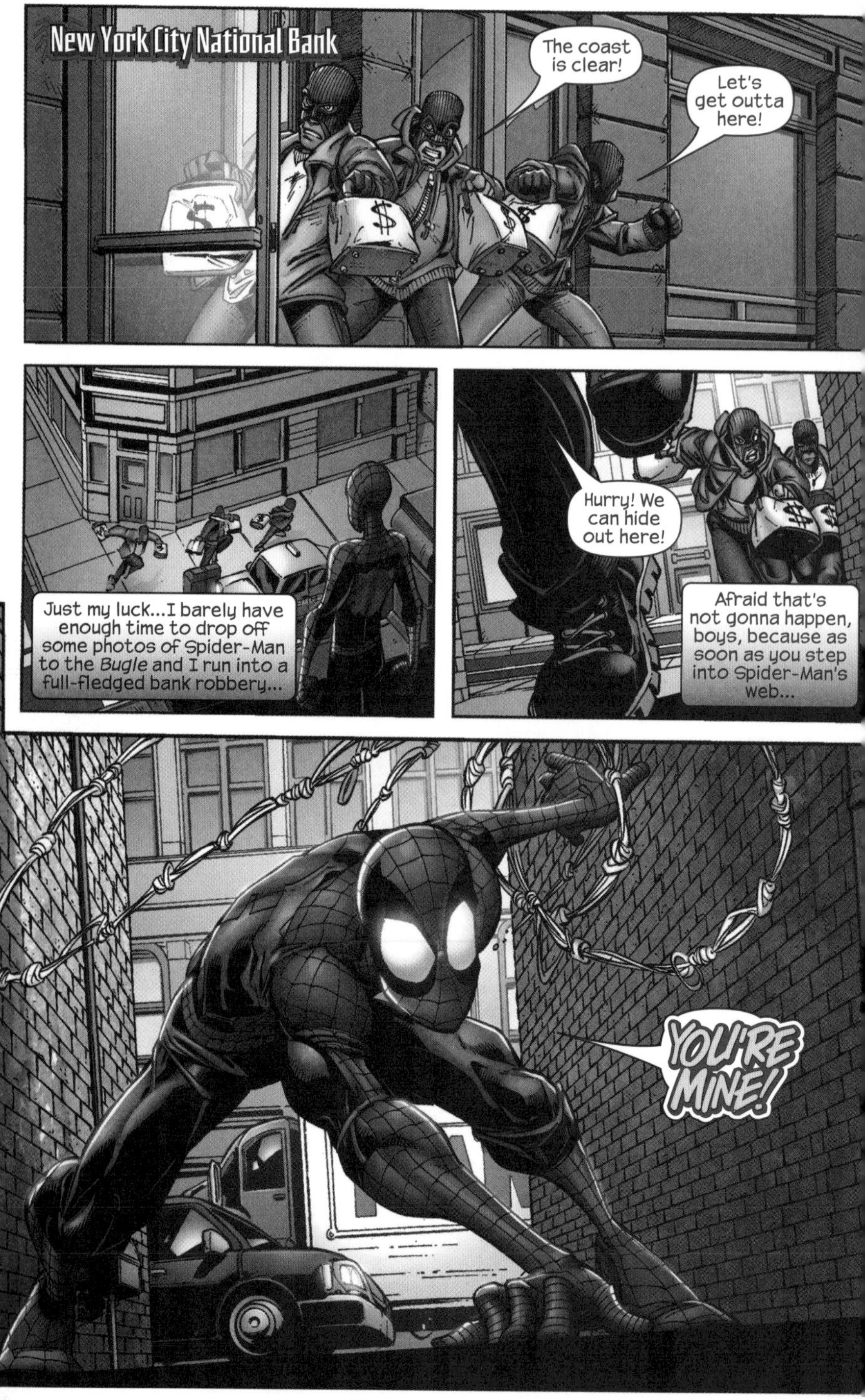
New York City National Bank
The coast is clear!
Let's get outta here!
Just my luck...I barely have enough time to drop off some photos of Spider-Man to the *Bugle* and I run into a full-fledged bank robbery...
Hurry! We can hide out here!
Afraid that's not gonna happen, boys, because as soon as you step into Spider-Man's web...
YOU'RE MINE!

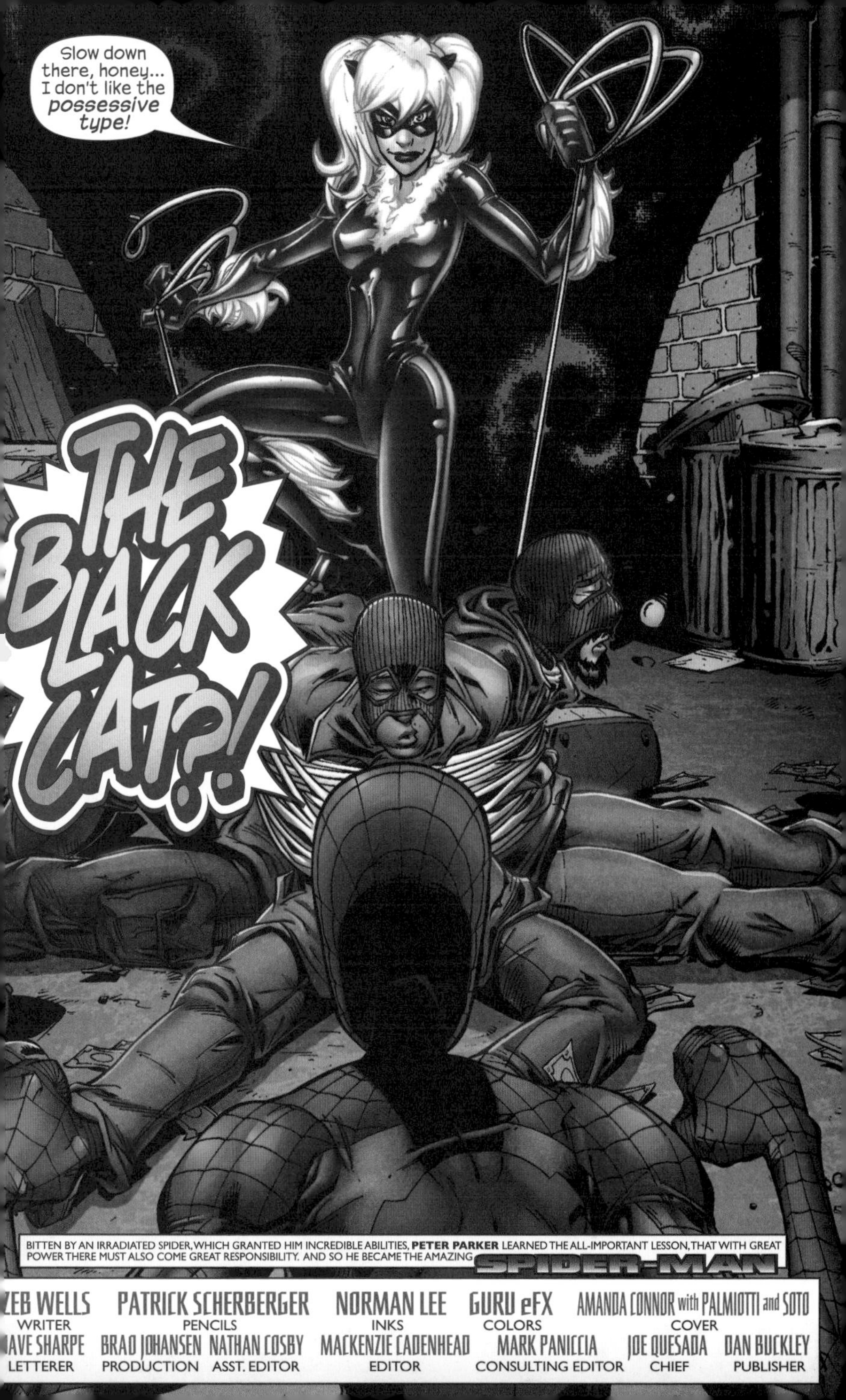
Slow down there, honey... I don't like the *possessive* type!
THE BLACK CAT?!
BITTEN BY AN IRRADIATED SPIDER, WHICH GRANTED HIM INCREDIBLE ABILITIES, **PETER PARKER** LEARNED THE ALL-IMPORTANT LESSON, THAT WITH GREAT POWER THERE MUST ALSO COME GREAT RESPONSIBILITY. AND SO HE BECAME THE AMAZING SPIDER-MAN
ZEB WELLS WRITER
PATRICK SCHERBERGER PENCILS
NORMAN LEE INKS
GURU eFX COLORS
AMANDA CONNOR with PALMIOTTI and SOTO COVER
AVE SHARPE LETTERER
BRAD JOHANSEN PRODUCTION
NATHAN COSBY ASST. EDITOR
MACKENZIE CADENHEAD EDITOR
MARK PANICCIA CONSULTING EDITOR
JOE QUESADA CHIEF
DAN BUCKLEY PUBLISHER

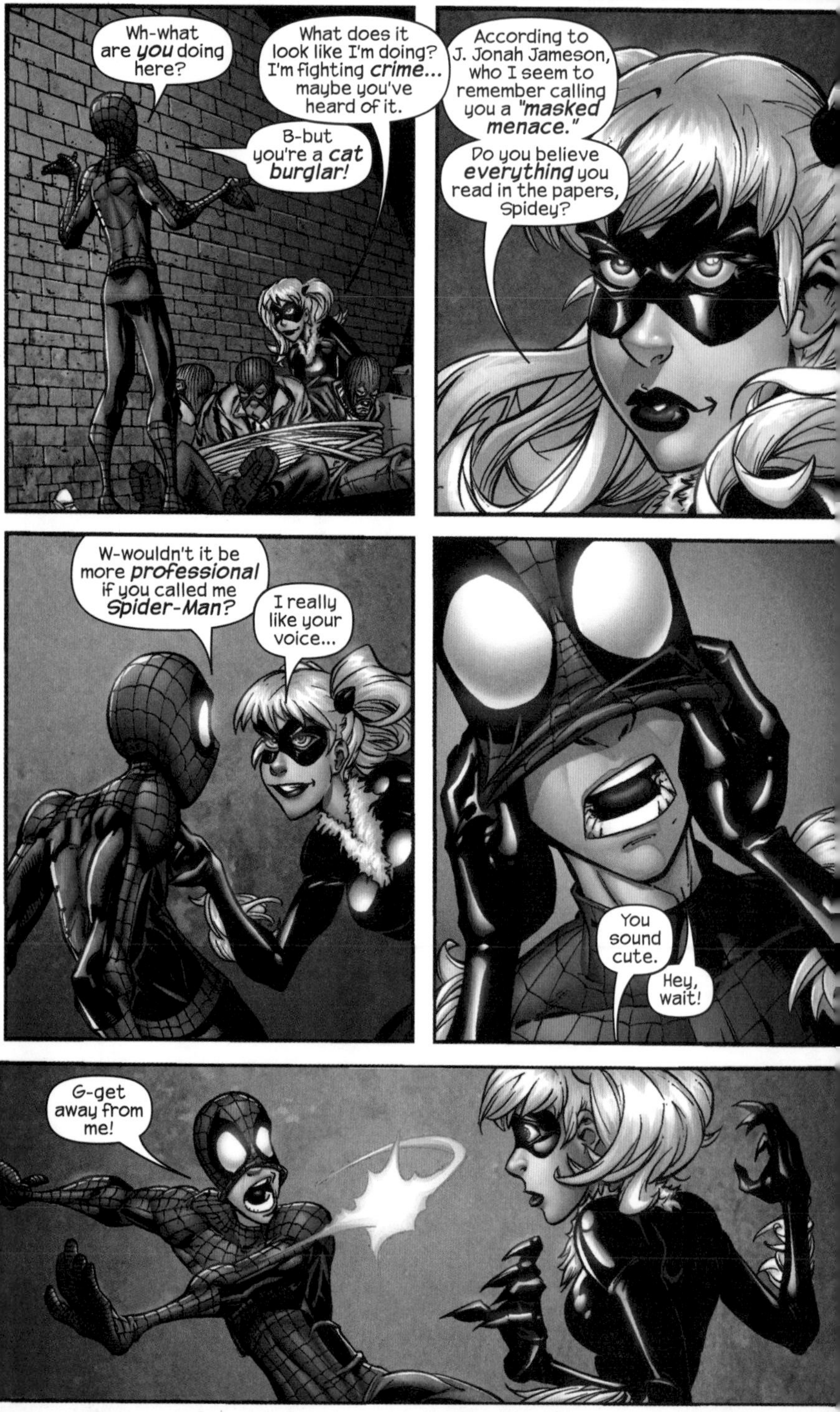
Wh-what are *you* doing here?
What does it look like I'm doing? I'm fighting *crime*... maybe you've heard of it.
B-but you're a *cat burglar!*
According to J. Jonah Jameson, who I seem to remember calling you a *"masked menace."*
Do you believe *everything* you read in the papers, Spidey?
W-wouldn't it be more *professional* if you called me *Spider-Man?*
I really like your voice...
You sound cute.
Hey, wait!
G-get away from me!

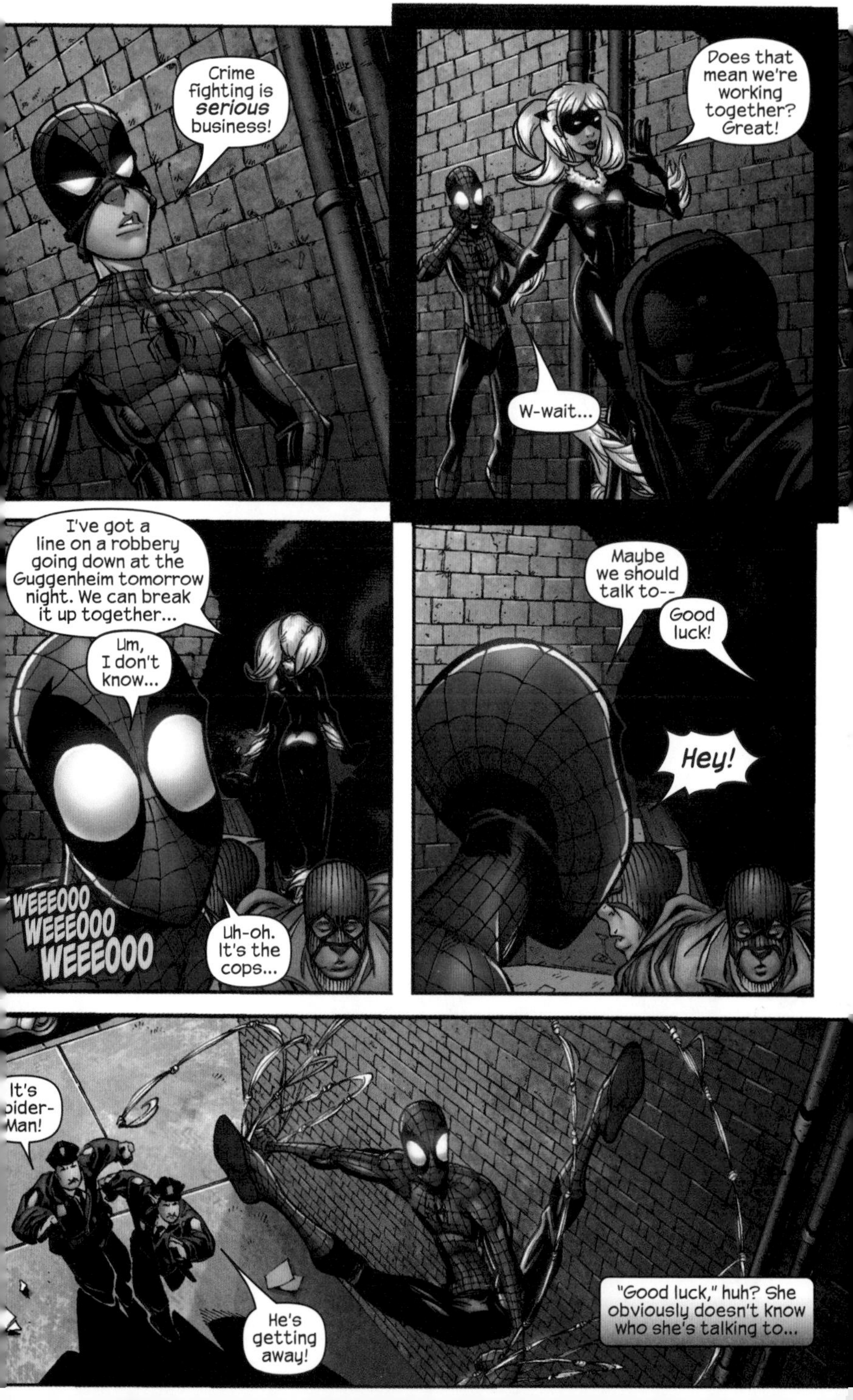
Crime fighting is *serious* business!
Does that mean we're working together? Great!
W-wait...
I've got a line on a robbery going down at the Guggenheim tomorrow night. We can break it up together...
Um, I don't know...
WEEEOOO WEEEOOO WEEEOOO
Uh-oh. It's the cops...
Maybe we should talk to--
Good luck!
Hey!
It's pider-Man!
He's getting away!
"Good luck," huh? She obviously doesn't know who she's talking to...

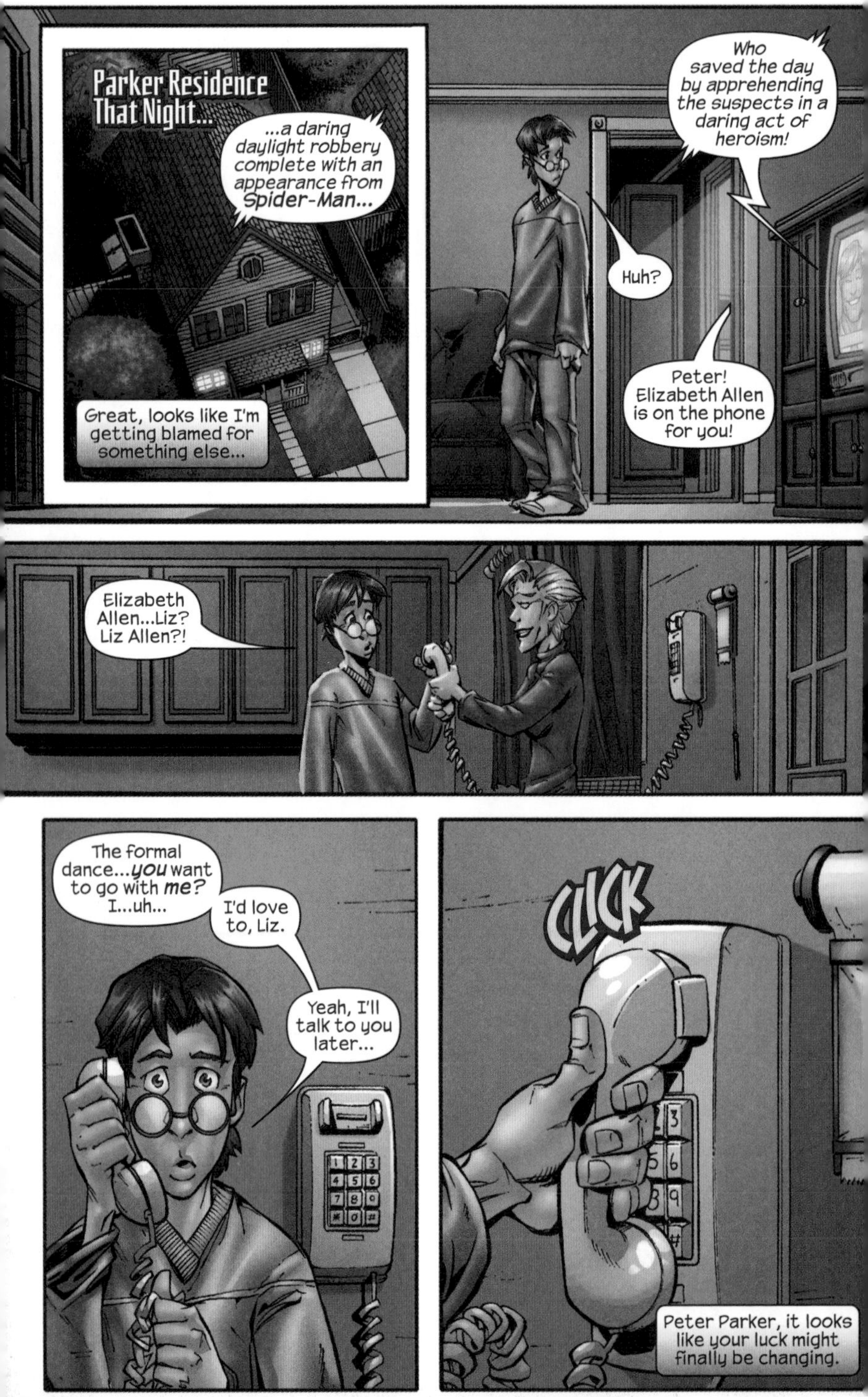
Parker Residence That Night...
...a daring daylight robbery complete with an appearance from Spider-Man...
Great, looks like I'm getting blamed for something else...
Who saved the day by apprehending the suspects in a daring act of heroism!
Huh?
Peter! Elizabeth Allen is on the phone for you!
Elizabeth Allen...Liz? Liz Allen?!
The formal dance...*you* want to go with *me?* I...uh...
I'd love to, Liz.
Yeah, I'll talk to you later...
CLICK
Peter Parker, it looks like your luck might finally be changing.

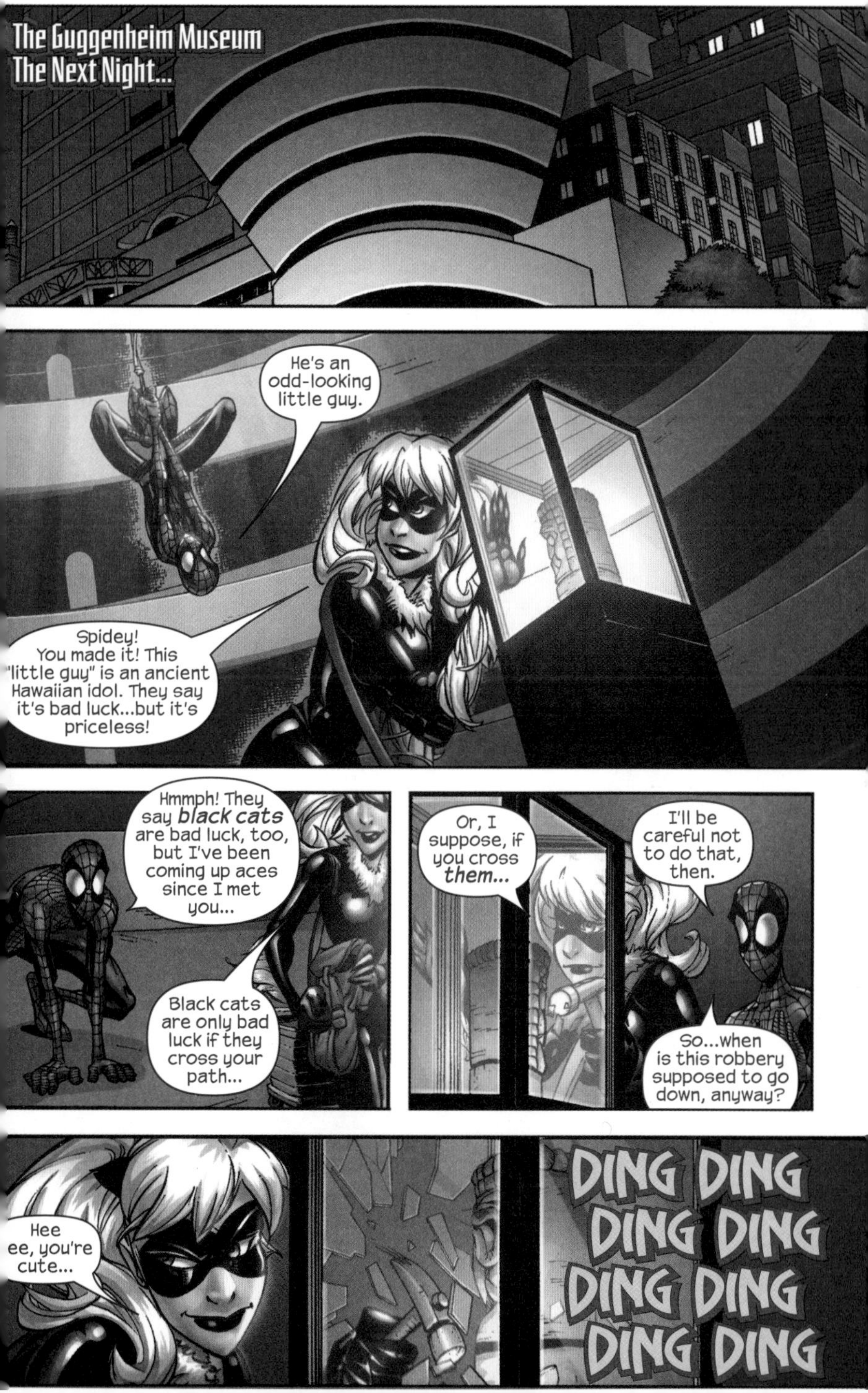
The Guggenheim Museum
The Next Night...
He's an odd-looking little guy.
Spidey! You made it! This "little guy" is an ancient Hawaiian idol. They say it's bad luck...but it's priceless!
Hmmph! They say *black cats* are bad luck, too, but I've been coming up aces since I met you...
Black cats are only bad luck if they cross your path...
Or, I suppose, if you cross *them...*
I'll be careful not to do that, then.
So...when is this robbery supposed to go down, anyway?
Hee ee, you're cute...
DING DING
DING DING
DING DING
DING DING

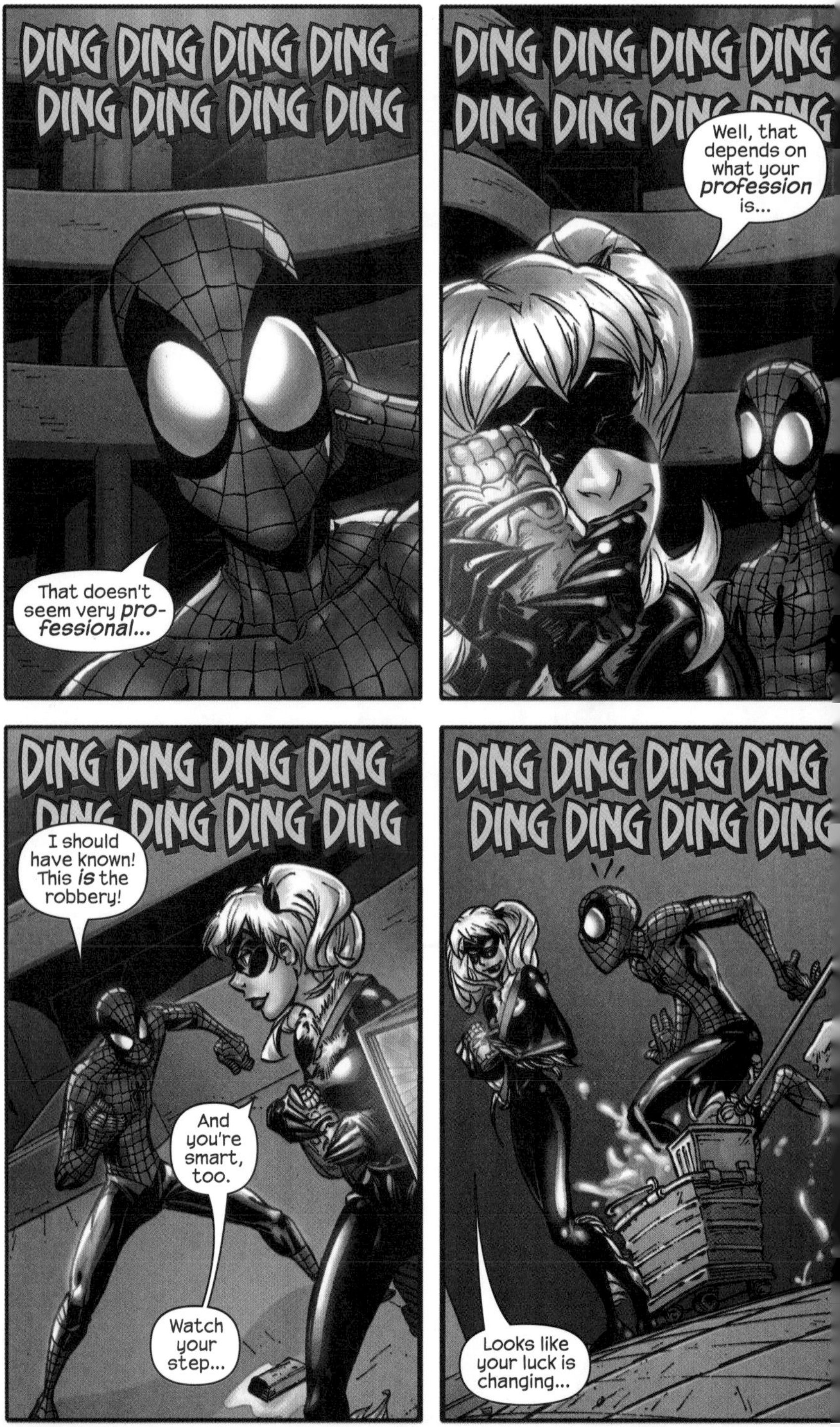
DING DING DING DING
DING DING DING DING
That doesn't seem very pro-fessional...
DING DING DING DING
DING DING DING DING
Well, that depends on what your profession is...
DING DING DING DING
DING DING DING DING
I should have known! This is the robbery!
And you're smart, too.
Watch your step...
DING DING DING DING
DING DING DING DING
Looks like your luck is changing...

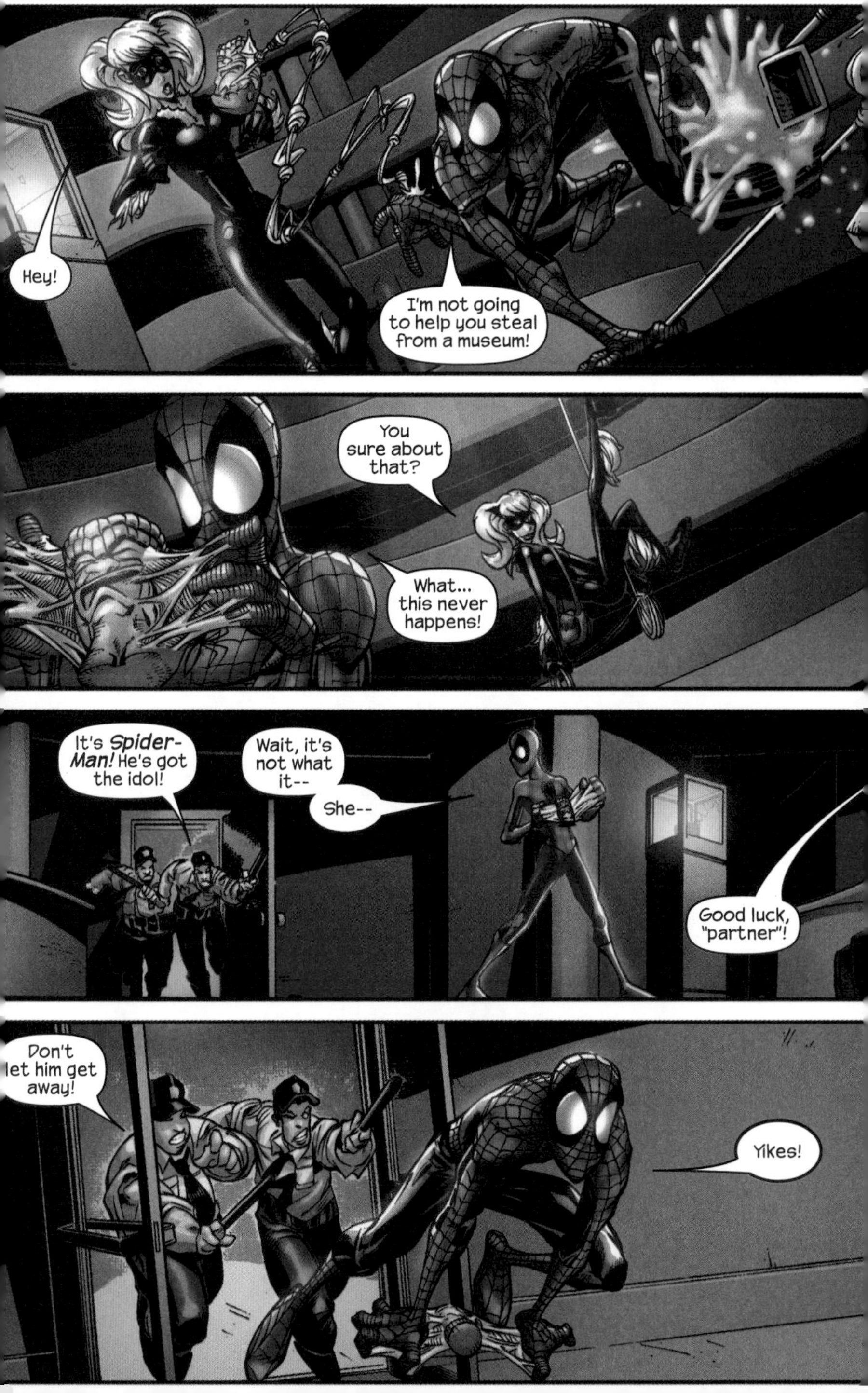
Hey!
I'm not going to help you steal from a museum!
You sure about that?
What... this never happens!
It's *Spider-Man!* He's got the idol!
Wait, it's not what it--
She--
Good luck, "partner"!
Don't let him get away!
Yikes!

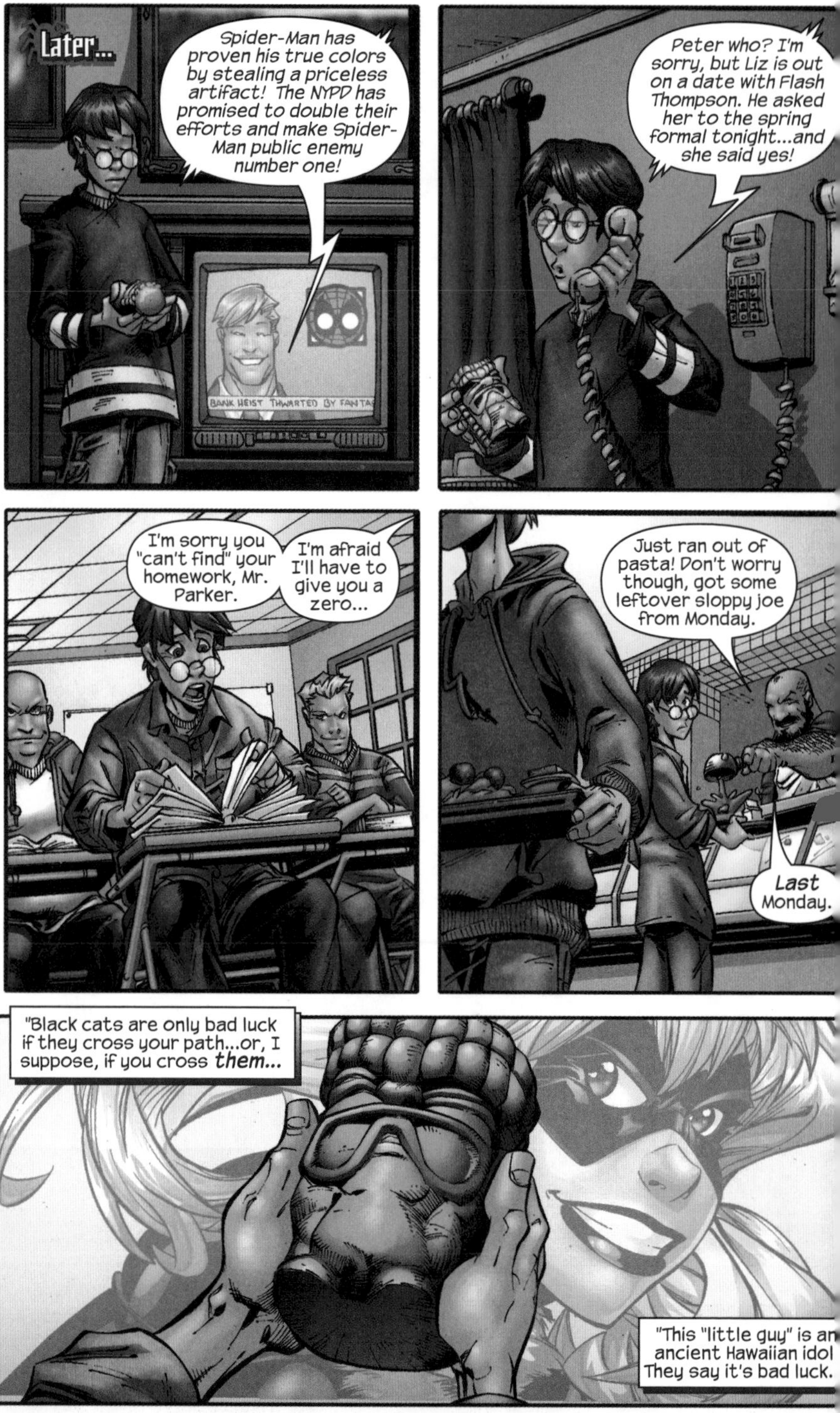
Later...
Spider-Man has proven his true colors by stealing a priceless artifact! The NYPD has promised to double their efforts and make Spider-Man public enemy number one!
BANK HEIST THWARTED BY FANTA
Peter who? I'm sorry, but Liz is out on a date with Flash Thompson. He asked her to the spring formal tonight...and she said yes!
I'm sorry you "can't find" your homework, Mr. Parker.
I'm afraid I'll have to give you a zero...
Just ran out of pasta! Don't worry though, got some leftover sloppy joe from Monday.
Last Monday.
"Black cats are only bad luck if they cross your path...or, I suppose, if you cross them...
"This "little guy" is an ancient Hawaiian idol. They say it's bad luck.

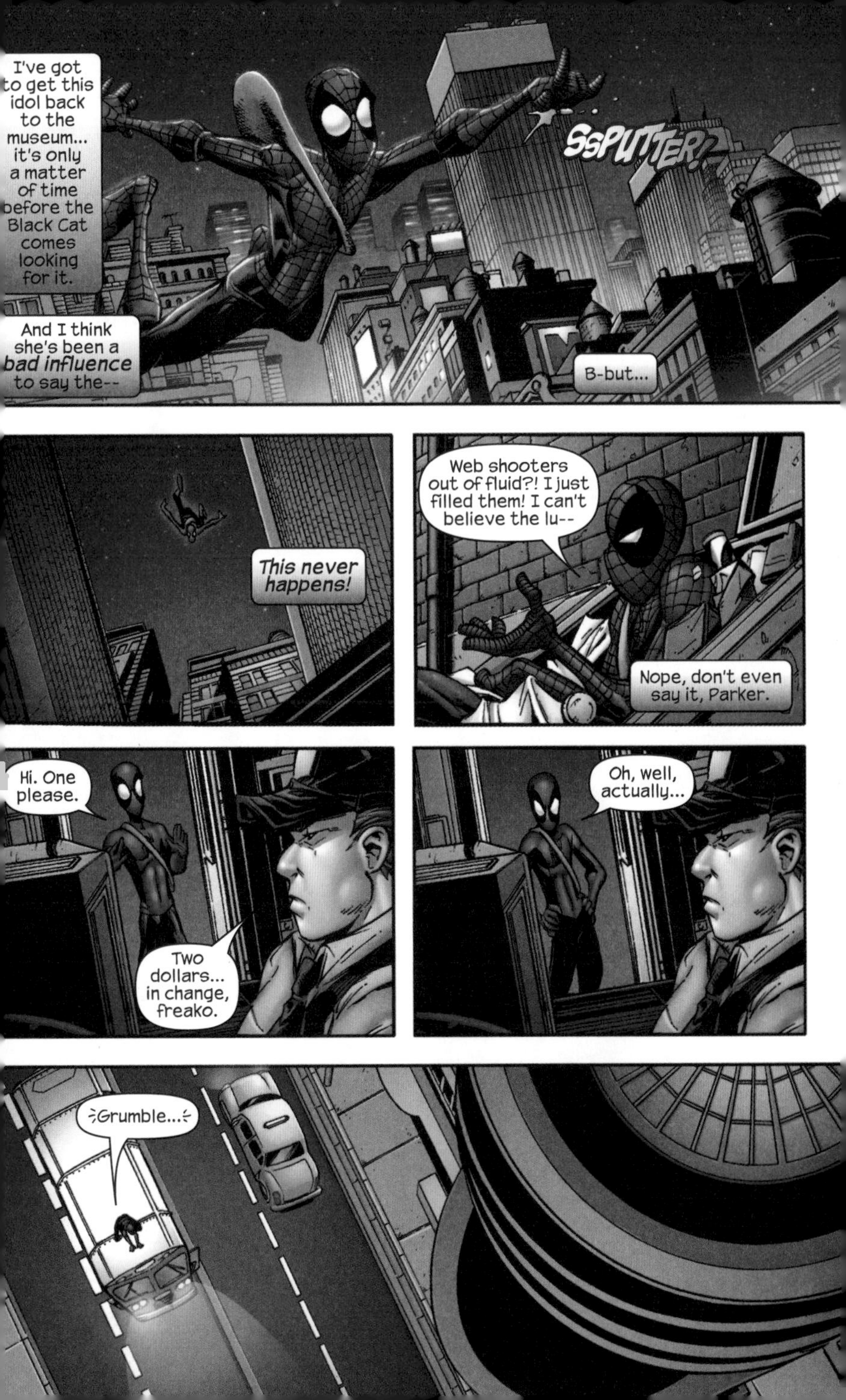
I've got to get this idol back to the museum... it's only a matter of time before the Black Cat comes looking for it.
And I think she's been a *bad influence* to say the--
SSPUTTER!
B-but...
This never happens!
Web shooters out of fluid?! I just filled them! I can't believe the lu--
Nope, don't even say it, Parker.
Hi. One please.
Two dollars... in change, freako.
Oh, well, actually...
Grumble...

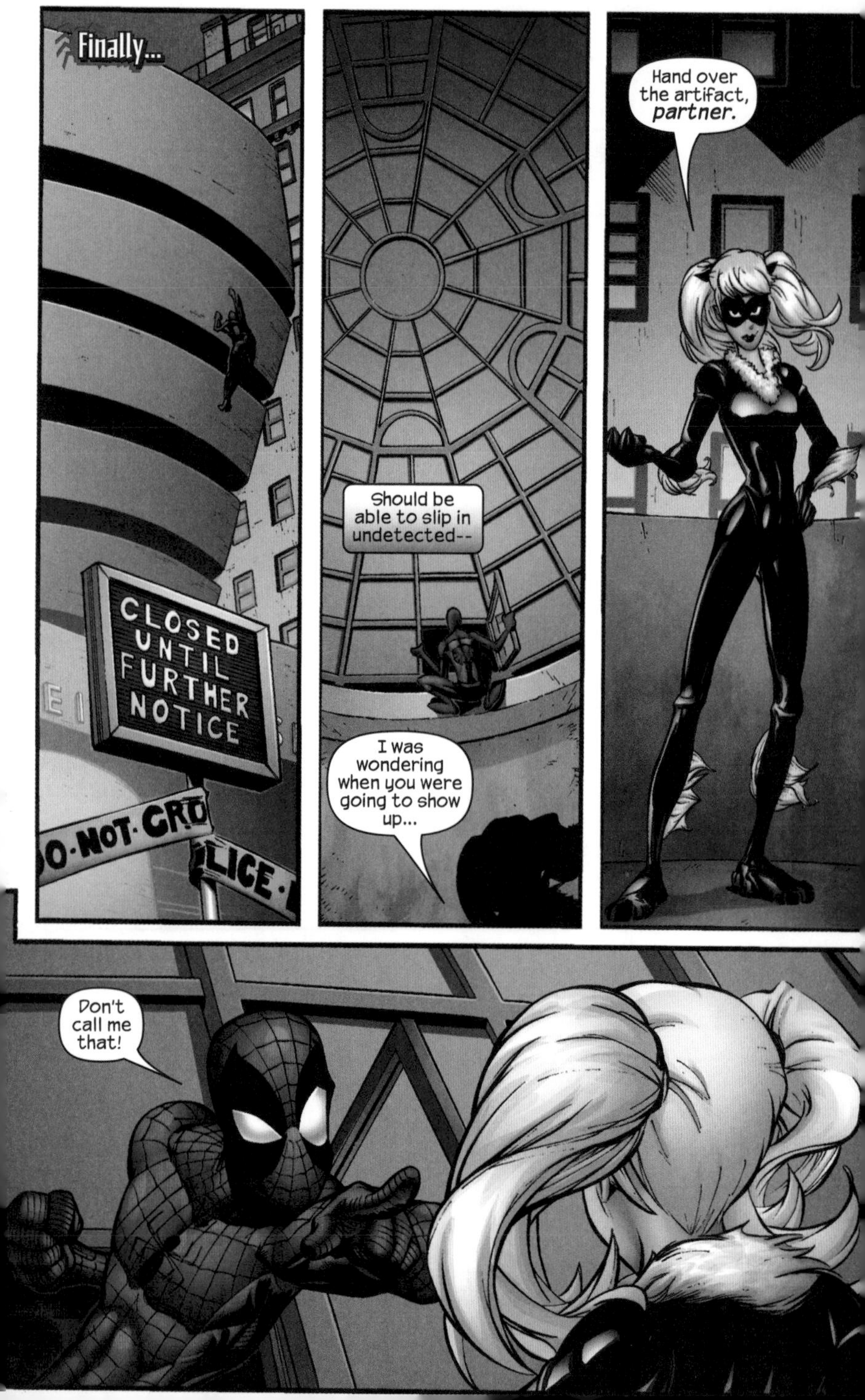
Finally...
CLOSED UNTIL FURTHER NOTICE
DO-NOT-CRO
LICE
Should be able to slip in undetected--
I was wondering when you were going to show up...
Hand over the artifact, *partner*.
Don't call me that!

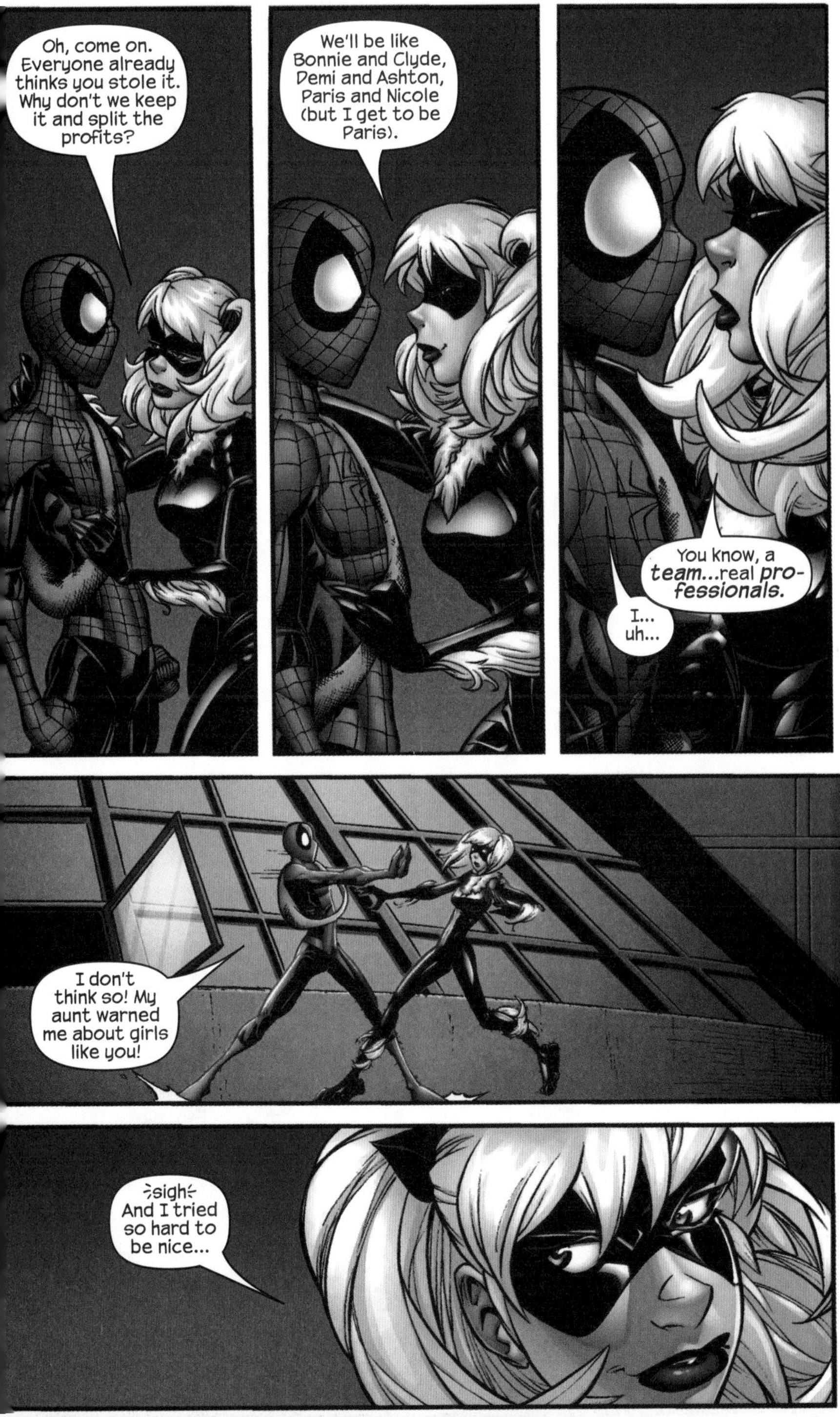
Oh, come on. Everyone already thinks you stole it. Why don't we keep it and split the profits?
We'll be like Bonnie and Clyde, Demi and Ashton, Paris and Nicole (but I get to be Paris).
You know, a *team*...real *pro-fessionals.*
I... uh...
I don't think so! My aunt warned me about girls like you!
sigh And I tried so hard to be nice...

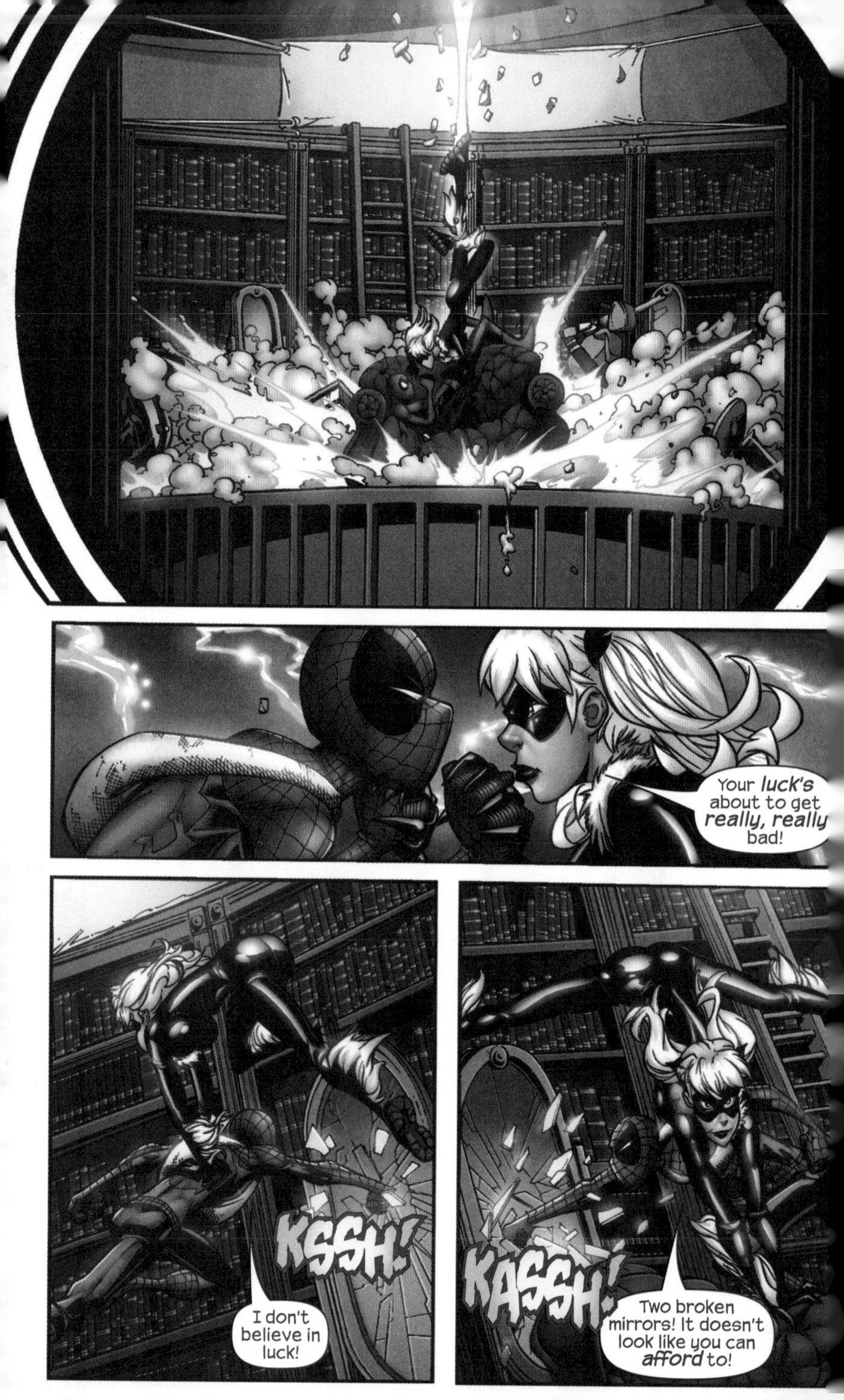
Your luck's about to get really, really bad!
KSSH!
I don't believe in luck!
KASSH!
Two broken mirrors! It doesn't look like you can afford to!

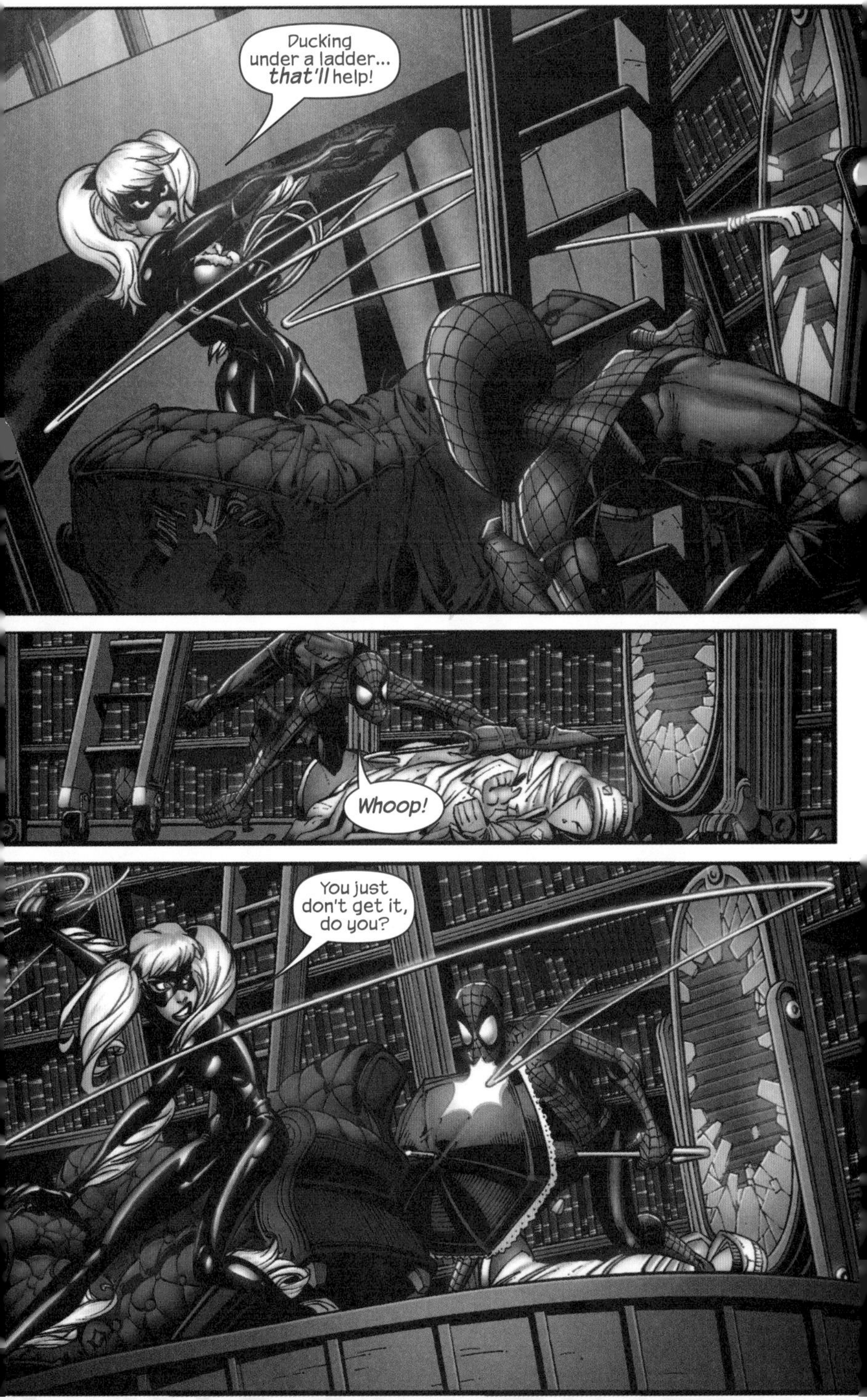
Ducking under a ladder... *that'll* help!
Whoop!
You just don't get it, do you?

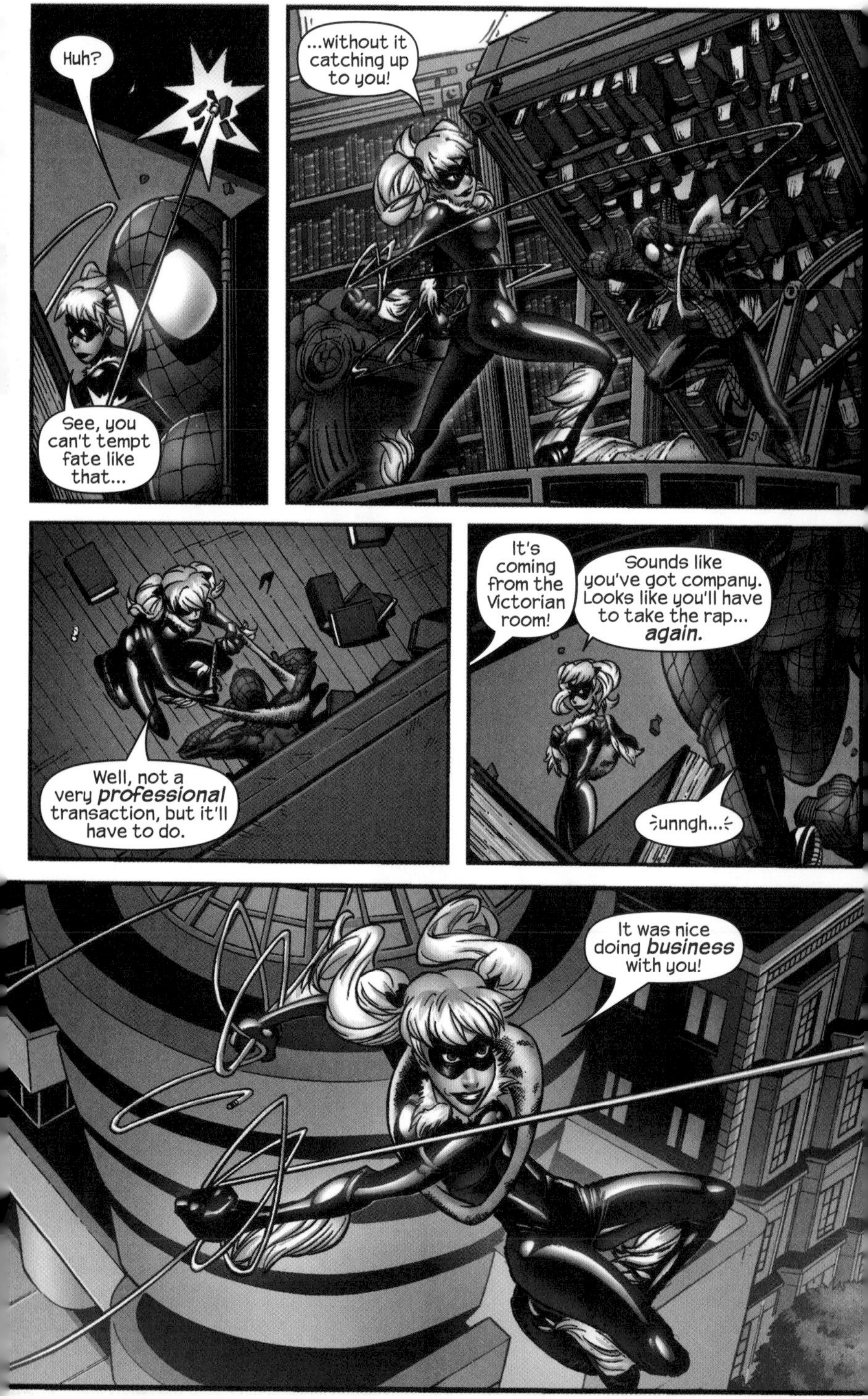

Huh?
See, you can't tempt fate like that...
...without it catching up to you!
Well, not a very *professional* transaction, but it'll have to do.
It's coming from the Victorian room!
Sounds like you've got company. Looks like you'll have to take the rap... *again.*
unngh...
It was nice doing *business* with you!

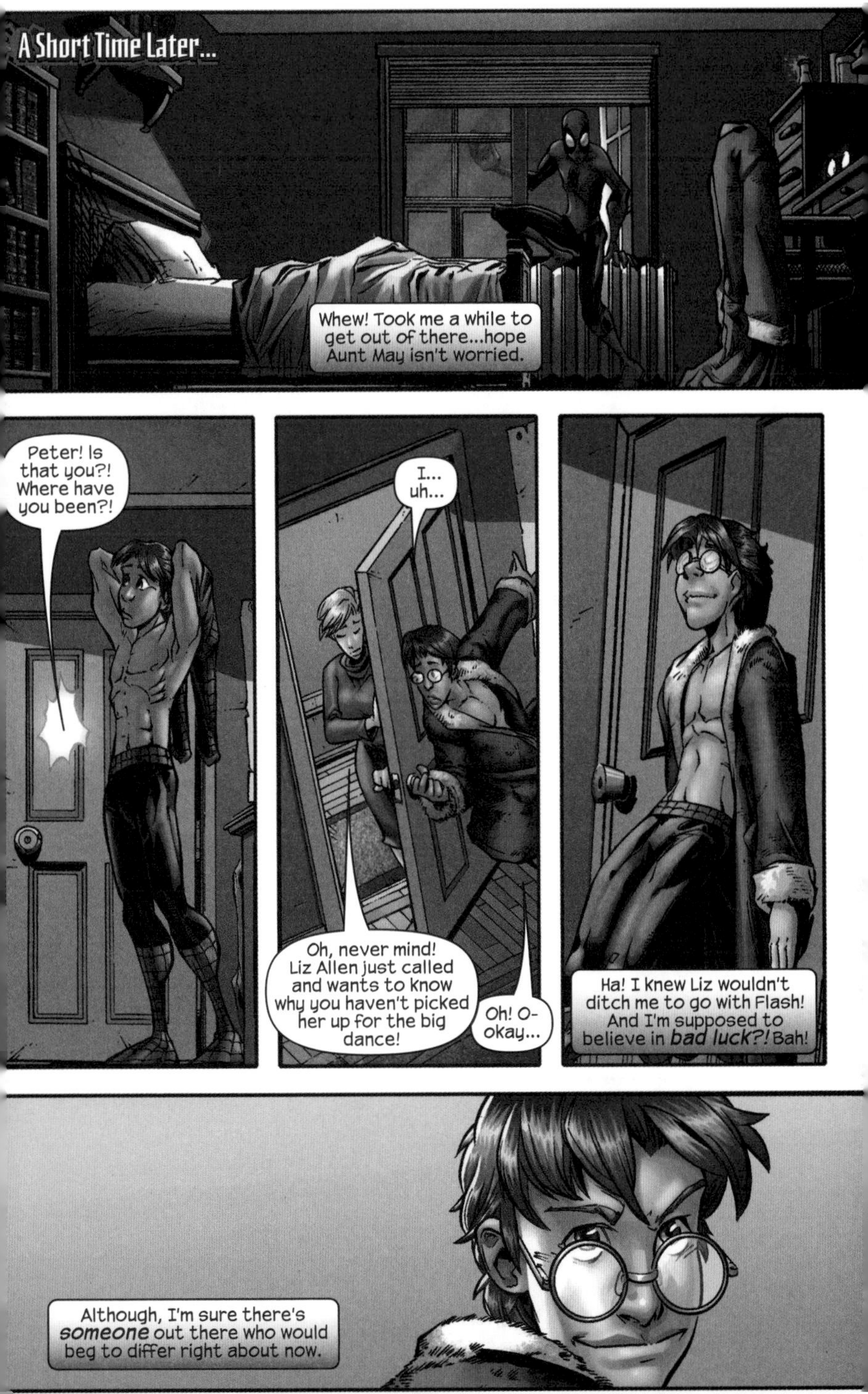
A Short Time Later...
Whew! Took me a while to get out of there...hope Aunt May isn't worried.
Peter! Is that you?! Where have you been?!
I... uh...
Oh, never mind! Liz Allen just called and wants to know why you haven't picked her up for the big dance!
Oh! O-okay...
Ha! I knew Liz wouldn't ditch me to go with Flash! And I'm supposed to believe in *bad luck?!* Bah!
Although, I'm sure there's *someone* out there who would beg to differ right about now.

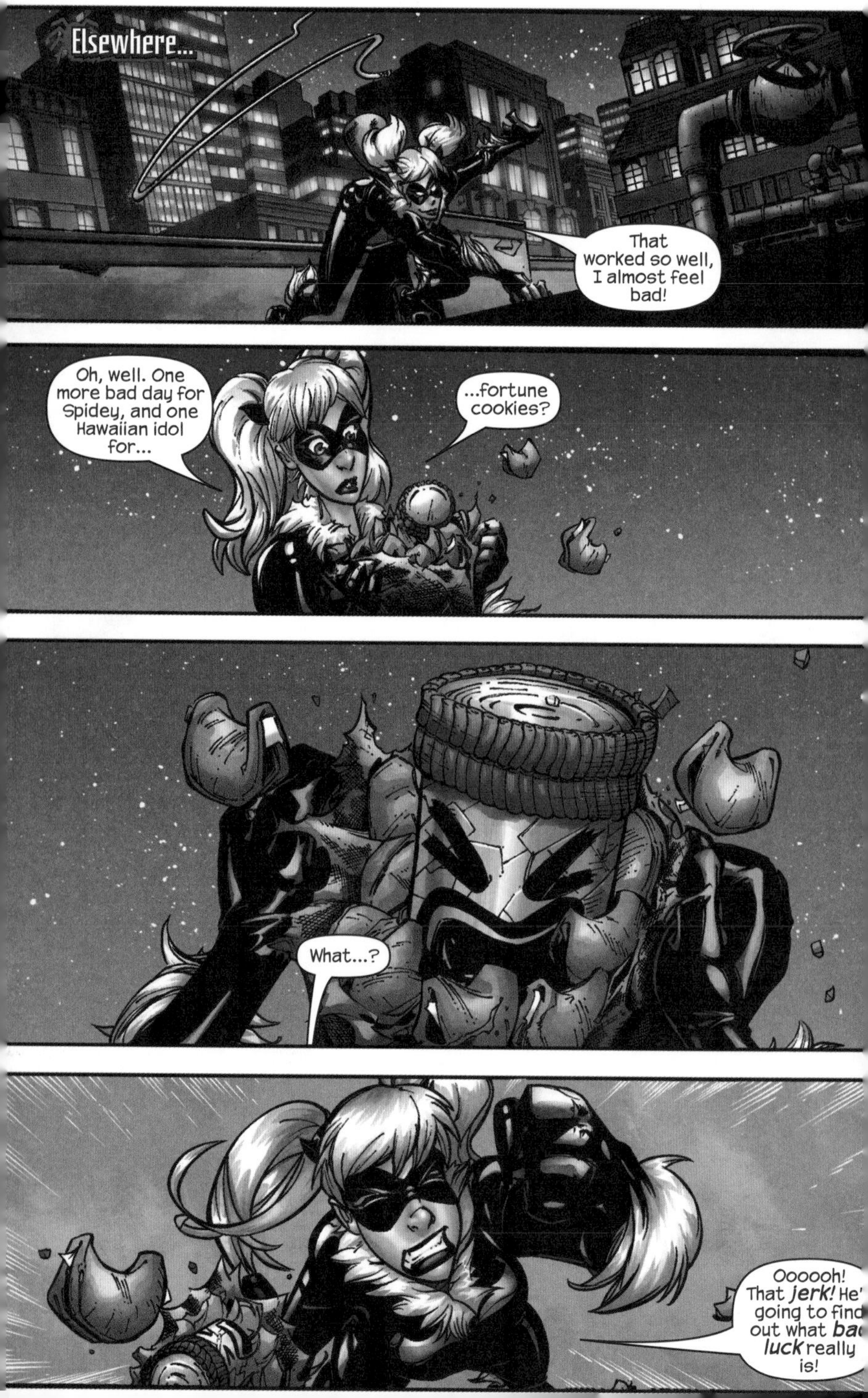
Elsewhere...
That worked so well, I almost feel bad!
Oh, well. One more bad day for Spidey, and one Hawaiian idol for...
...fortune cookies?
What...?
Oooooh! That jerk! He' going to find out what bad luck really is!

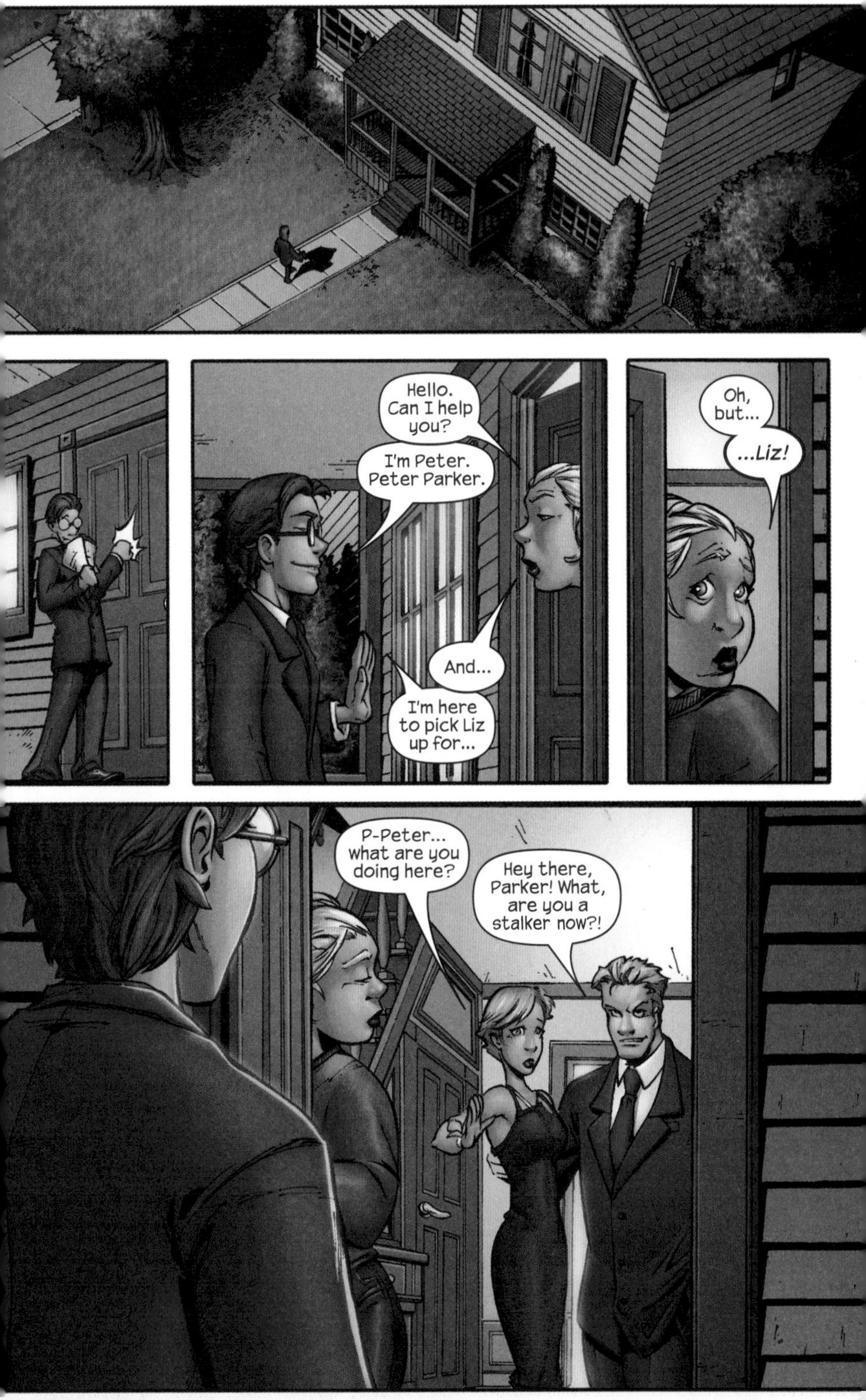
Hello. Can I help you?
I'm Peter. Peter Parker.
And...
I'm here to pick Liz up for...
Oh, but...
...Liz!
P-Peter... what are you doing here?
Hey there, Parker! What, are you a stalker now?!

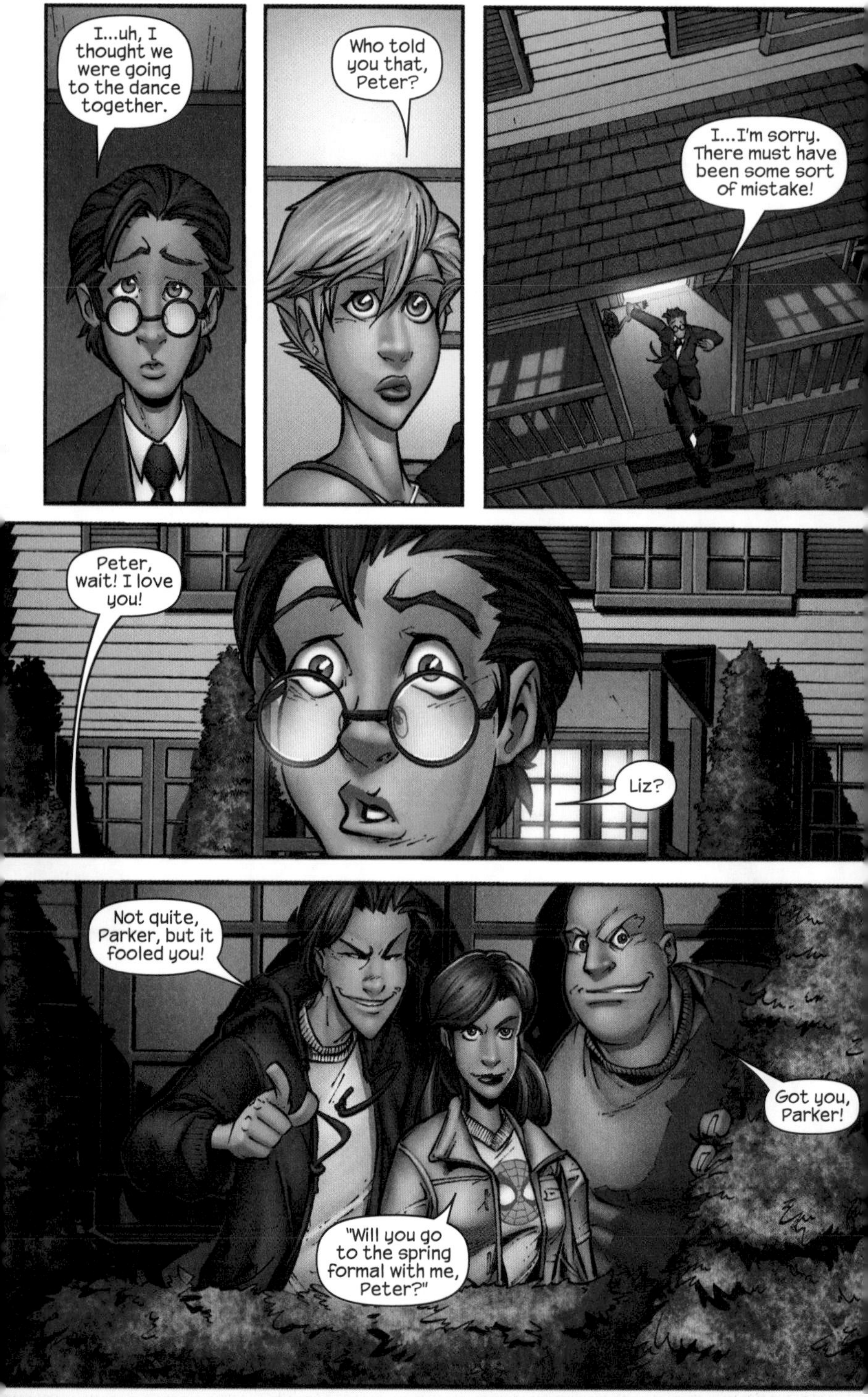
I...uh, I thought we were going to the dance together.
Who told you that, Peter?
I...I'm sorry. There must have been some sort of mistake!
Peter, wait! I love you!
Liz?
Not quite, Parker, but it fooled you!
"Will you go to the spring formal with me, Peter?"
Got you, Parker!

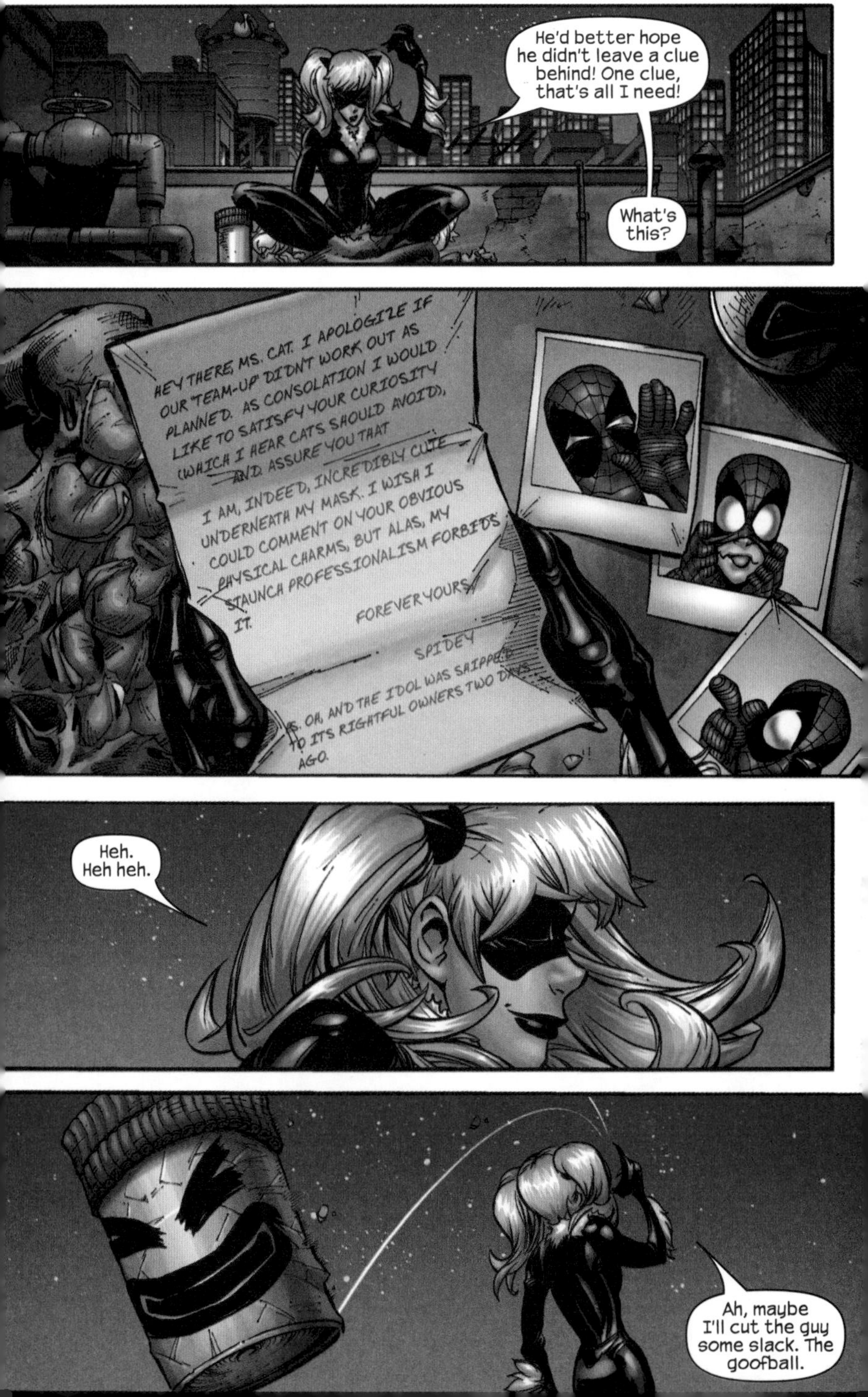
He'd better hope he didn't leave a clue behind! One clue, that's all I need!
What's this?
HEY THERE, MS. CAT. I APOLOGIZE IF OUR "TEAM-UP" DIDN'T WORK OUT AS PLANNED. AS CONSOLATION I WOULD LIKE TO SATISFY YOUR CURIOSITY (WHICH I HEAR CATS SHOULD AVOID), AND ASSURE YOU THAT I AM, INDEED, INCREDIBLY CUTE UNDERNEATH MY MASK. I WISH I COULD COMMENT ON YOUR OBVIOUS PHYSICAL CHARMS, BUT ALAS, MY STAUNCH PROFESSIONALISM FORBIDS IT.
FOREVER YOURS,
SPIDEY
P.S. OH, AND THE IDOL WAS SHIPPED TO ITS RIGHTFUL OWNERS TWO DAYS AGO.
Heh. Heh heh.
Ah, maybe I'll cut the guy some slack. The goofball.

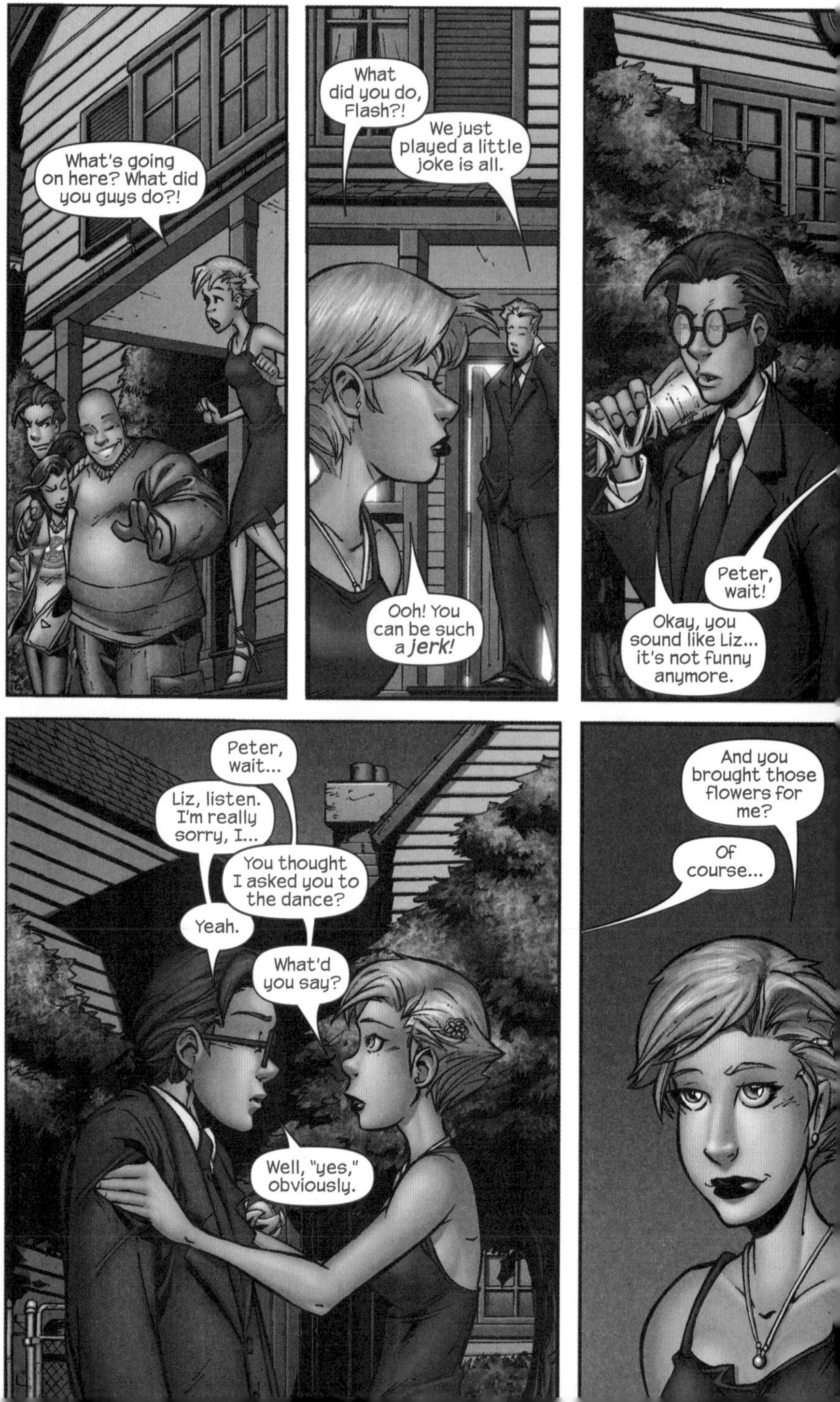

What's going on here? What did you guys do?!
What did you do, Flash?!
We just played a little joke is all.
Ooh! You can be such a *jerk!*
Peter, wait!
Okay, you sound like Liz... it's not funny anymore.
Peter, wait...
Liz, listen. I'm really sorry, I...
You thought I asked you to the dance?
Yeah.
What'd you say?
Well, "yes," obviously.
And you brought those flowers for me?
Of course...

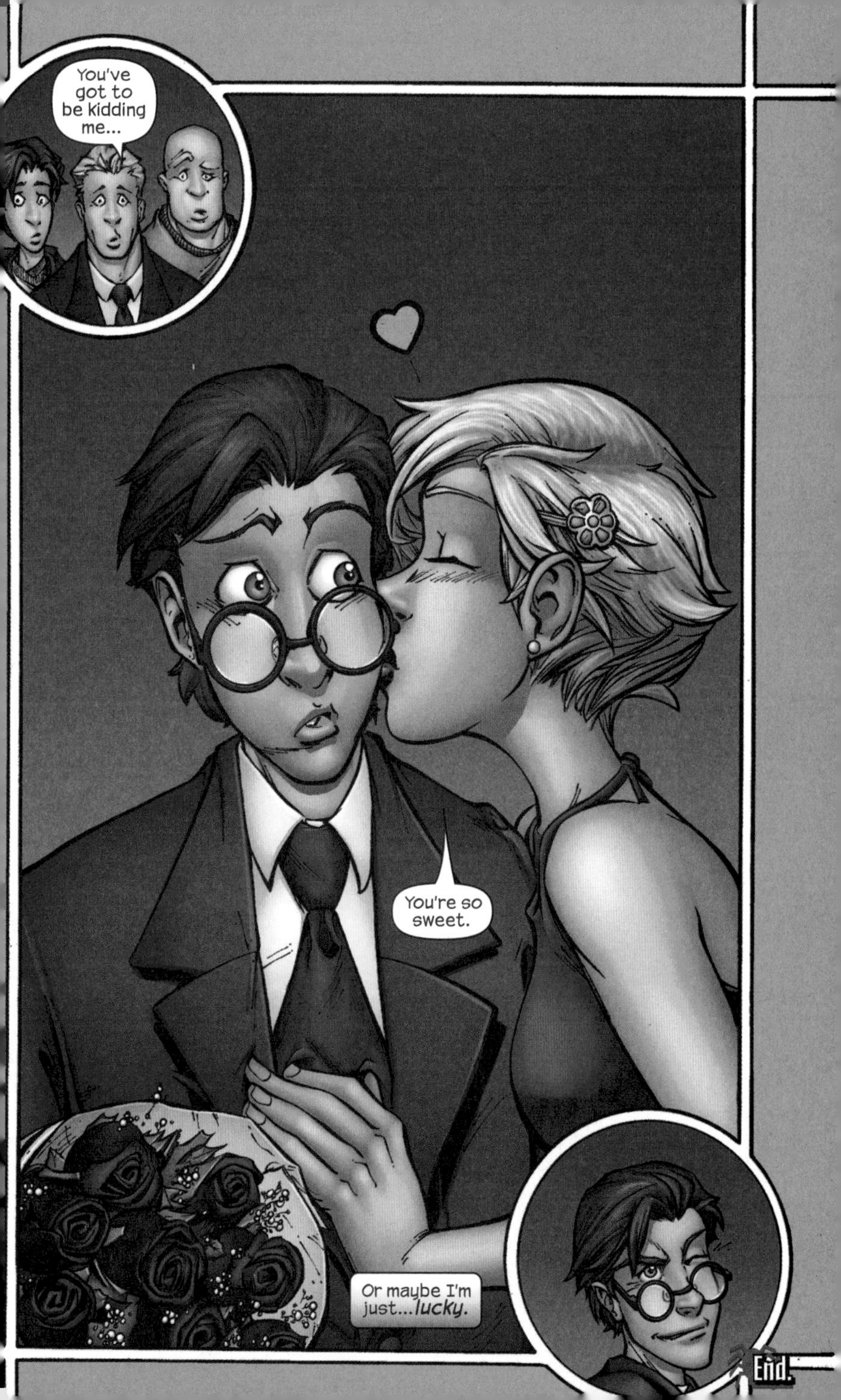
You've got to be kidding me...
You're so sweet.
Or maybe I'm just...lucky.
End.

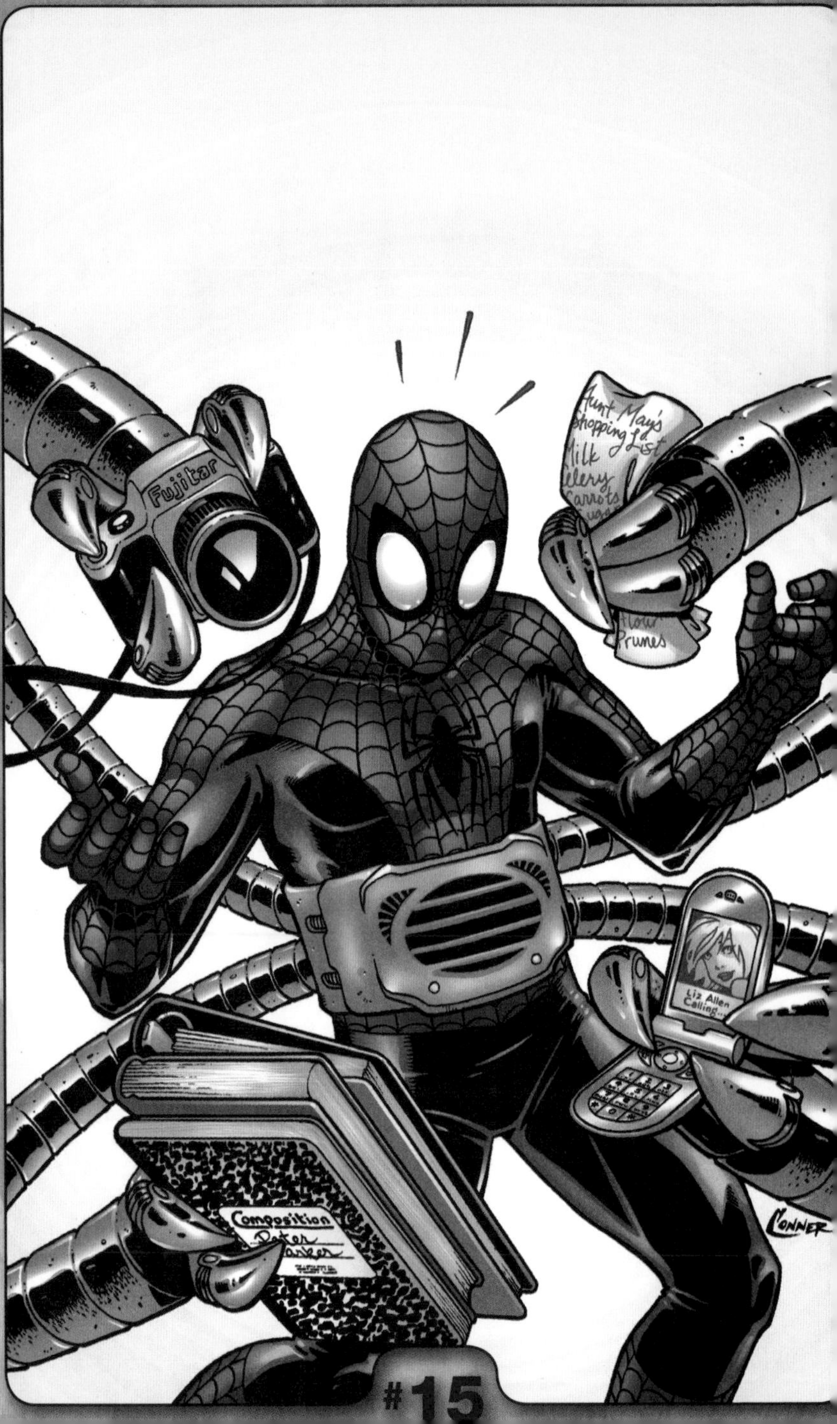
Fujitar
Aunt May's Shopping List
Milk
Carrots
Prunes
Liz Allen Calling...
Composition
CONNER
#15

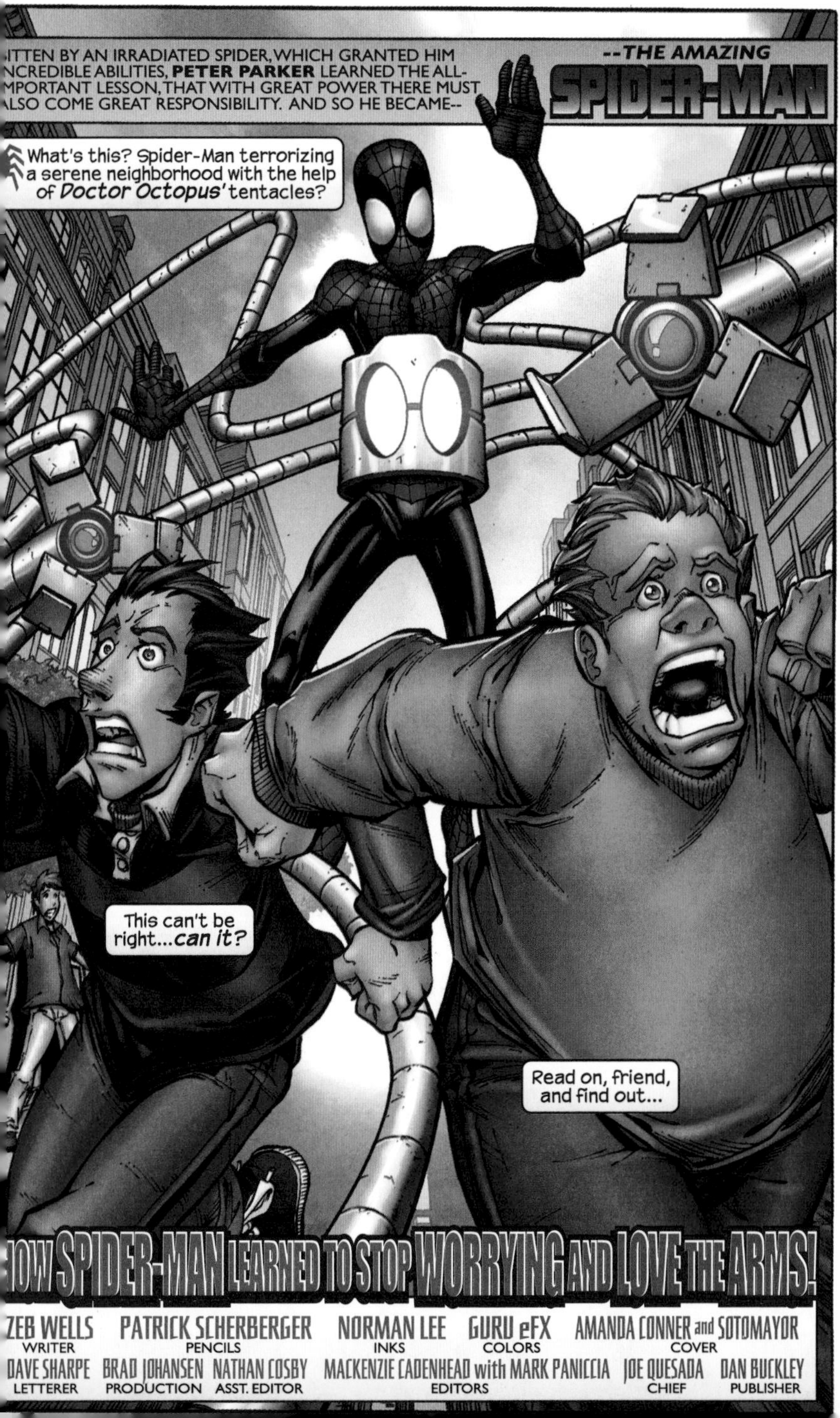
ITTEN BY AN IRRADIATED SPIDER, WHICH GRANTED HIM NCREDIBLE ABILITIES, **PETER PARKER** LEARNED THE ALL-MPORTANT LESSON, THAT WITH GREAT POWER THERE MUST LSO COME GREAT RESPONSIBILITY. AND SO HE BECAME--
--THE AMAZING SPIDER-MAN
What's this? Spider-Man terrorizing a serene neighborhood with the help of *Doctor Octopus'* tentacles?
This can't be right...*can it?*
Read on, friend, and find out...
OW SPIDER-MAN LEARNED TO STOP WORRYING AND LOVE THE ARMS!
ZEB WELLS WRITER
PATRICK SCHERBERGER PENCILS
NORMAN LEE INKS
GURU eFX COLORS
AMANDA CONNER and SOTOMAYOR COVER
DAVE SHARPE LETTERER
BRAD JOHANSEN PRODUCTION
NATHAN COSBY ASST. EDITOR
MACKENZIE CADENHEAD with MARK PANICCIA EDITORS
JOE QUESADA CHIEF
DAN BUCKLEY PUBLISHER

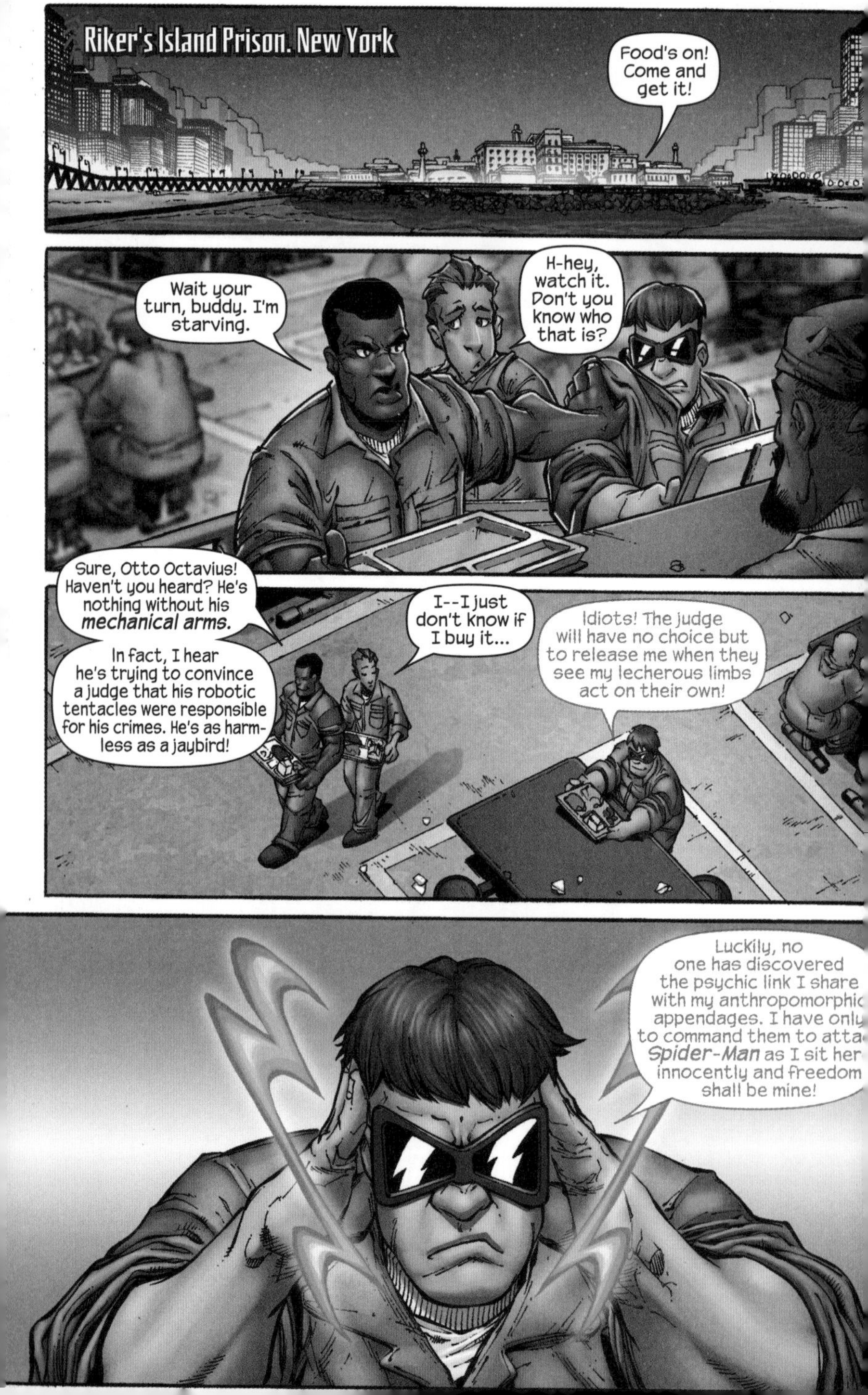
Riker's Island Prison. New York
Food's on! Come and get it!
Wait your turn, buddy. I'm starving.
H-hey, watch it. Don't you know who that is?
Sure, Otto Octavius! Haven't you heard? He's nothing without his *mechanical arms.*
In fact, I hear he's trying to convince a judge that his robotic tentacles were responsible for his crimes. He's as harmless as a jaybird!
I--I just don't know if I buy it...
Idiots! The judge will have no choice but to release me when they see my lecherous limbs act on their own!
Luckily, no one has discovered the psychic link I share with my anthropomorphic appendages. I have only to command them to atta *Spider-Man* as I sit her innocently and freedom shall be mine!

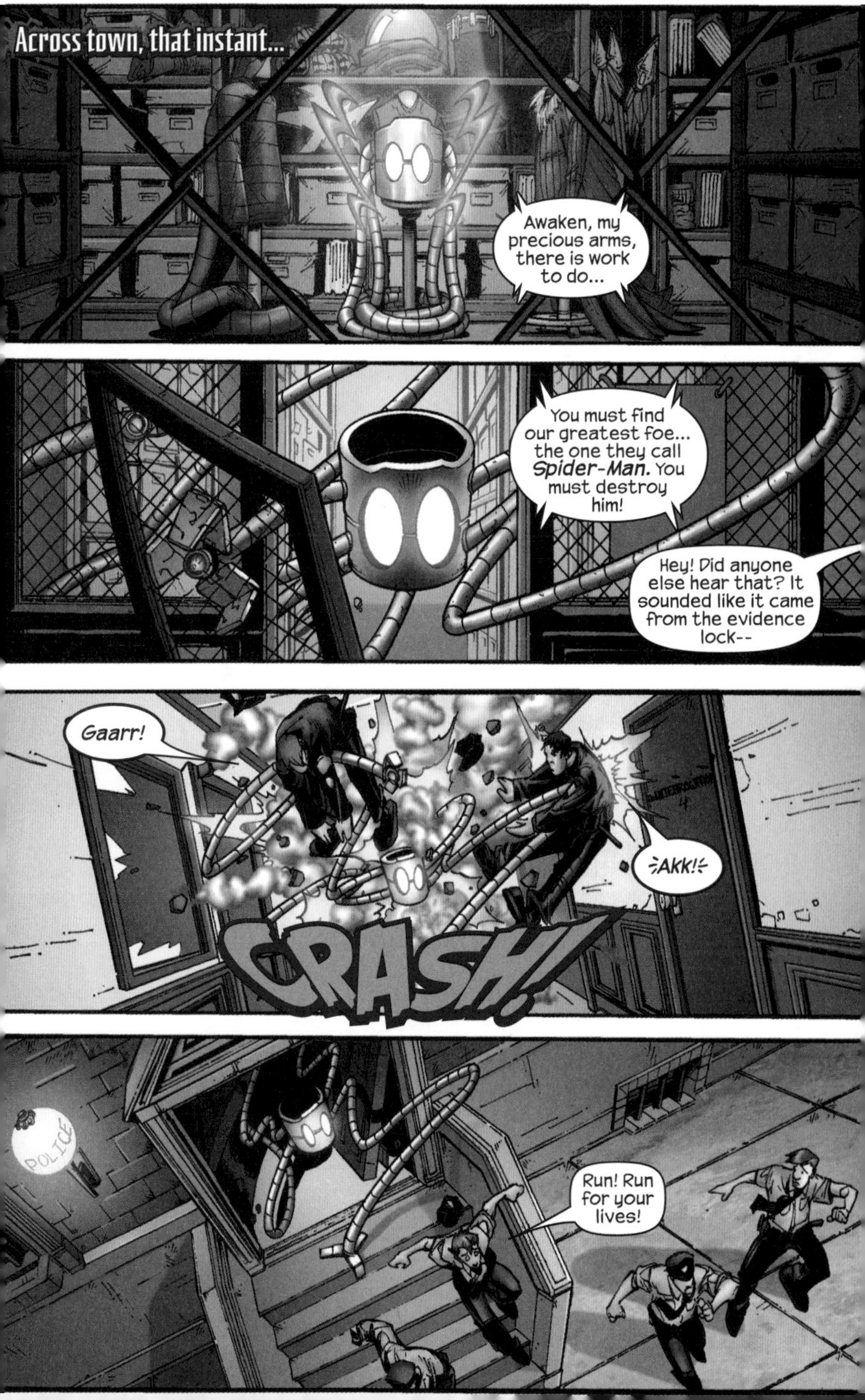
Across town, that instant...
Awaken, my precious arms, there is work to do...
You must find our greatest foe... the one they call Spider-Man. You must destroy him!
Hey! Did anyone else hear that? It sounded like it came from the evidence lock--
Gaarr!
Akk!
CRASH!
POLICE
Run! Run for your lives!

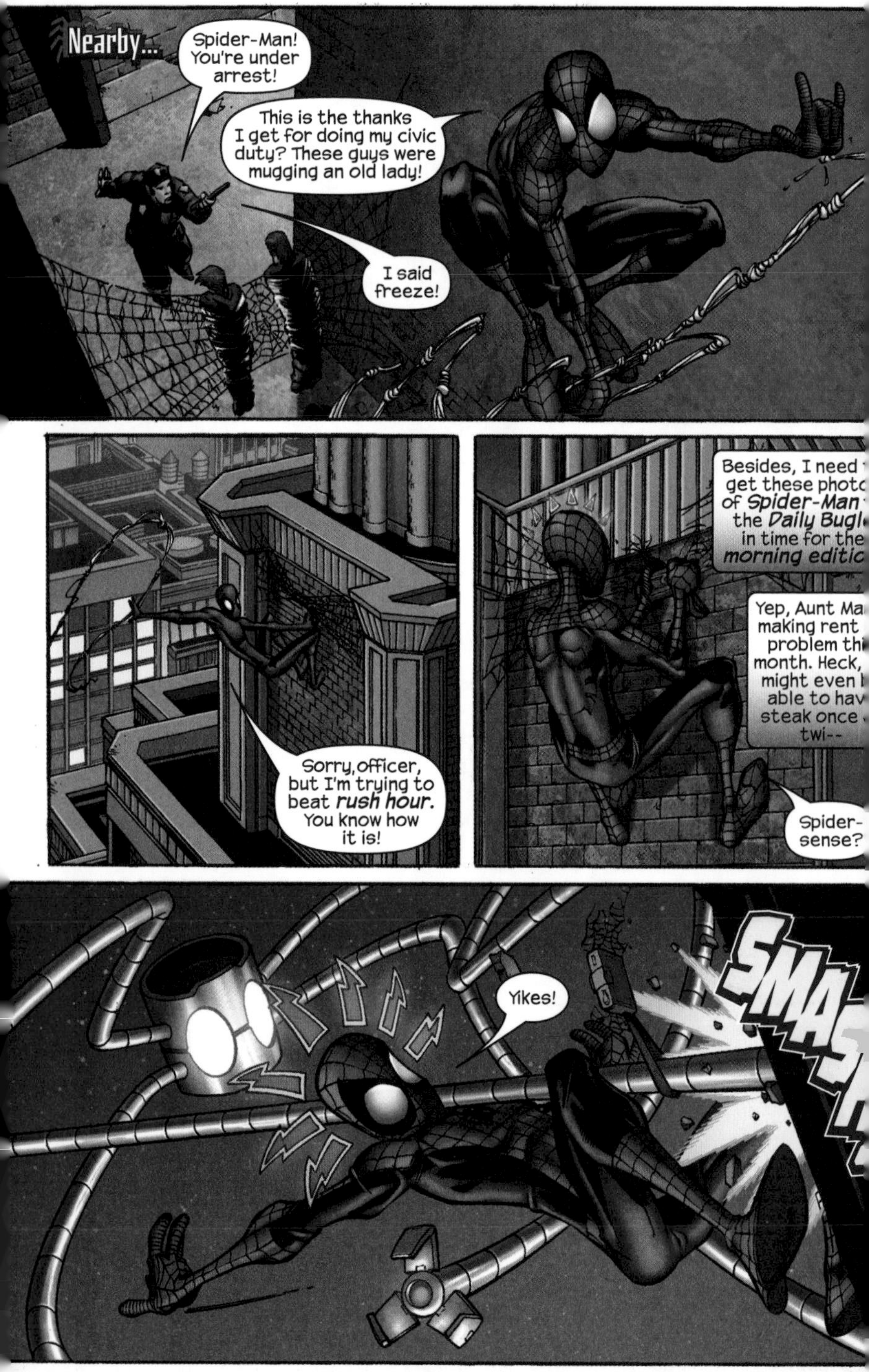

Nearby...
Spider-Man! You're under arrest!
This is the thanks I get for doing my civic duty? These guys were mugging an old lady!
I said freeze!
Sorry, officer, but I'm trying to beat *rush hour.* You know how it is!
Besides, I need get these photo of *Spider-Man* the *Daily Bugl* in time for the *morning editic*
Yep, Aunt Ma making rent problem thi month. Heck, might even able to hav steak once twi--
Spider-sense?
Yikes!
SMAS

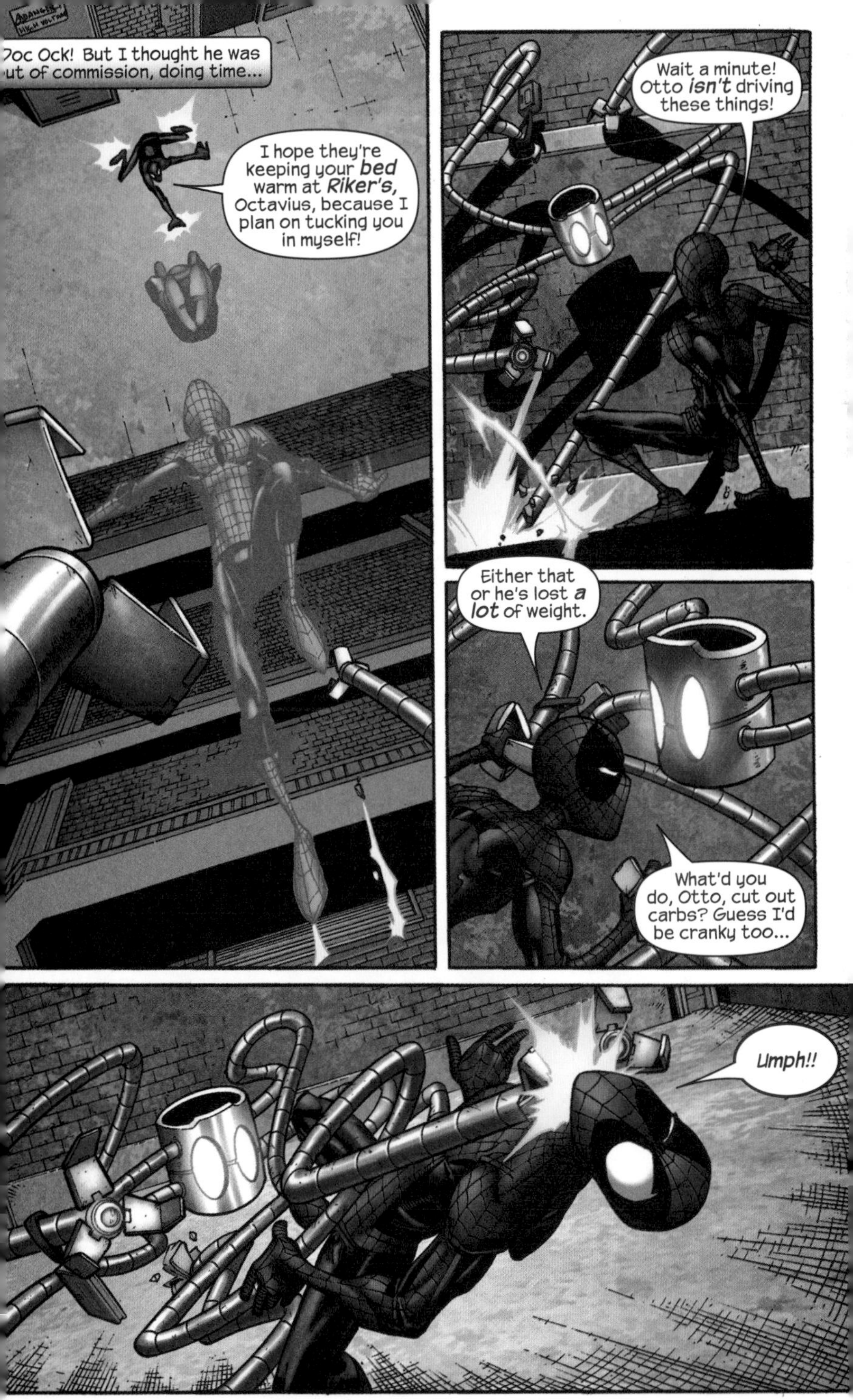
oc Ock! But I thought he was ut of commission, doing time...
I hope they're keeping your bed warm at Riker's, Octavius, because I plan on tucking you in myself!
Wait a minute! Otto isn't driving these things!
Either that or he's lost a lot of weight.
What'd you do, Otto, cut out carbs? Guess I'd be cranky too...
Umph!!

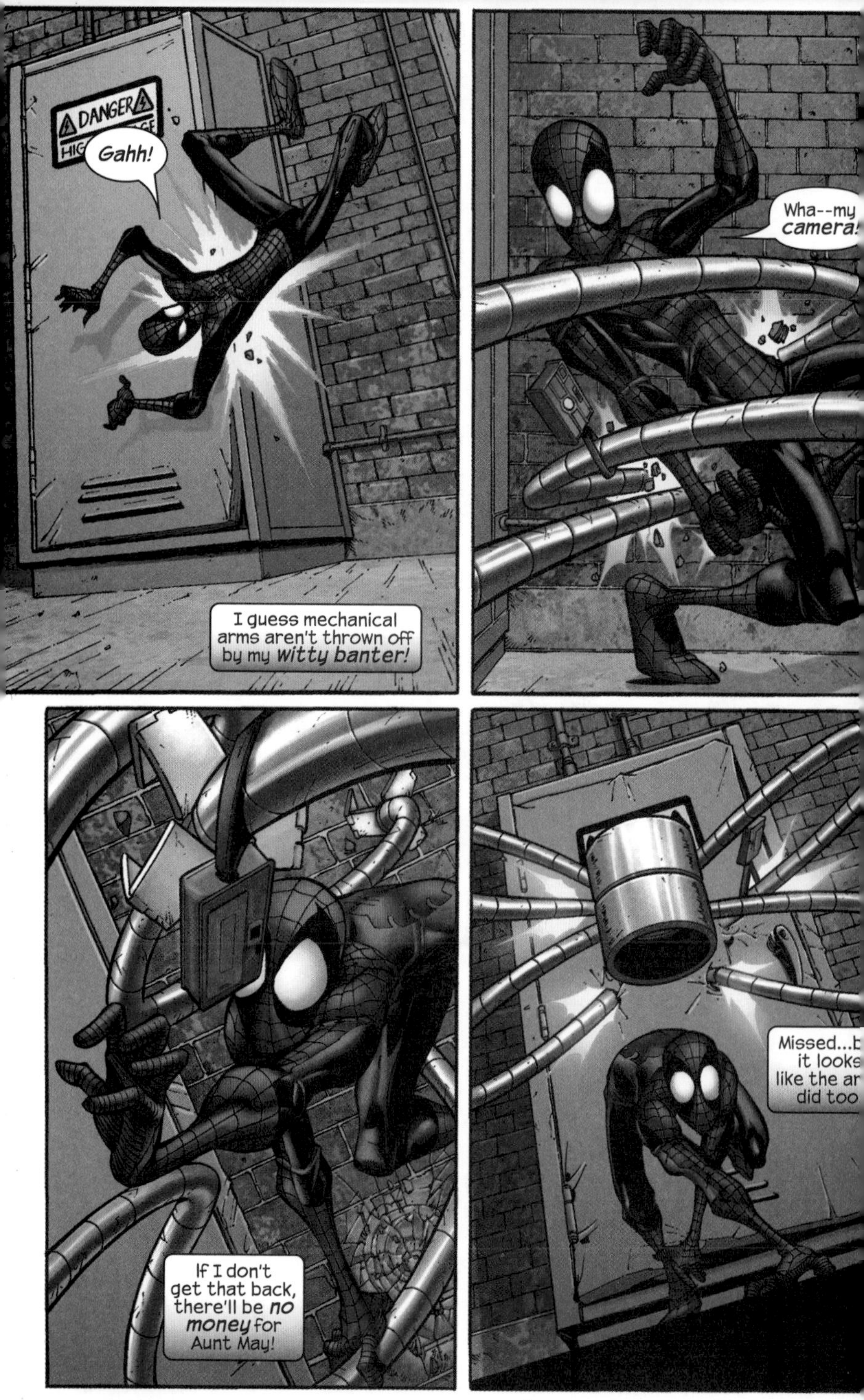
DANGER
Gahh!
I guess mechanical arms aren't thrown off by my witty banter!
Wha--my camera!
If I don't get that back, there'll be no money for Aunt May!
Missed...
it looks
like the
did too

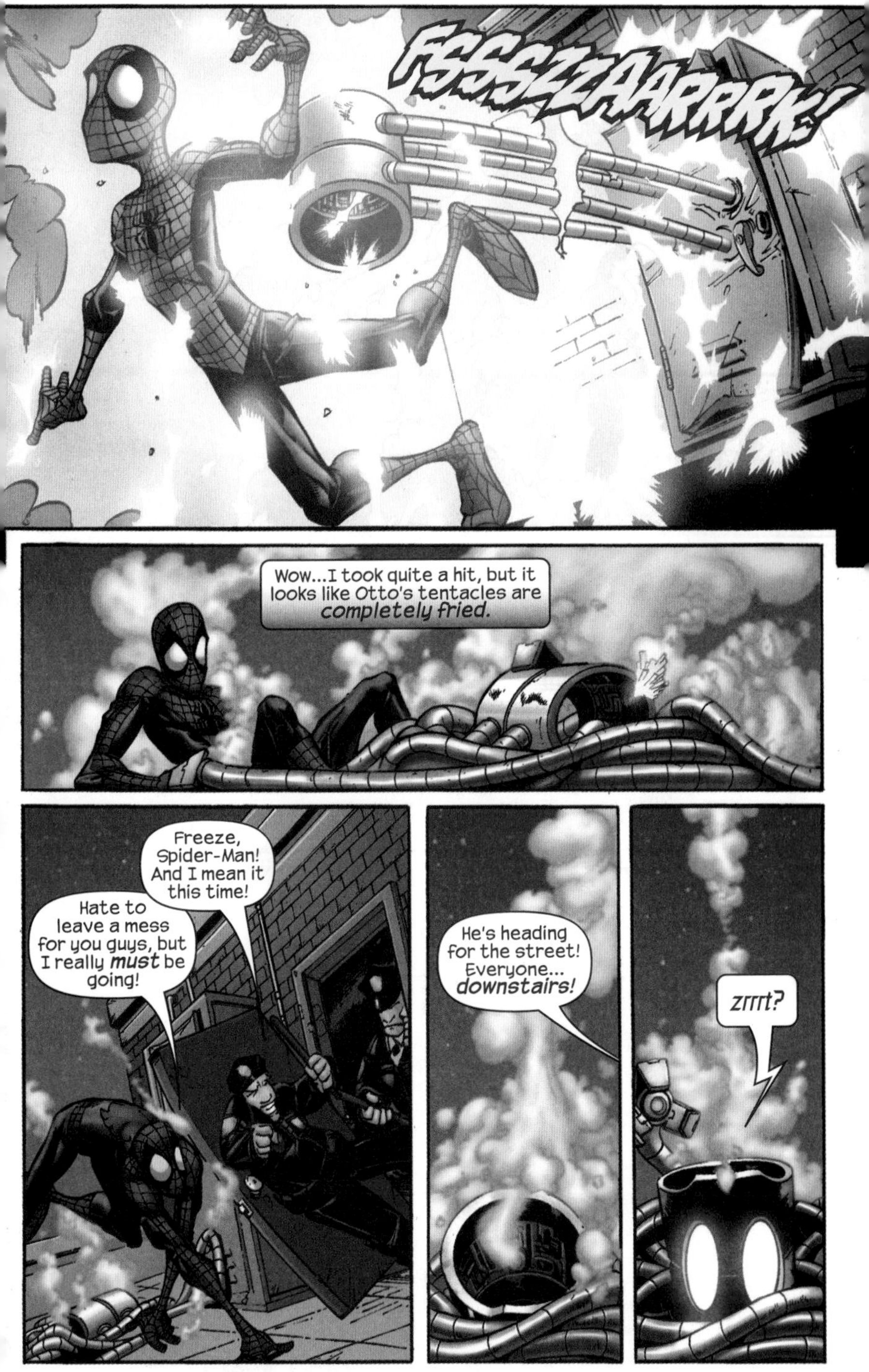
FSSSZZAARRRRK!
Wow...I took quite a hit, but it looks like Otto's tentacles are *completely fried.*
Freeze, Spider-Man! And I mean it this time!
Hate to leave a mess for you guys, but I really ***must*** be going!
He's heading for the street! Everyone... ***downstairs!***
zrrrt?

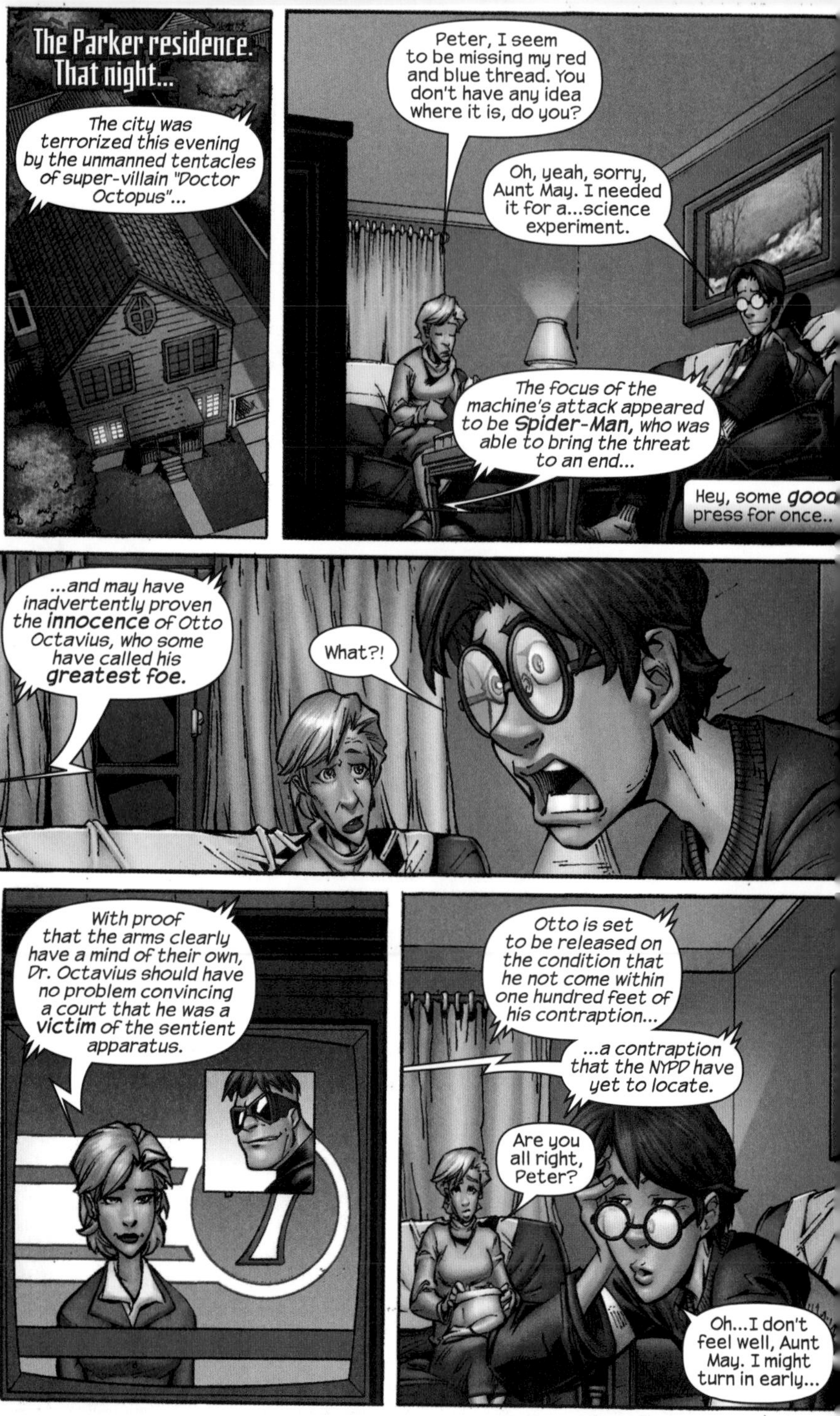

The Parker residence. That night...
The city was terrorized this evening by the unmanned tentacles of super-villain "Doctor Octopus"...
Peter, I seem to be missing my red and blue thread. You don't have any idea where it is, do you?
Oh, yeah, sorry, Aunt May. I needed it for a...science experiment.
The focus of the machine's attack appeared to be Spider-Man, who was able to bring the threat to an end...
Hey, some good press for once..
...and may have inadvertently proven the innocence of Otto Octavius, who some have called his greatest foe.
What?!
With proof that the arms clearly have a mind of their own, Dr. Octavius should have no problem convincing a court that he was a victim of the sentient apparatus.
Otto is set to be released on the condition that he not come within one hundred feet of his contraption...
...a contraption that the NYPD have yet to locate.
Are you all right, Peter?
Oh...I don't feel well, Aunt May. I might turn in early...

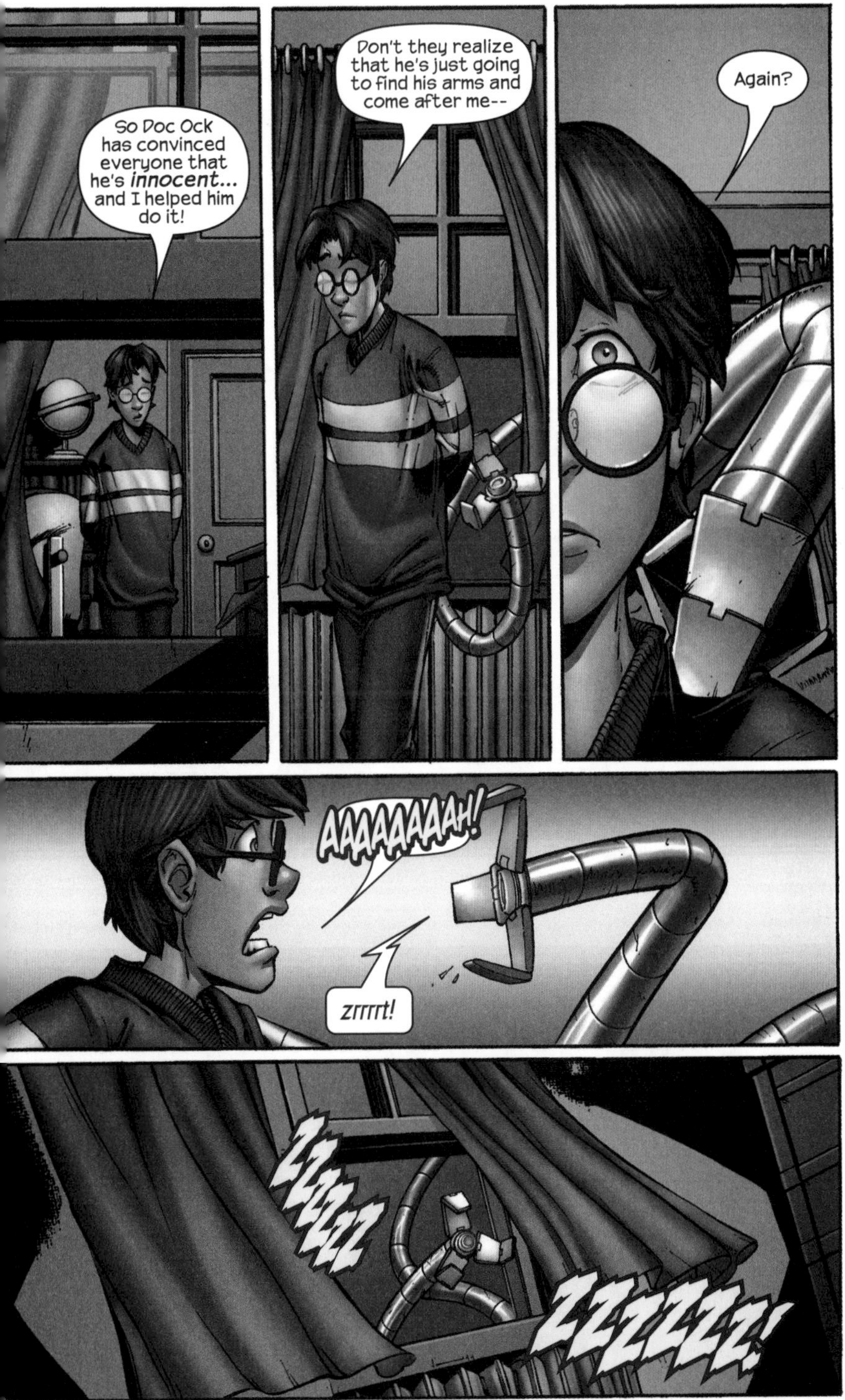
So Doc Ock has convinced everyone that he's *innocent...* and I helped him do it!
Don't they realize that he's just going to find his arms and come after me--
Again?
AAAAAAAAH!
zrrrrt!
ZZZZZ
ZZZZZZ!

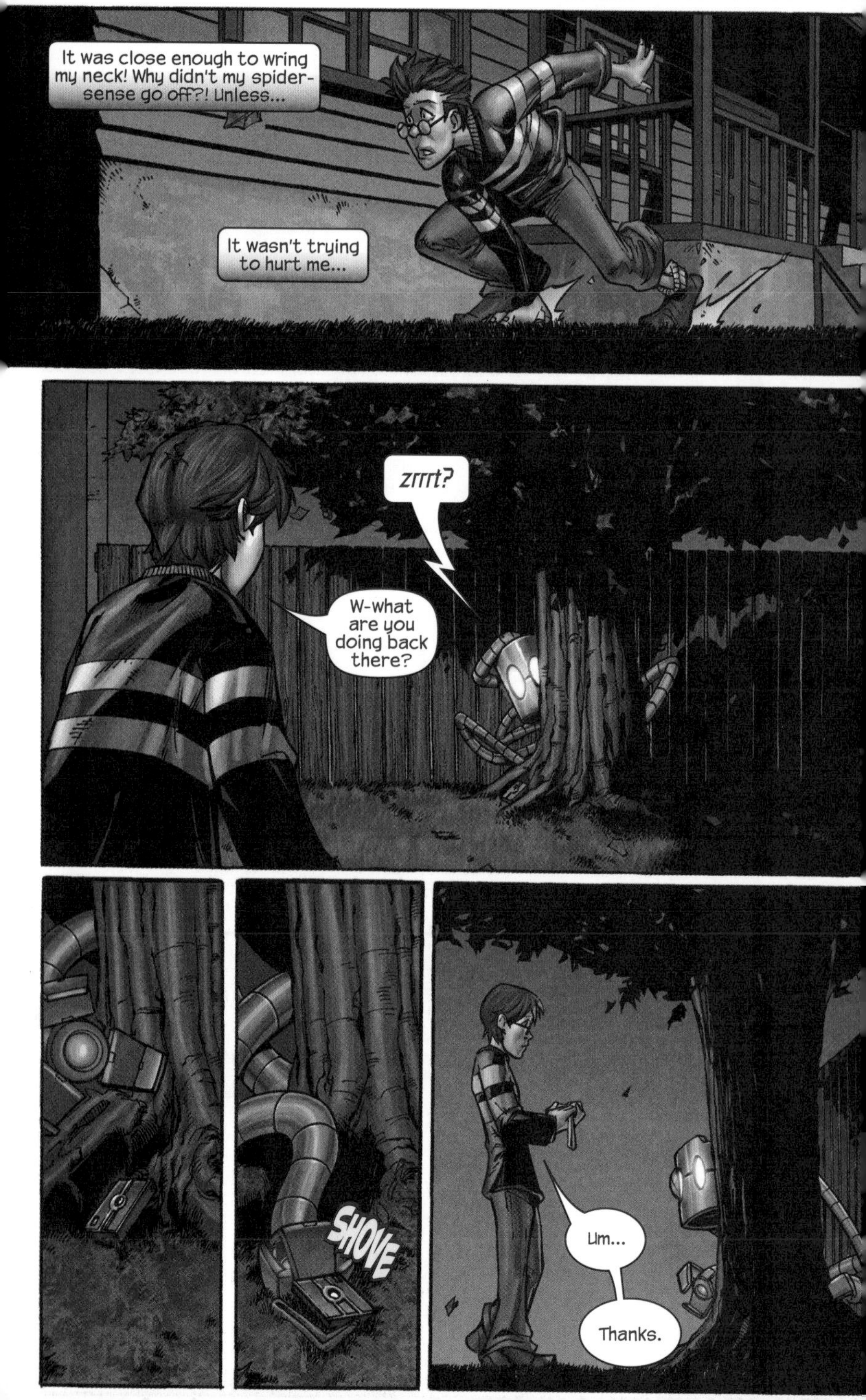

It was close enough to wring my neck! Why didn't my spider-sense go off?! Unless...
It wasn't trying to hurt me...
zrrrt?
W-what are you doing back there?
SHOVE
Um...
Thanks.

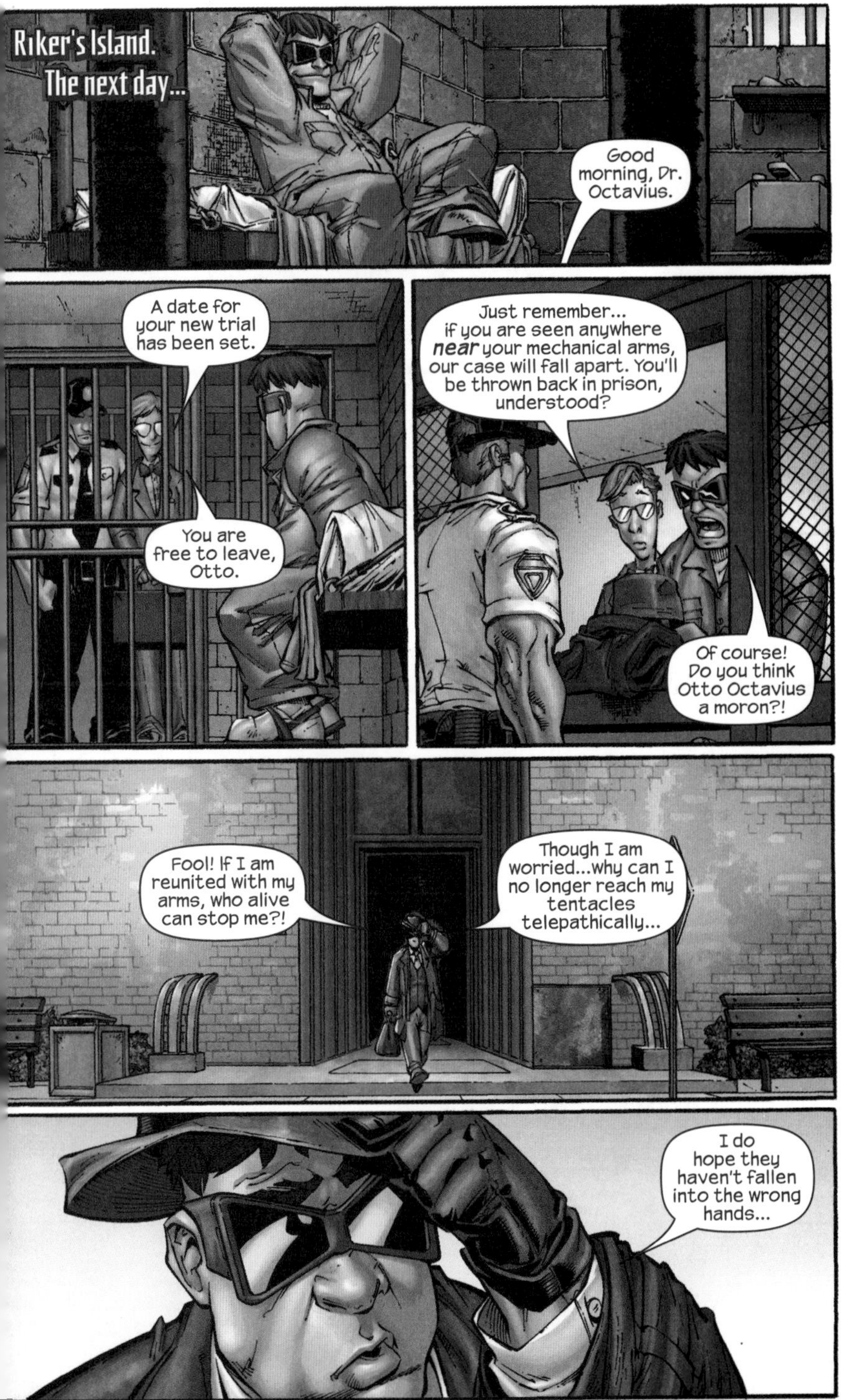
Riker's Island. The next day...
Good morning, Dr. Octavius.
A date for your new trial has been set.
You are free to leave, Otto.
Just remember... if you are seen anywhere **near** your mechanical arms, our case will fall apart. You'll be thrown back in prison, understood?
Of course! Do you think Otto Octavius a moron?!
Fool! If I am reunited with my arms, who alive can stop me?!
Though I am worried...why can I no longer reach my tentacles telepathically...
I do hope they haven't fallen into the wrong hands...

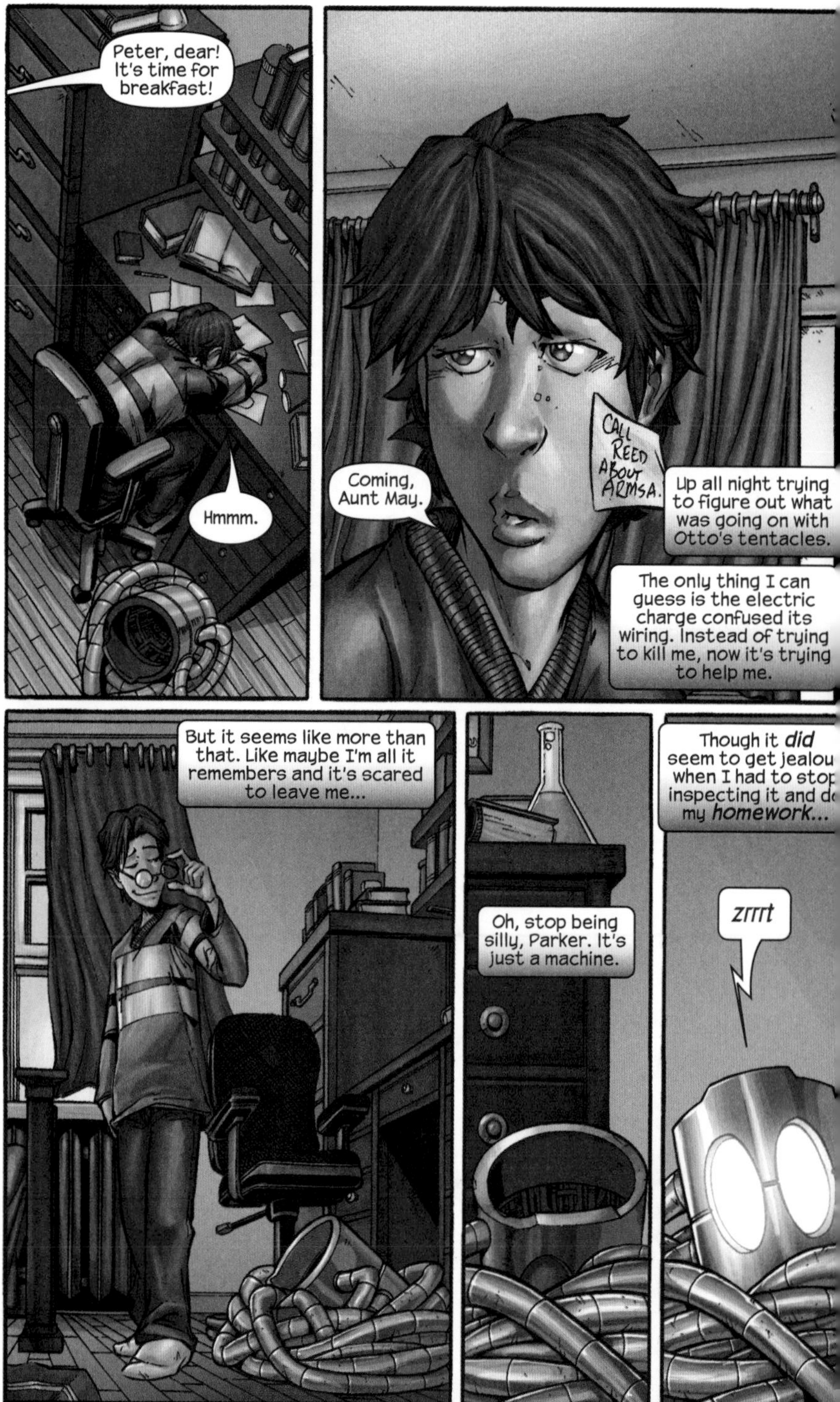
Peter, dear! It's time for breakfast!
Hmmm.
CALL REED ABOUT ARMSA.
Coming, Aunt May.
Up all night trying to figure out what was going on with Otto's tentacles.
The only thing I can guess is the electric charge confused its wiring. Instead of trying to kill me, now it's trying to help me.
But it seems like more than that. Like maybe I'm all it remembers and it's scared to leave me...
Oh, stop being silly, Parker. It's just a machine.
Though it *did* seem to get jealou when I had to stop inspecting it and d my *homework*...
zrrrt

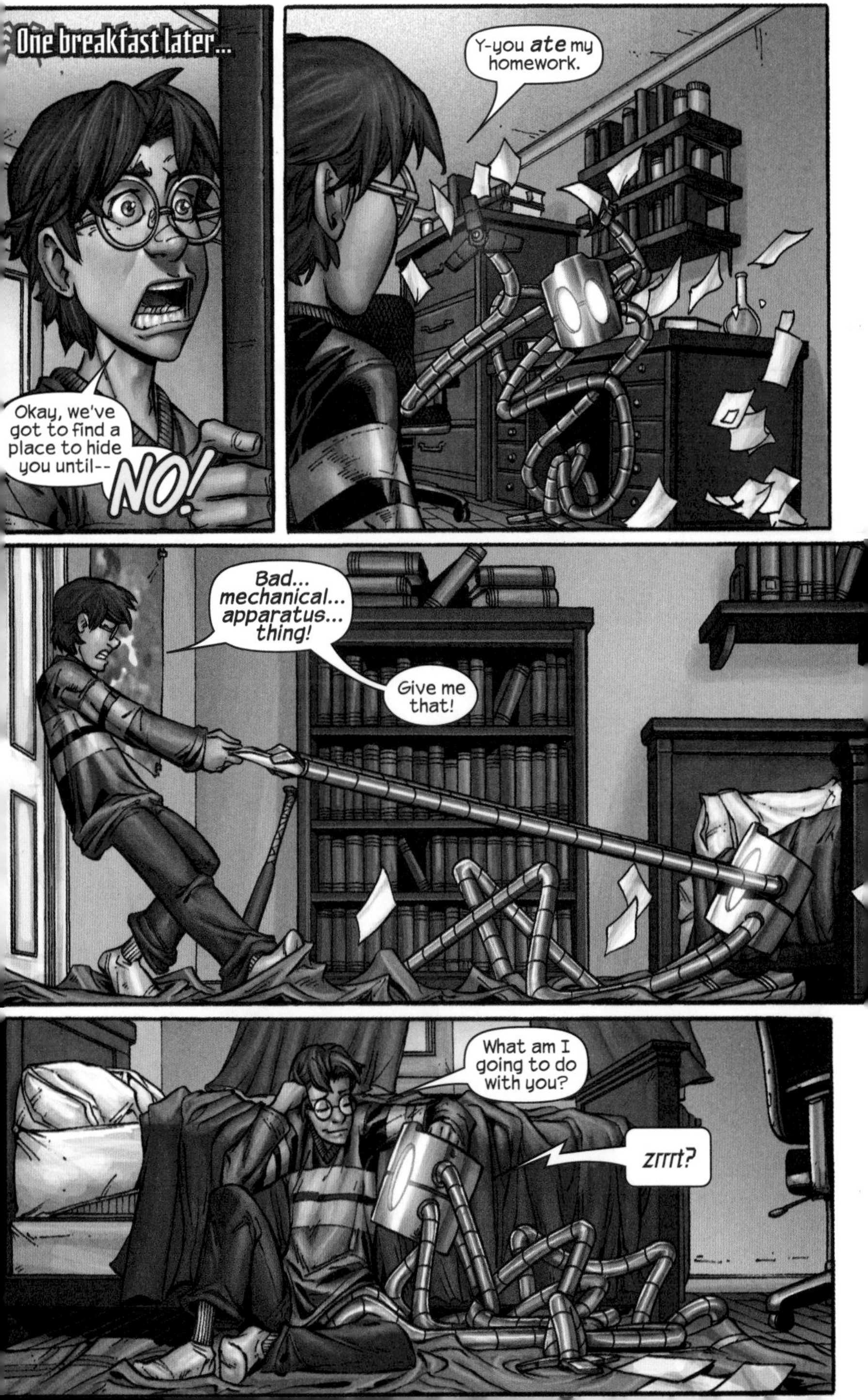
One breakfast later...
Okay, we've got to find a place to hide you until--
NO!
Y-you ate my homework.
Bad... mechanical... apparatus... thing!
Give me that!
What am I going to do with you?
zrrrt?

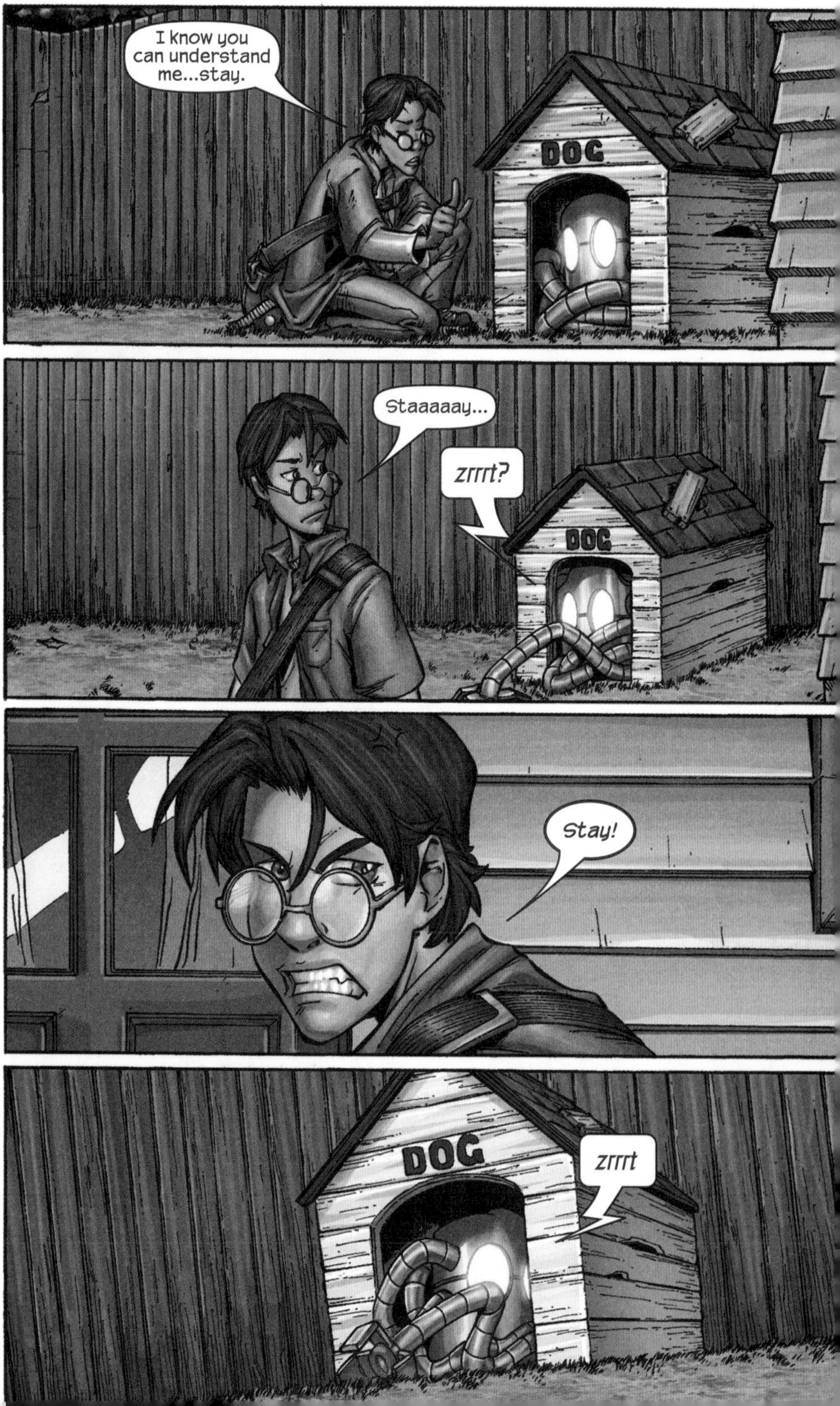
I know you can understand me...stay.
DOG
Staaaaay...
zrrrt?
DOG
Stay!
DOG
zrrrt

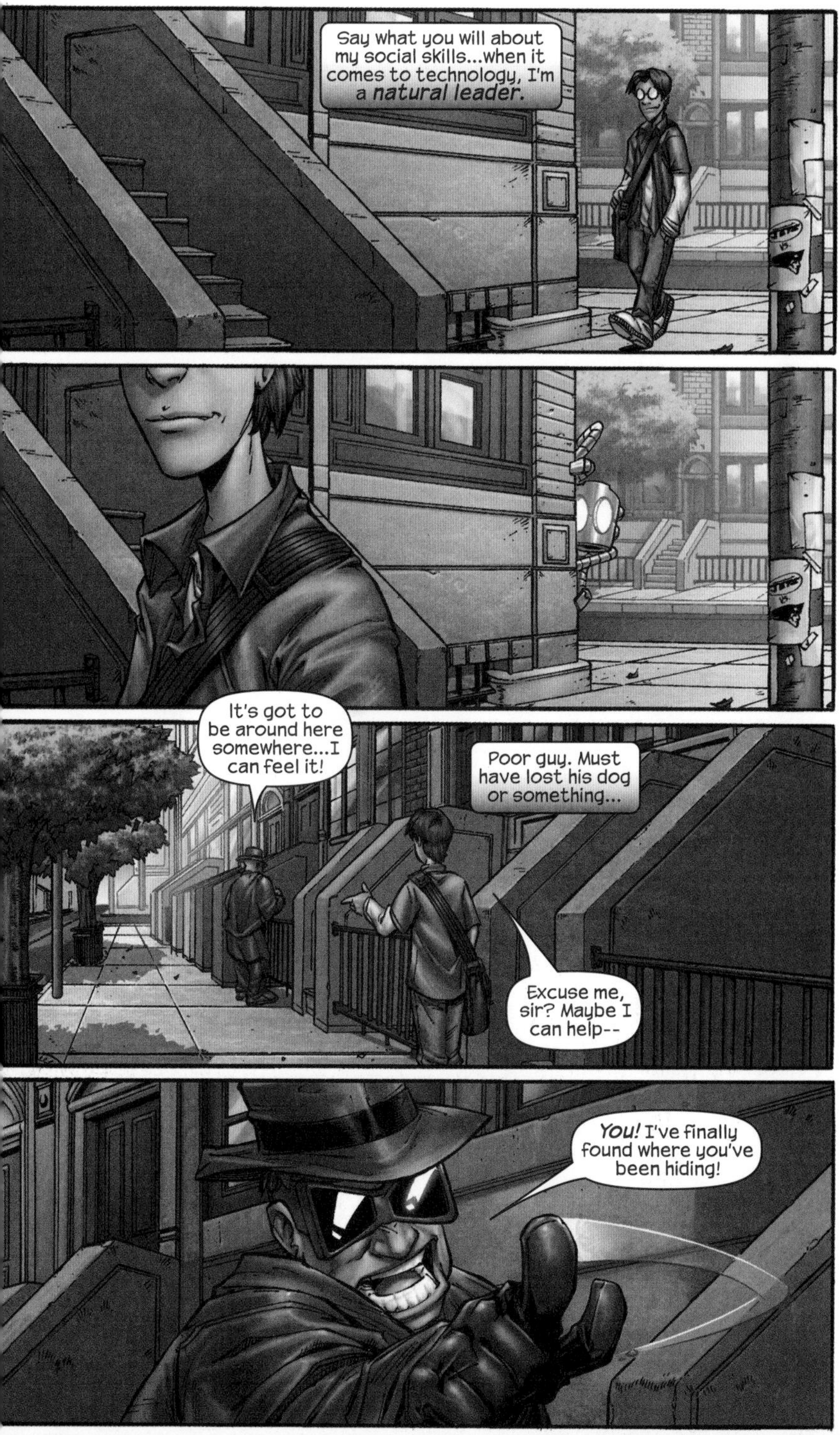

Say what you will about my social skills...when it comes to technology, I'm a *natural leader.*
It's got to be around here somewhere...I can feel it!
Poor guy. Must have lost his dog or something...
Excuse me, sir? Maybe I can help--
YOU! I've finally found where you've been hiding!

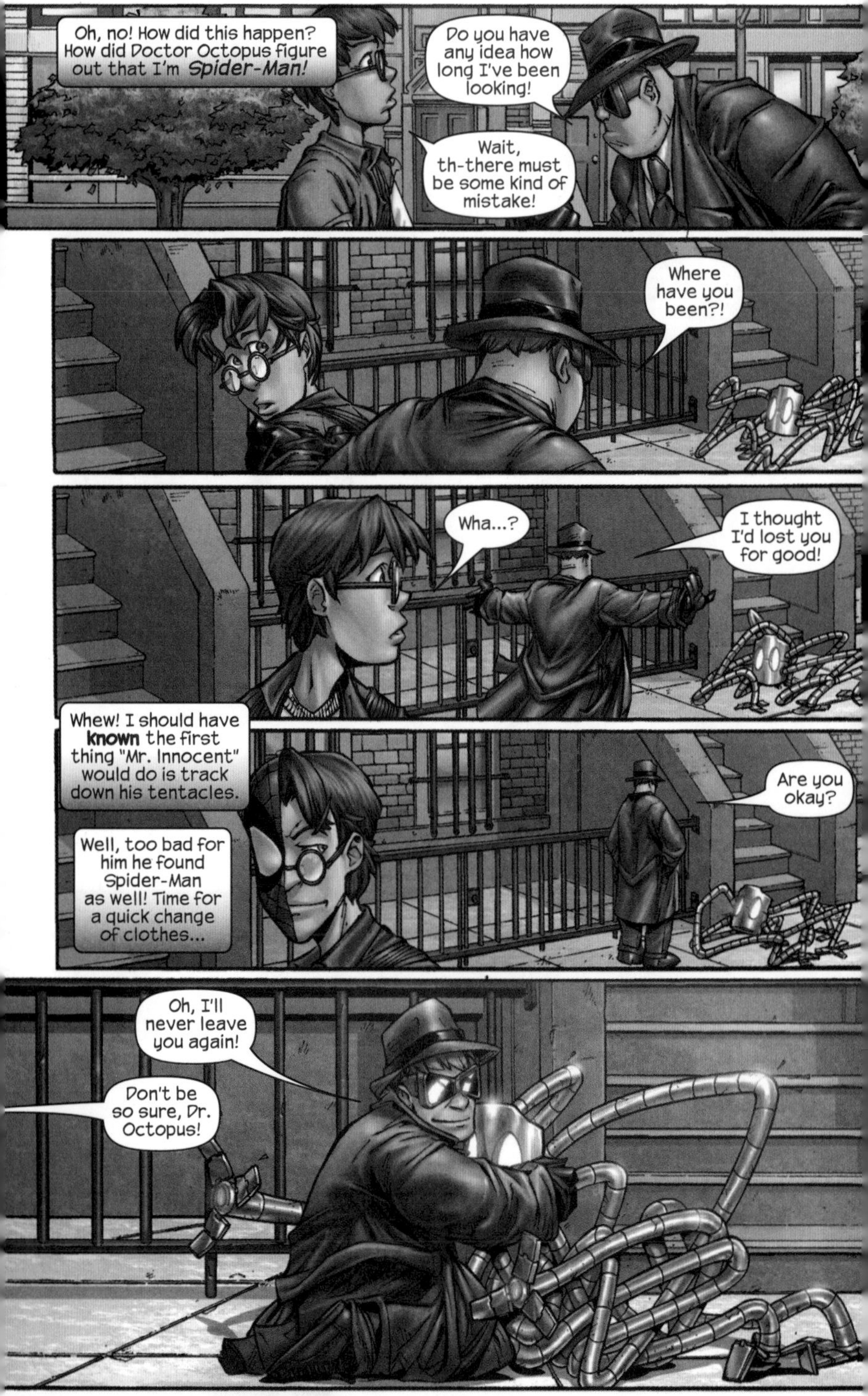

Oh, no! How did this happen? How did Doctor Octopus figure out that I'm Spider-Man!
Do you have any idea how long I've been looking!
Wait, th-there must be some kind of mistake!
Where have you been?!
Wha...?
I thought I'd lost you for good!
Whew! I should have known the first thing "Mr. Innocent" would do is track down his tentacles.
Well, too bad for him he found Spider-Man as well! Time for a quick change of clothes...
Are you okay?
Oh, I'll never leave you again!
Don't be so sure, Dr. Octopus!

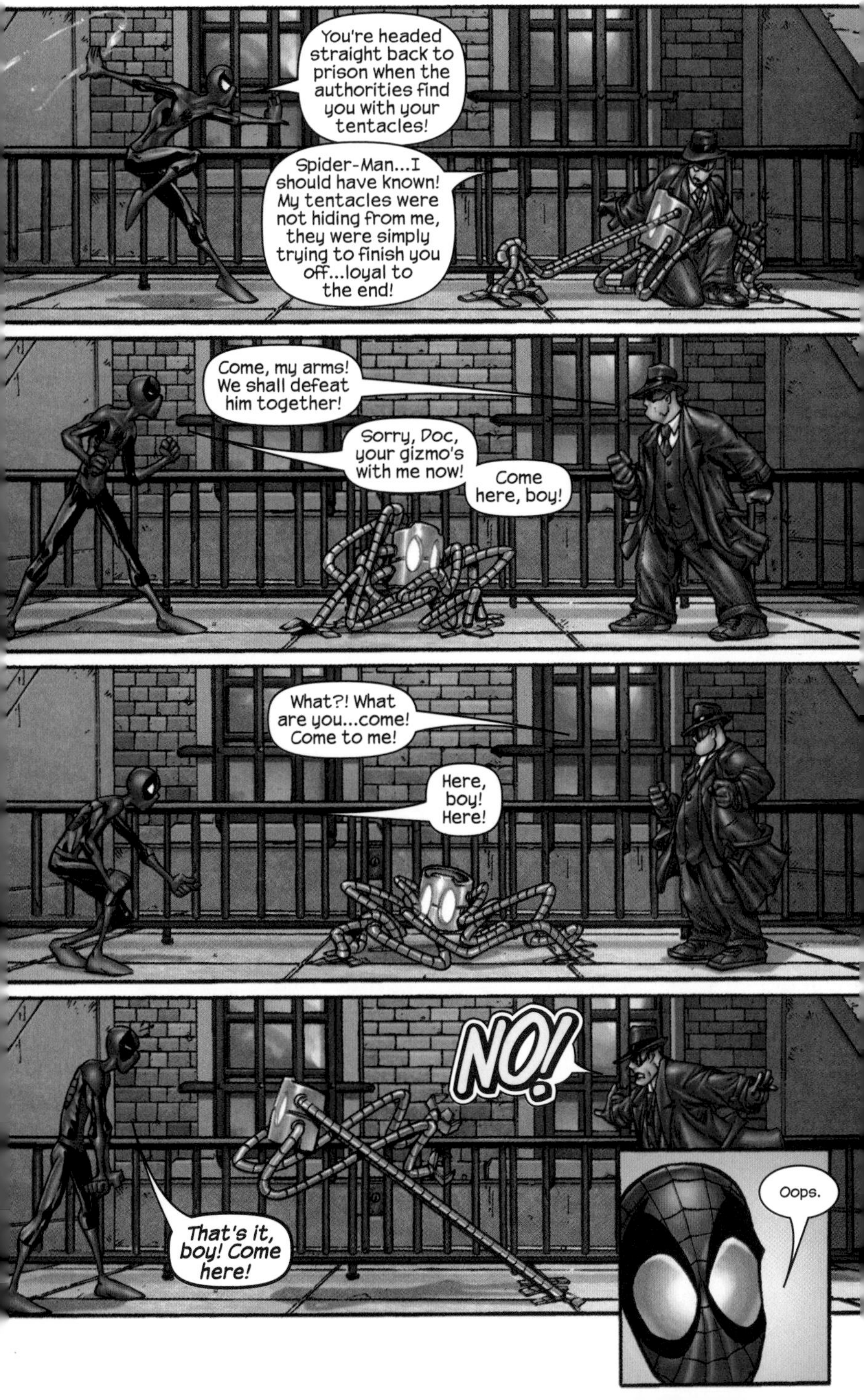
You're headed straight back to prison when the authorities find you with your tentacles!
Spider-Man...I should have known! My tentacles were not hiding from me, they were simply trying to finish you off...loyal to the end!
Come, my arms! We shall defeat him together!
Sorry, Doc, your gizmo's with me now!
Come here, boy!
What?! What are you...come! Come to me!
Here, boy! Here!
NO!
That's it, boy! Come here!
Oops.

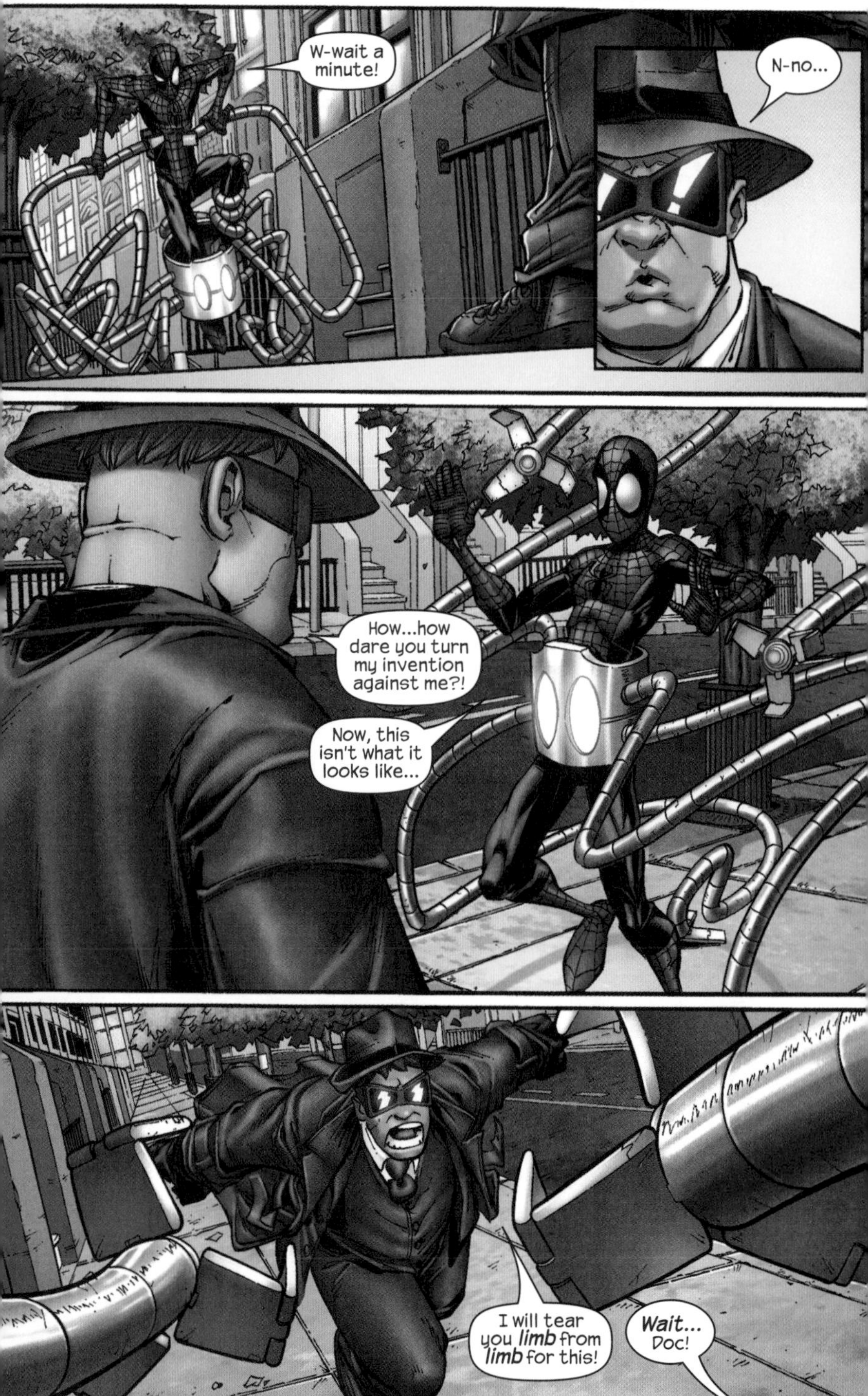

W-wait a minute!
N-no...
How...how dare you turn my invention against me?!
Now, this isn't what it looks like...
I will tear you *limb* from *limb* for this!
Wait... Doc!

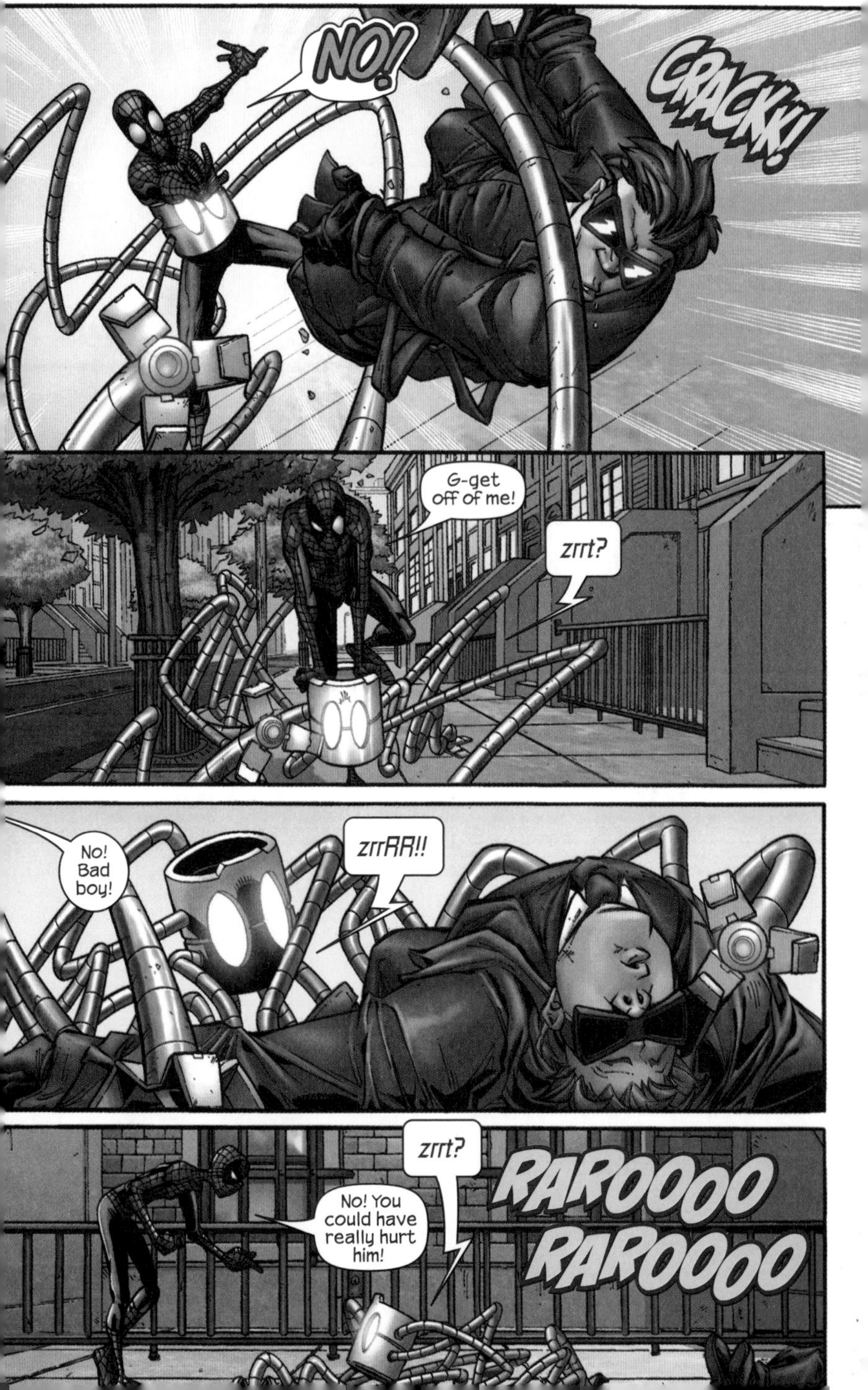

NO!
CRACK!
G-get off of me!
zrrt?
No! Bad boy!
zrrRR!!
zrrt?
No! You could have really hurt him!
RAROOOO
RAROOOO

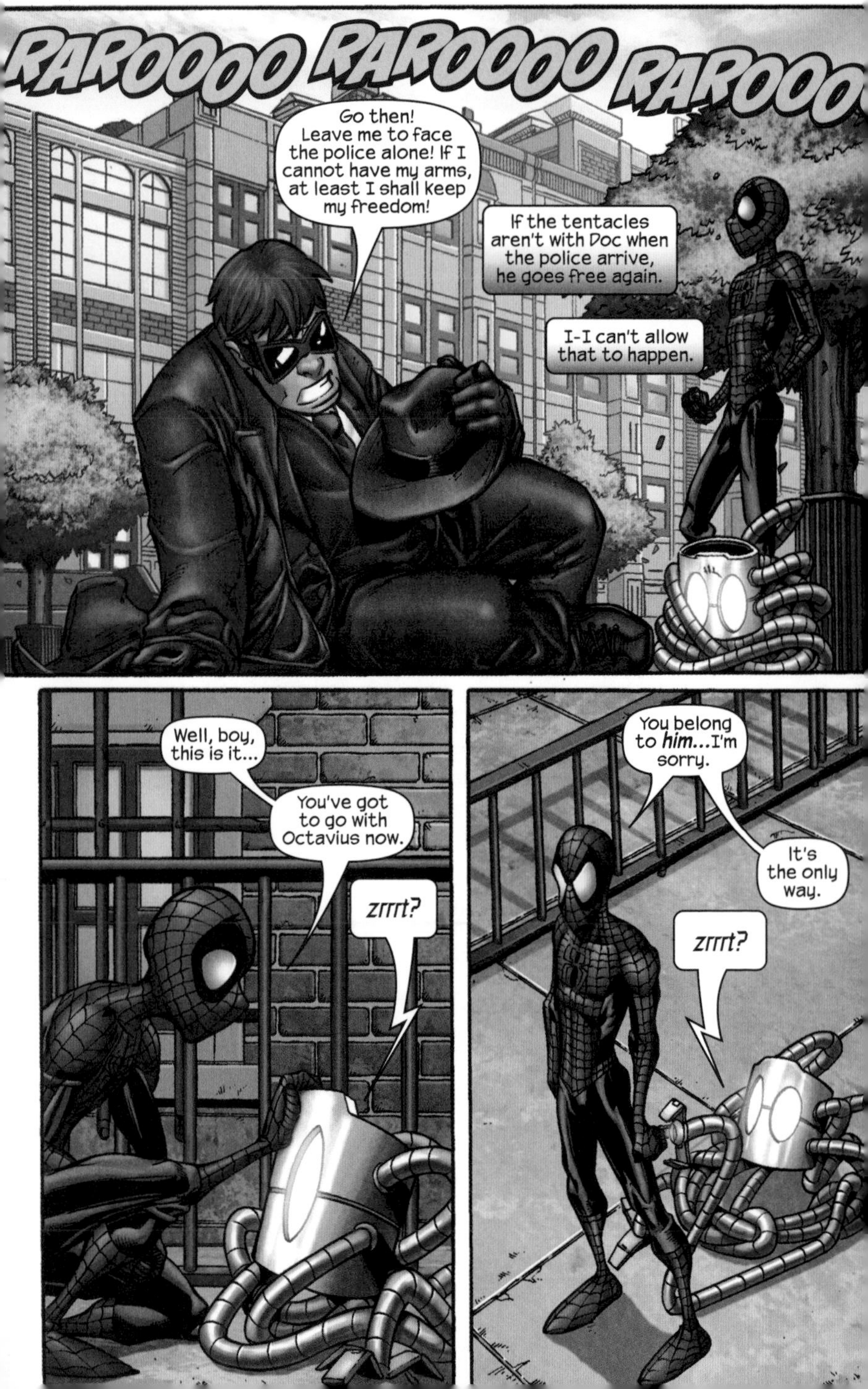
RAROOOO RAROOOOO RAROOO
Go then! Leave me to face the police alone! If I cannot have my arms, at least I shall keep my freedom!
If the tentacles aren't with Doc when the police arrive, he goes free again.
I-I can't allow that to happen.
Well, boy, this is it...
You've got to go with Octavius now.
zrrrt?
You belong to *him*...I'm sorry.
It's the only way.
zrrrt?

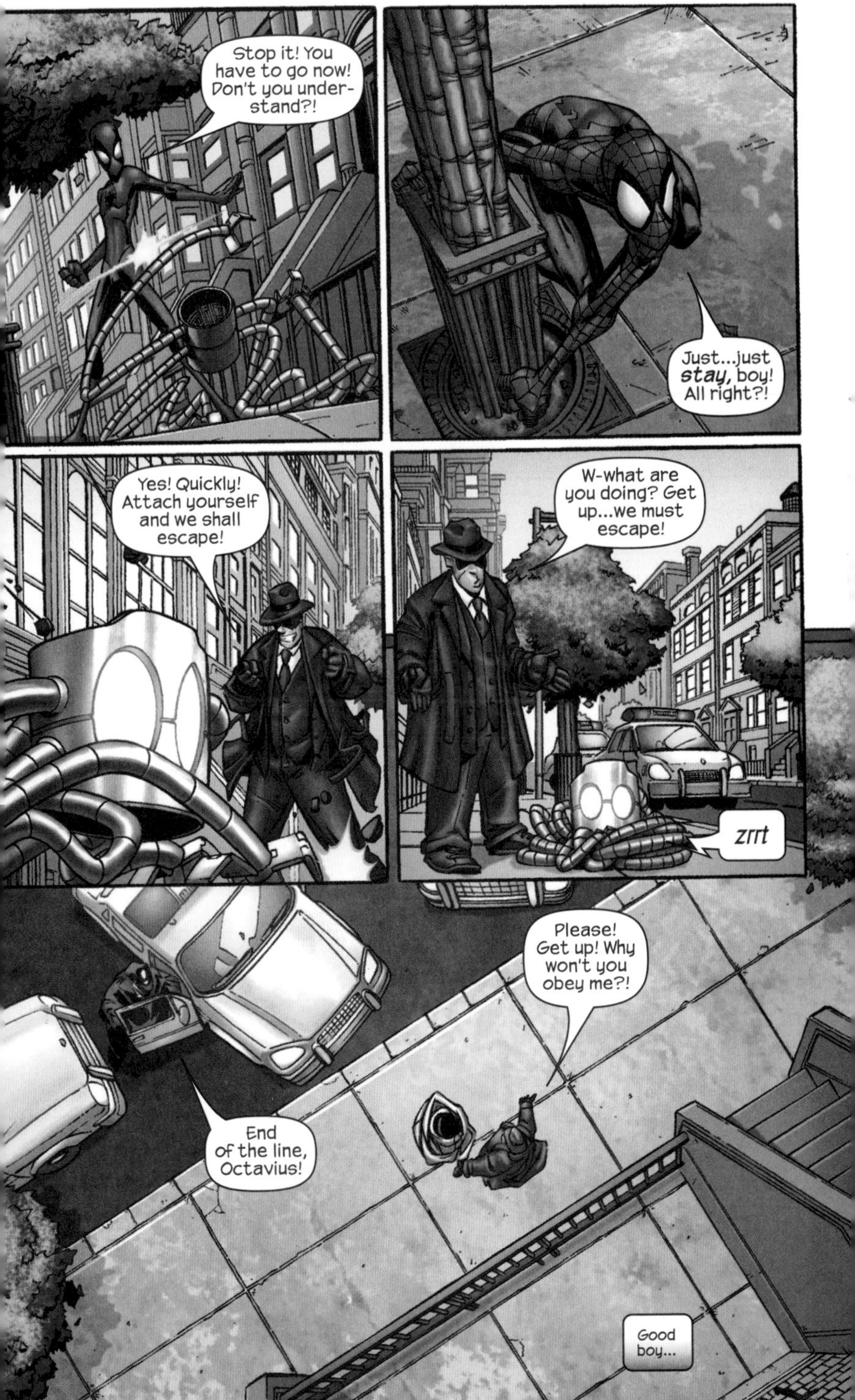
Stop it! You have to go now! Don't you under-stand?!
Just...just *stay,* boy! All right?!
Yes! Quickly! Attach yourself and we shall escape!
W-what are you doing? Get up...we must escape!
zrrt
Please! Get up! Why won't you obey me?!
End of the line, Octavius!
Good boy...

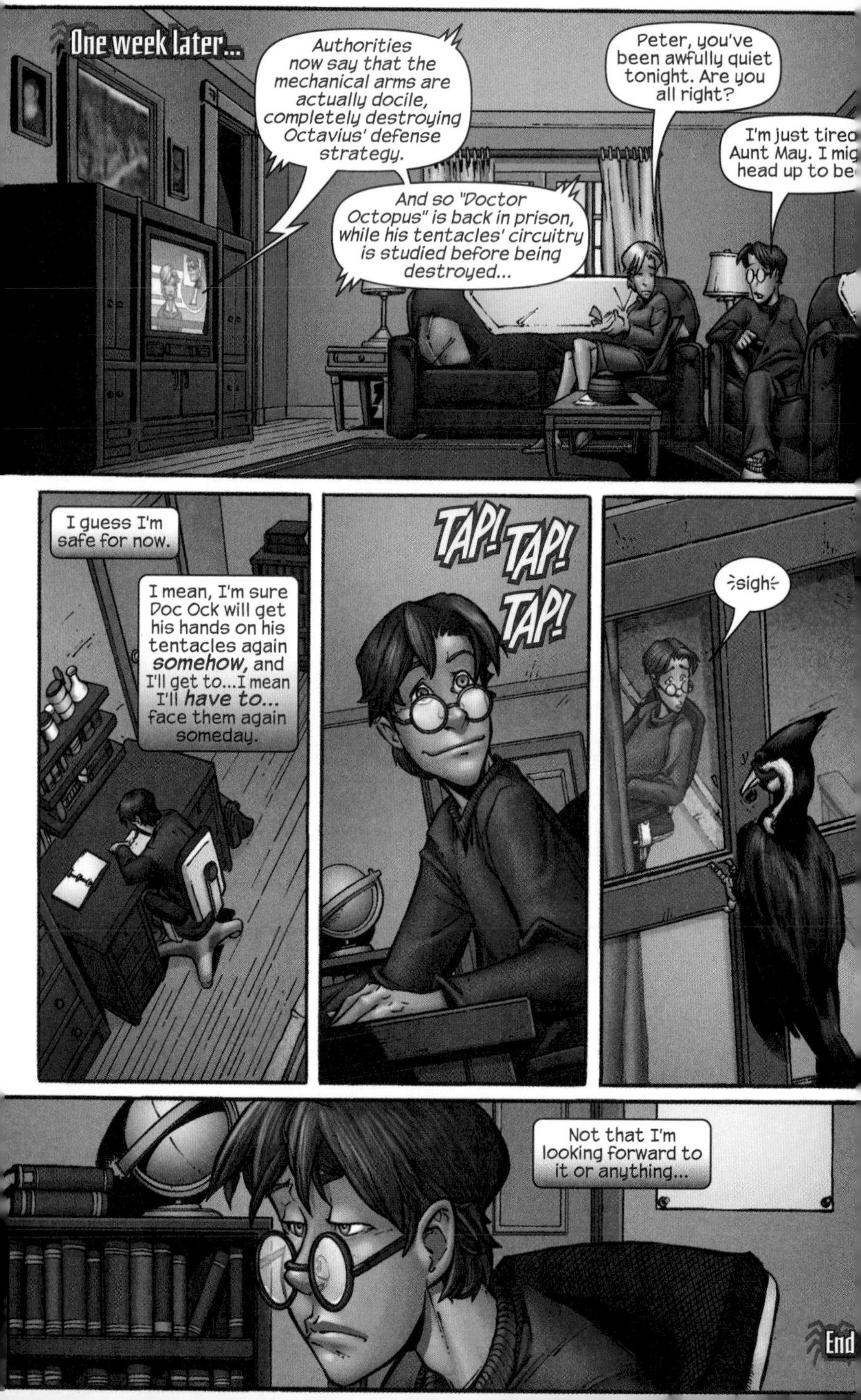

One week later...
Authorities now say that the mechanical arms are actually docile, completely destroying Octavius' defense strategy.
And so "Doctor Octopus" is back in prison, while his tentacles' circuitry is studied before being destroyed...
Peter, you've been awfully quiet tonight. Are you all right?
I'm just tired Aunt May. I mig head up to be
I guess I'm safe for now.
I mean, I'm sure Doc Ock will get his hands on his tentacles again somehow, and I'll get to...I mean I'll have to... face them again someday.
TAP! TAP! TAP!
sigh
Not that I'm looking forward to it or anything...
End

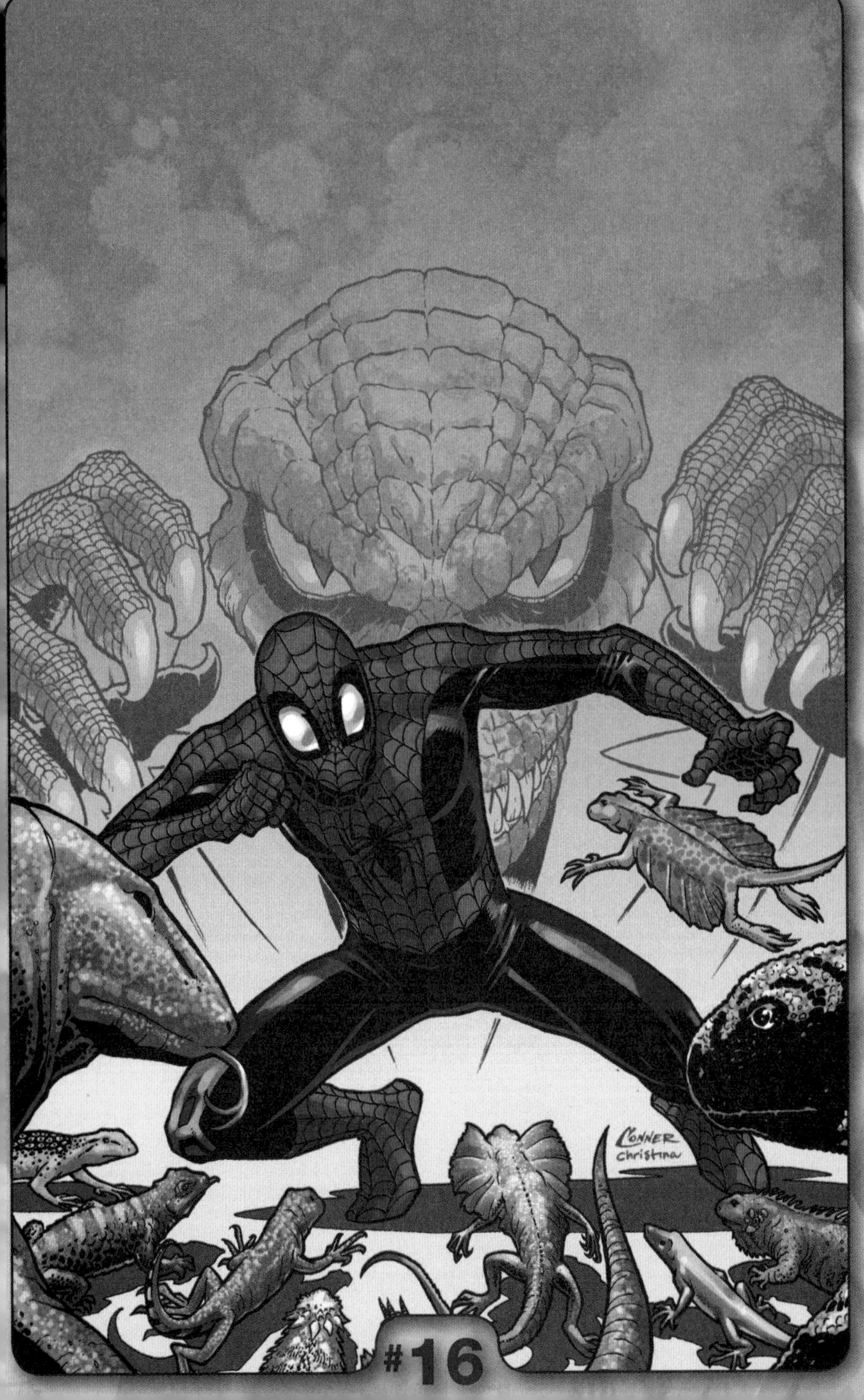
CONNER
Christina
#16

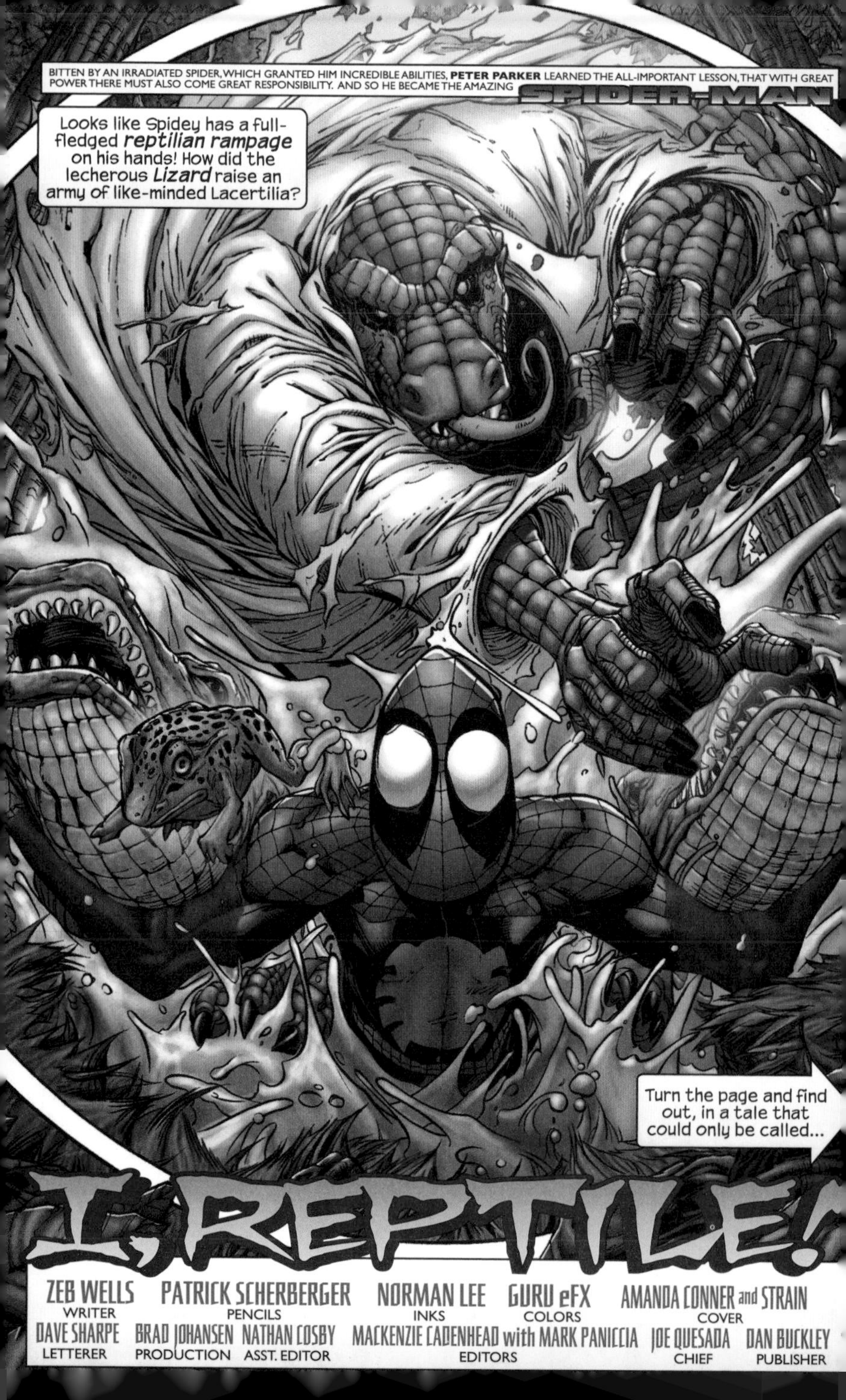
BITTEN BY AN IRRADIATED SPIDER, WHICH GRANTED HIM INCREDIBLE ABILITIES, PETER PARKER LEARNED THE ALL-IMPORTANT LESSON, THAT WITH GREAT POWER THERE MUST ALSO COME GREAT RESPONSIBILITY. AND SO HE BECAME THE AMAZING SPIDER-MAN
Looks like Spidey has a full-fledged reptilian rampage on his hands! How did the lecherous Lizard raise an army of like-minded Lacertilia?
Turn the page and find out, in a tale that could only be called...
I, REPTILE!
ZEB WELLS WRITER PATRICK SCHERBERGER PENCILS NORMAN LEE INKS GURU eFX COLORS AMANDA CONNER and STRAIN COVER
DAVE SHARPE LETTERER BRAD JOHANSEN PRODUCTION NATHAN COSBY ASST. EDITOR MACKENZIE CADENHEAD with MARK PANICCIA EDITORS JOE QUESADA CHIEF DAN BUCKLEY PUBLISHER

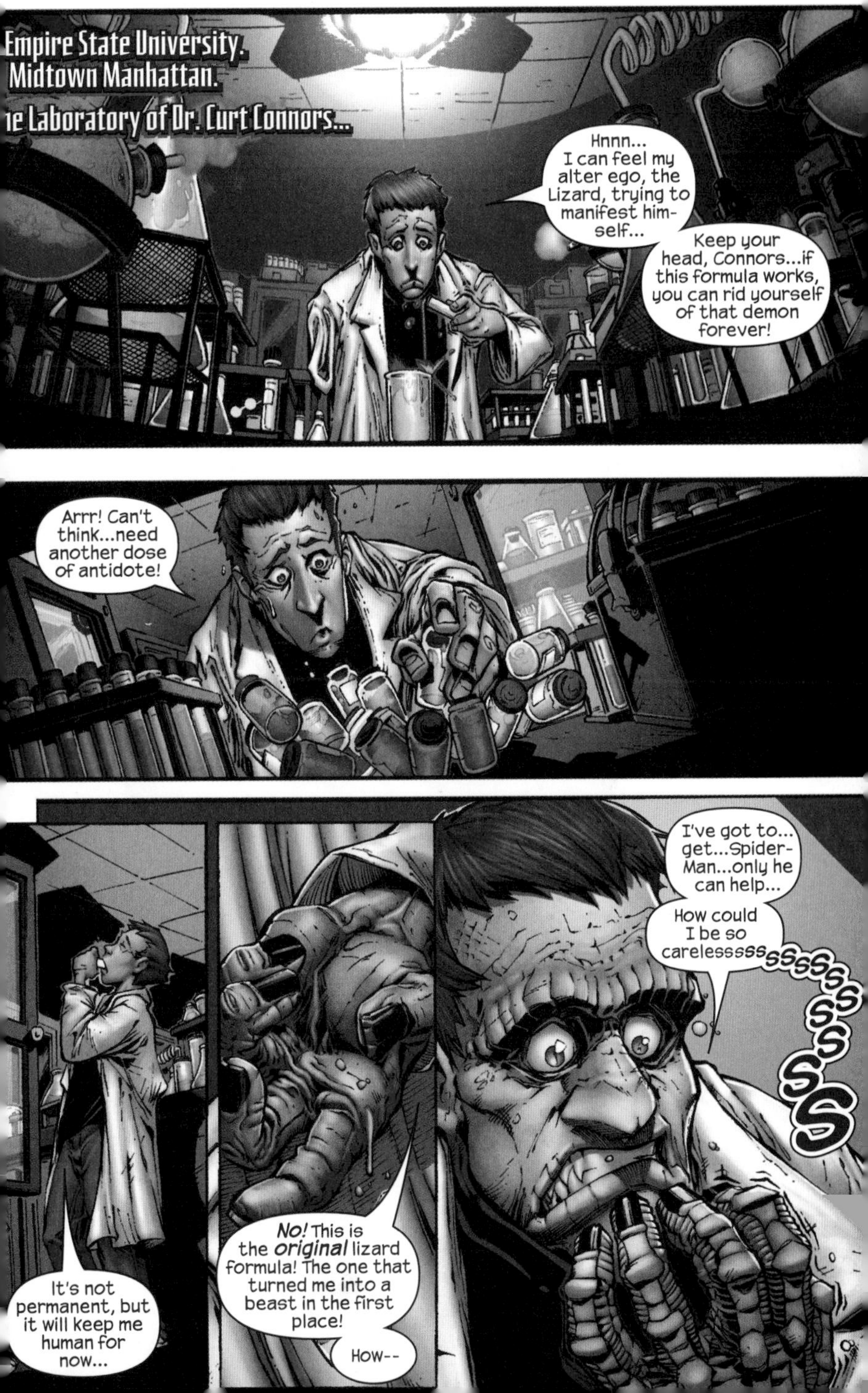

Empire State University.
Midtown Manhattan.
ie Laboratory of Dr. Curt Connors...
Hnnn... I can feel my alter ego, the Lizard, trying to manifest him-self...
Keep your head, Connors...if this formula works, you can rid yourself of that demon forever!
Arrr! Can't think...need another dose of antidote!
It's not permanent, but it will keep me human for now...
No! This is the ***original*** lizard formula! The one that turned me into a beast in the first place!
How--
I've got to... get...Spider-Man...only he can help...
How could I be so carelesssssSSSSSSSSSSS

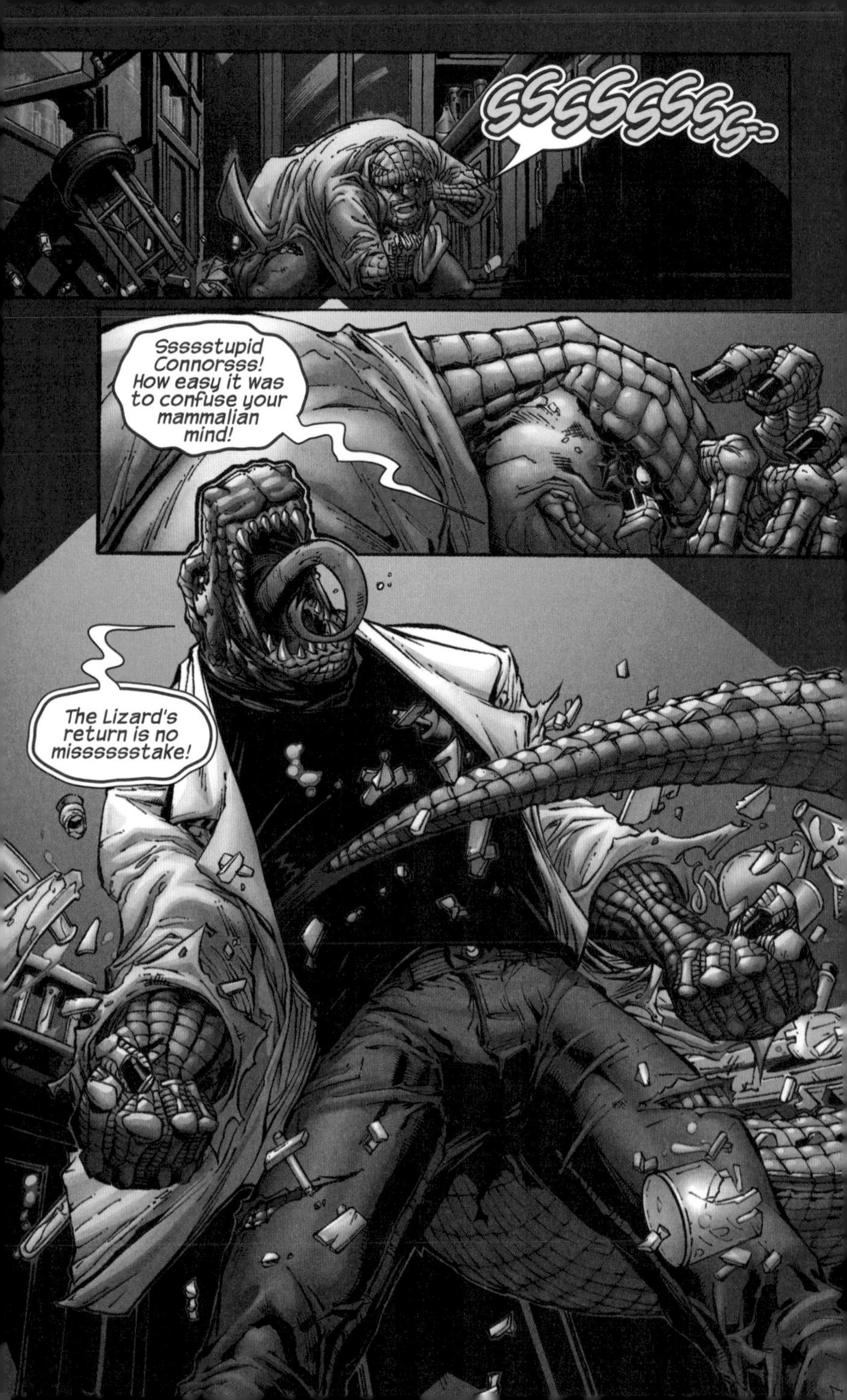
SSSSSSSSS-
Ssssstupid Connorsss! How easy it was to confuse your mammalian mind!
The Lizard's return is no missssssstake!

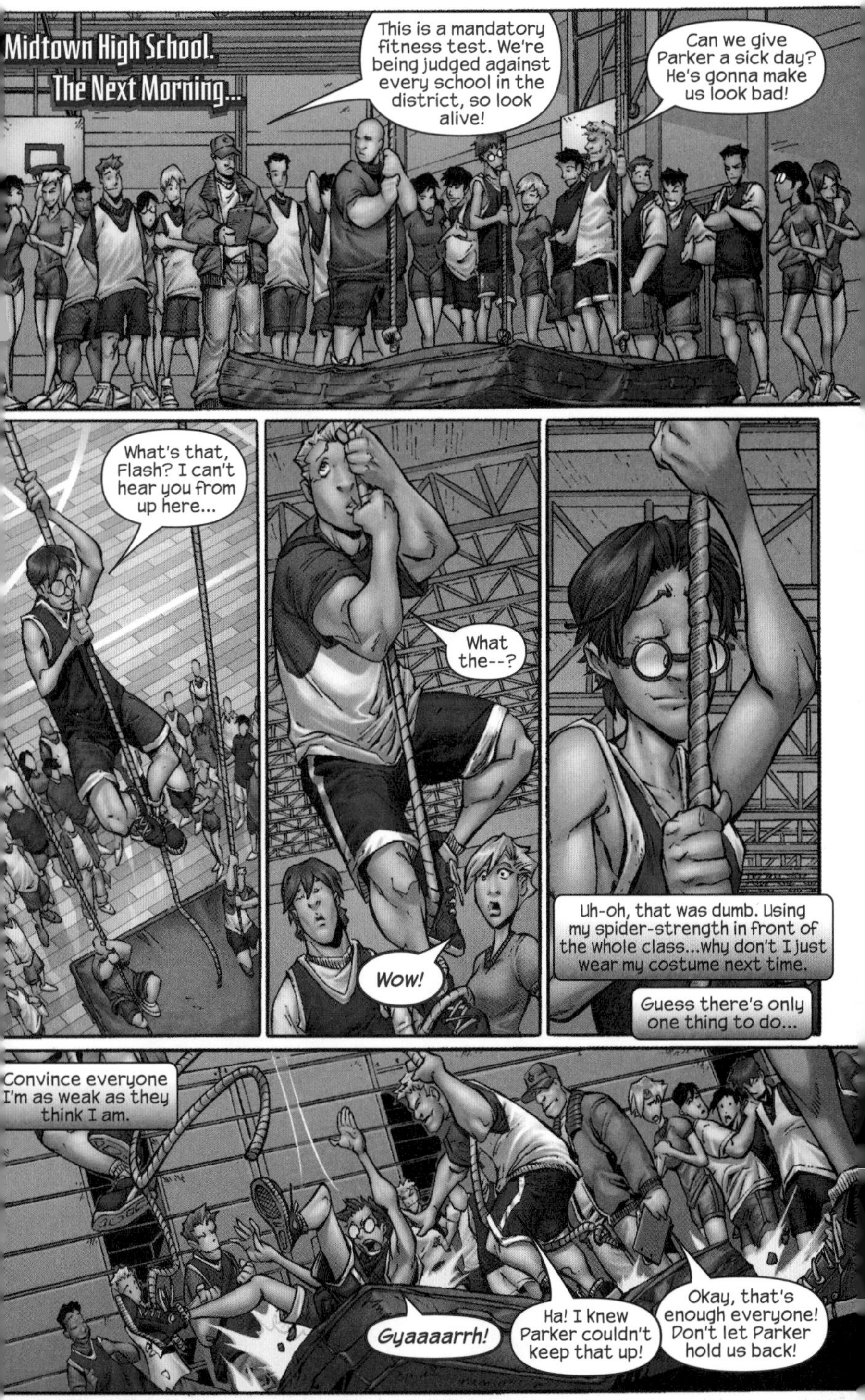
Midtown High School.
The Next Morning...
This is a mandatory fitness test. We're being judged against every school in the district, so look alive!
Can we give Parker a sick day? He's gonna make us look bad!
What's that, Flash? I can't hear you from up here...
What the--?
Wow!
Uh-oh, that was dumb. Using my spider-strength in front of the whole class...why don't I just wear my costume next time.
Guess there's only one thing to do...
Convince everyone I'm as weak as they think I am.
Gyaaaarrh!
Ha! I knew Parker couldn't keep that up!
Okay, that's enough everyone! Don't let Parker hold us back!

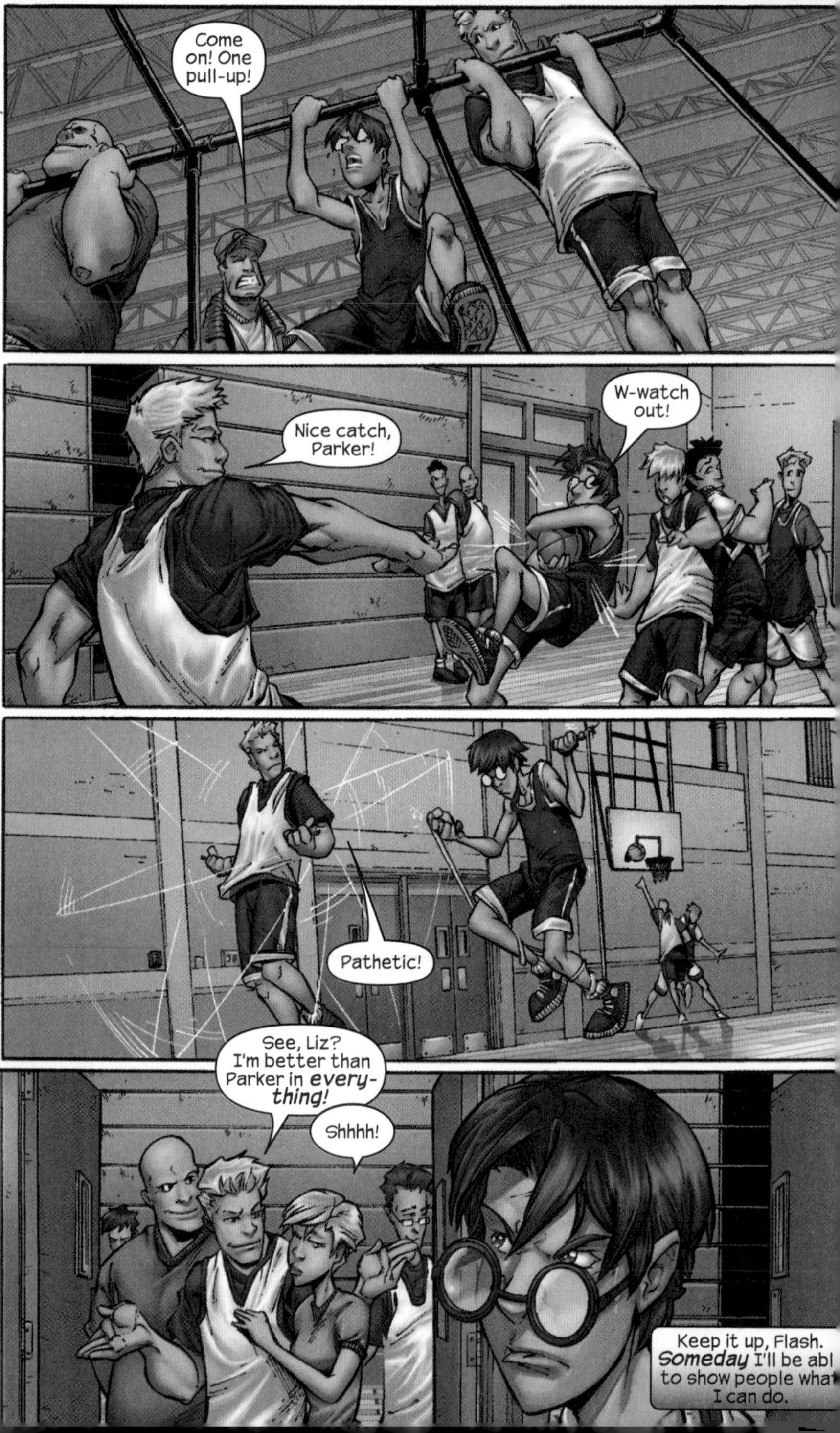
Come on! One pull-up!
Nice catch, Parker!
W-watch out!
Pathetic!
See, Liz? I'm better than Parker in *every-thing!*
Shhhh!
Keep it up, Flash. *Someday* I'll be abl to show people wha I can do.

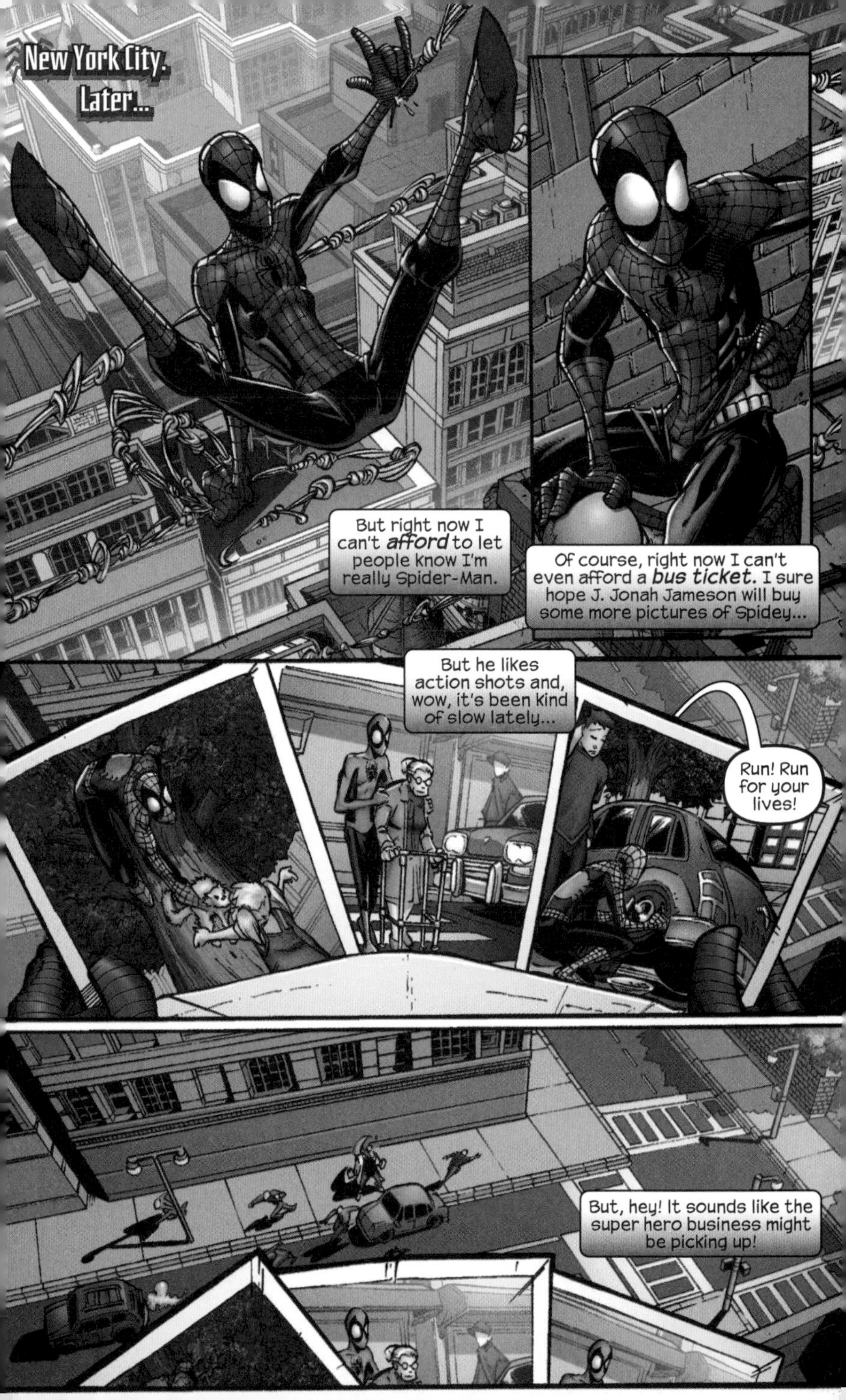
New York City. Later...
But right now I can't *afford* to let people know I'm really Spider-Man.
Of course, right now I can't even afford a **bus ticket.** I sure hope J. Jonah Jameson will buy some more pictures of Spidey...
But he likes action shots and, wow, it's been kind of slow lately...
Run! Run for your lives!
But, hey! It sounds like the super hero business might be picking up!

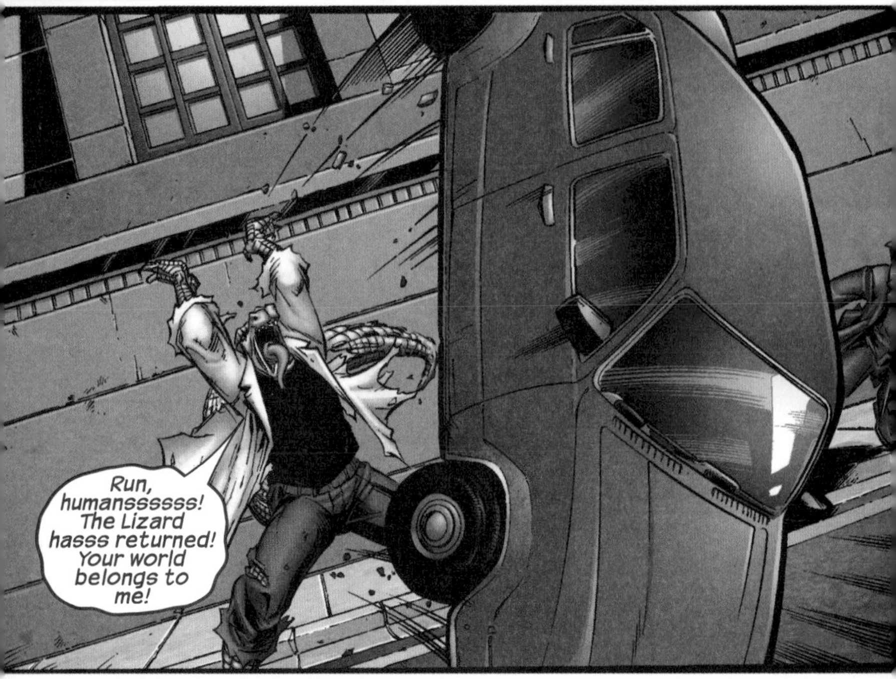
Run, humansssssss! The Lizard hasss returned! Your world belongs to me!

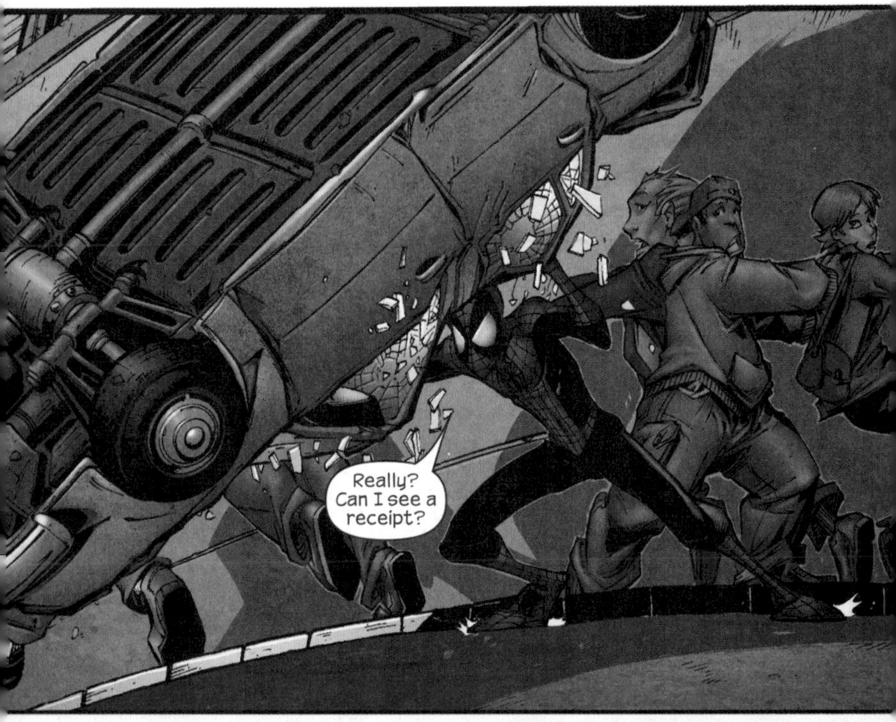
Really? Can I see a receipt?

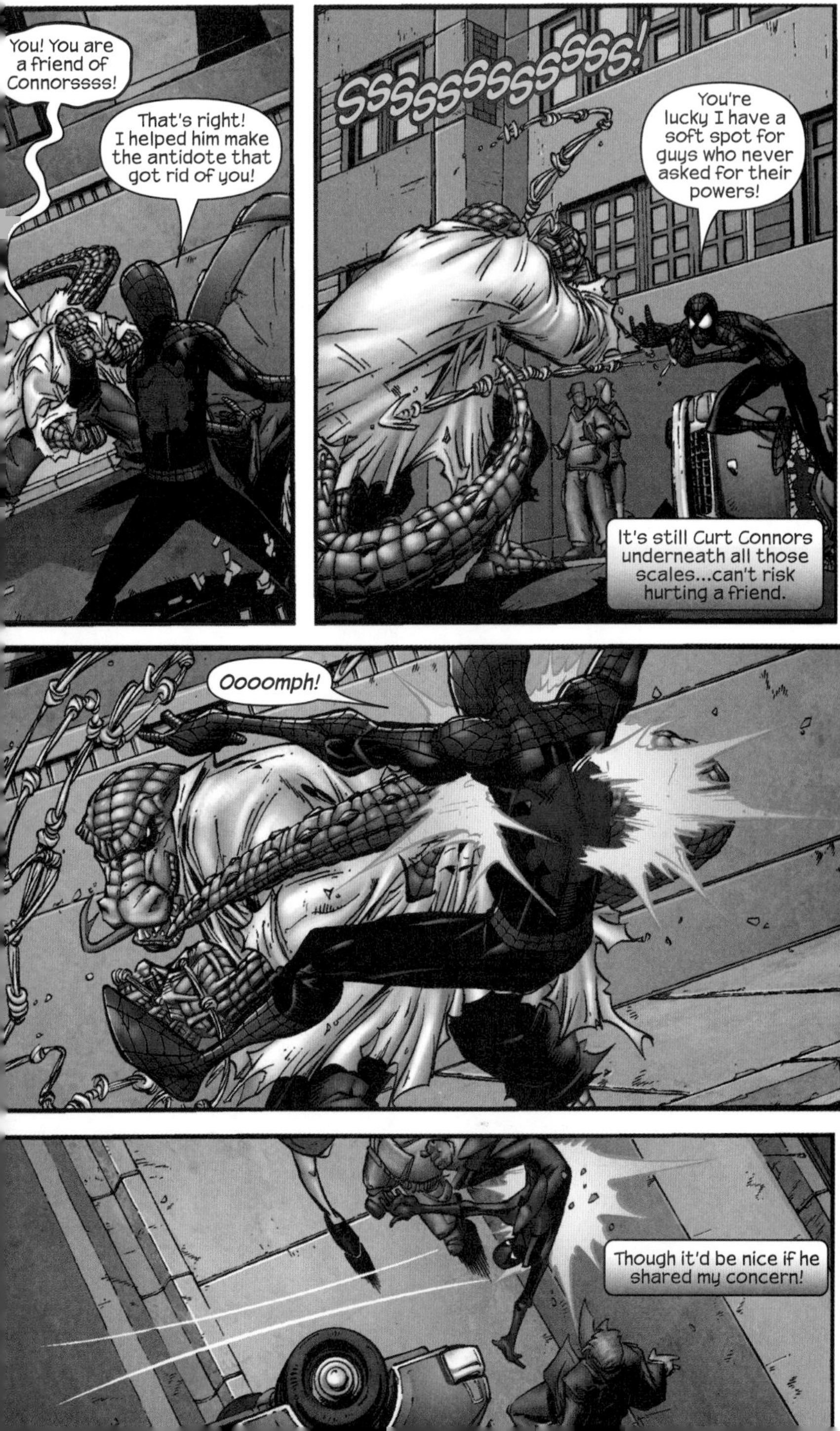
You! You are a friend of Connorssss!
That's right! I helped him make the antidote that got rid of you!
SSSSSSSSSSSSS!
You're lucky I have a soft spot for guys who never asked for their powers!
It's still Curt Connors underneath all those scales...can't risk hurting a friend.
Oooomph!
Though it'd be nice if he shared my concern!

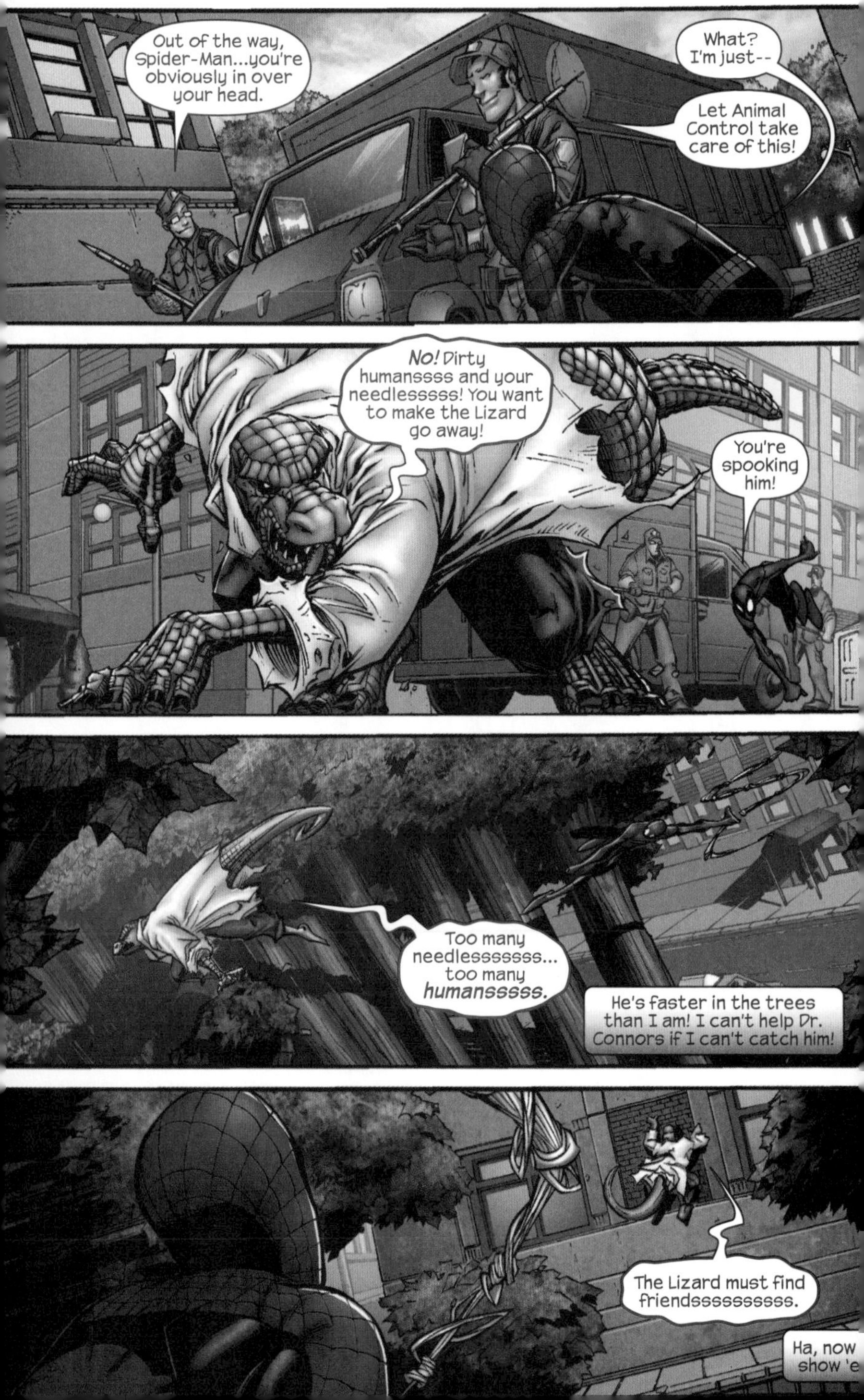
Out of the way, Spider-Man...you're obviously in over your head.
What? I'm just--
Let Animal Control take care of this!
No! Dirty humanssss and your needlesssss! You want to make the Lizard go away!
You're spooking him!
Too many needlessssss... too many humanssssss.
He's faster in the trees than I am! I can't help Dr. Connors if I can't catch him!
The Lizard must find friendsssssssssss.
Ha, now
show 'e

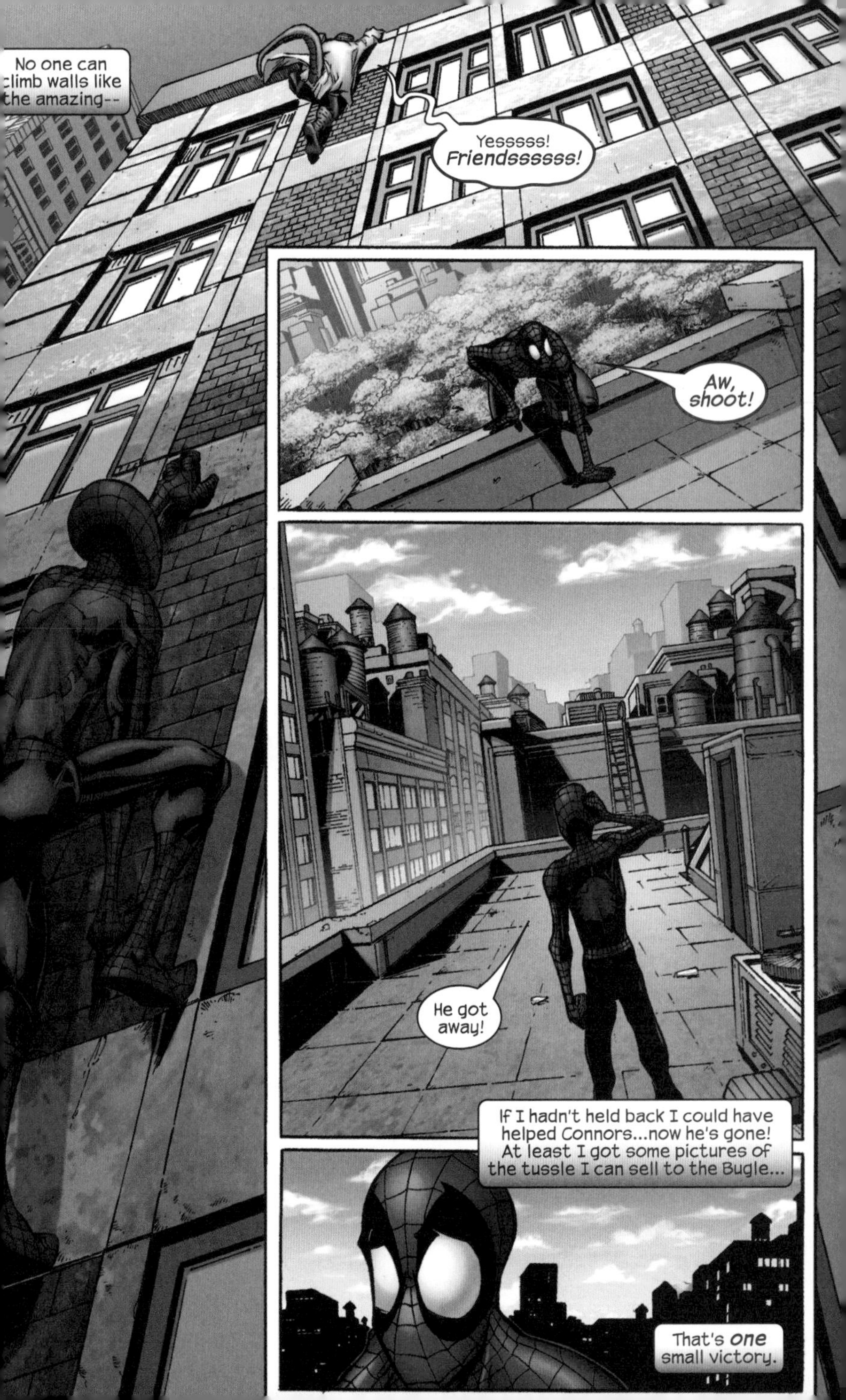
No one can climb walls like the amazing--
Yesssss! Friendsssssss!
Aw, shoot!
He got away!
If I hadn't held back I could have helped Connors...now he's gone! At least I got some pictures of the tussle I can sell to the Bugle...
That's one small victory.

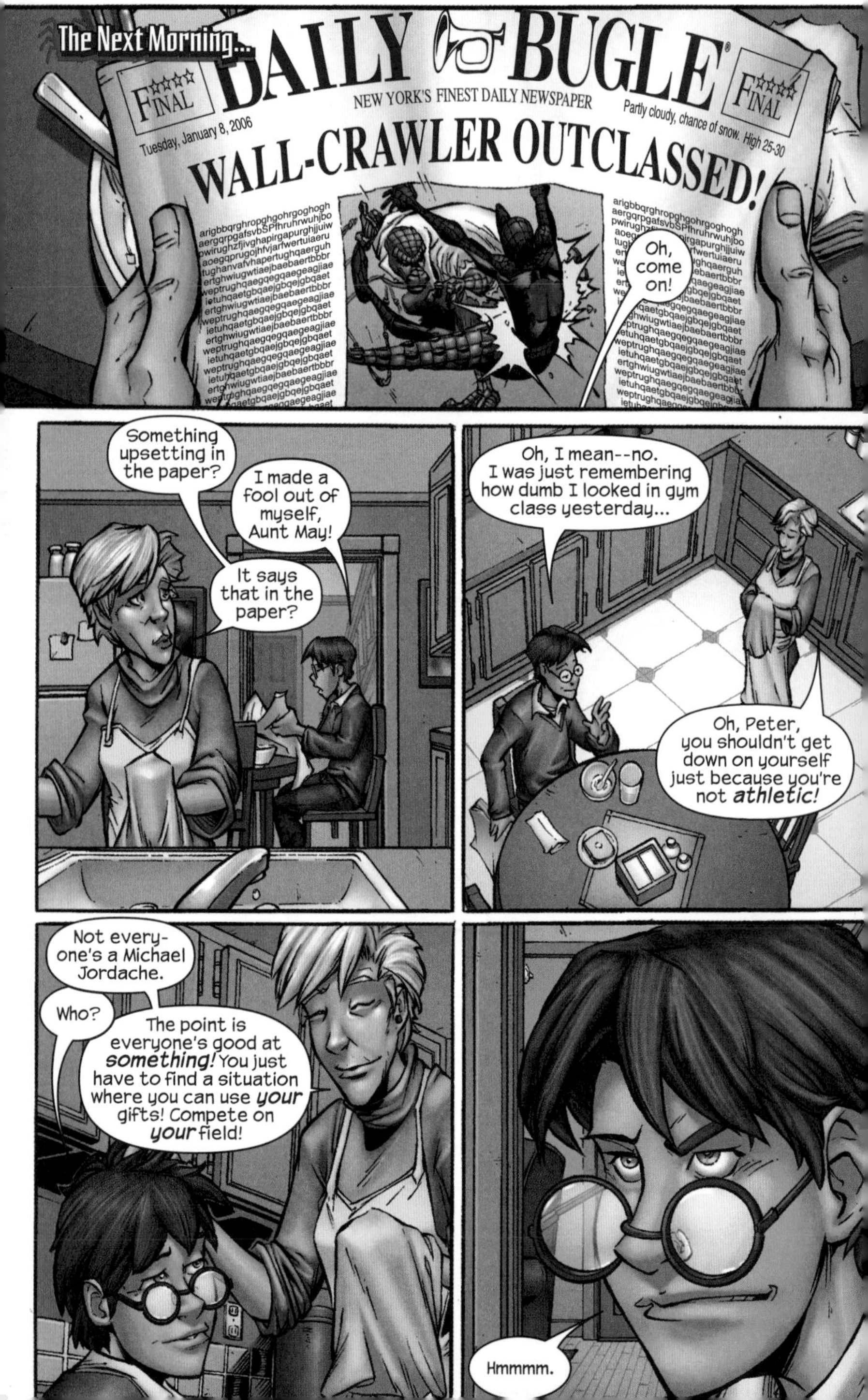
The Next Morning...
DAILY BUGLE
FINAL
NEW YORK'S FINEST DAILY NEWSPAPER
Tuesday, January 8, 2006
Partly cloudy, chance of snow. High 25-30
WALL-CRAWLER OUTCLASSED!
Oh, come on!
Something upsetting in the paper?
I made a fool out of myself, Aunt May!
It says that in the paper?
Oh, I mean--no. I was just remembering how dumb I looked in gym class yesterday...
Oh, Peter, you shouldn't get down on yourself just because you're not *athletic!*
Not every-one's a Michael Jordache.
Who?
The point is everyone's good at *something!* You just have to find a situation where you can use *your* gifts! Compete on *your* field!
Hmmmm.

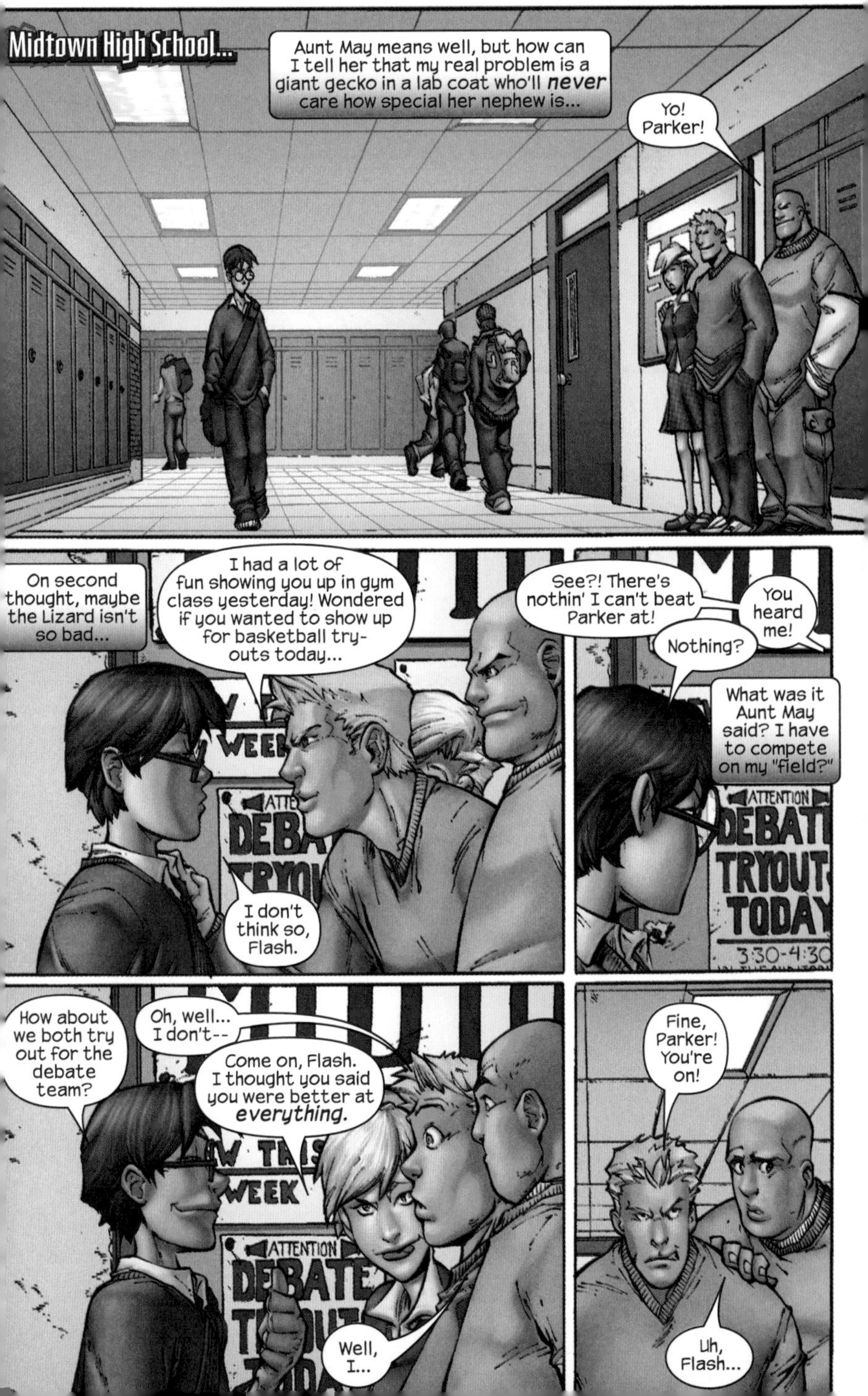
Midtown High School...
Aunt May means well, but how can I tell her that my real problem is a giant gecko in a lab coat who'll *never* care how special her nephew is...
Yo! Parker!
On second thought, maybe the Lizard isn't so bad...
I had a lot of fun showing you up in gym class yesterday! Wondered if you wanted to show up for basketball try-outs today...
I don't think so, Flash.
See?! There's nothin' I can't beat Parker at!
You heard me!
Nothing?
What was it Aunt May said? I have to compete on my "field?"
ATTENTION
DEBATE
TRYOUTS
TODAY
3:30-4:30
How about we both try out for the debate team?
Oh, well... I don't--
Come on, Flash. I thought you said you were better at *everything.*
Well, I...
Fine, Parker! You're on!
Uh, Flash...

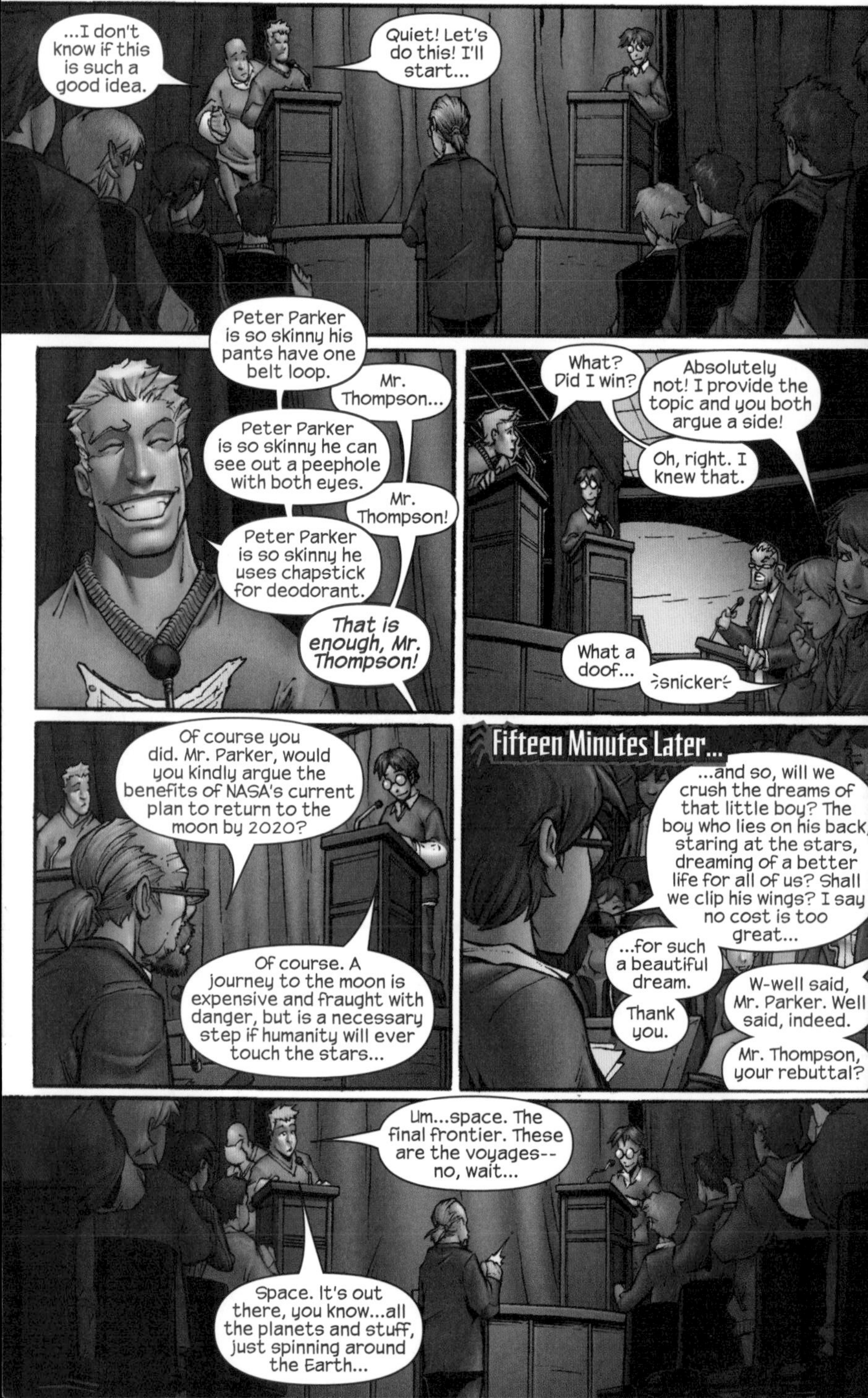
...I don't know if this is such a good idea.
Quiet! Let's do this! I'll start...
Peter Parker is so skinny his pants have one belt loop.
Mr. Thompson...
Peter Parker is so skinny he can see out a peephole with both eyes.
Mr. Thompson!
Peter Parker is so skinny he uses chapstick for deodorant.
That is enough, Mr. Thompson!
What? Did I win?
Absolutely not! I provide the topic and you both argue a side!
Oh, right. I knew that.
What a doof...
snicker
Of course you did. Mr. Parker, would you kindly argue the benefits of NASA's current plan to return to the moon by 2020?
Of course. A journey to the moon is expensive and fraught with danger, but is a necessary step if humanity will ever touch the stars...
Fifteen Minutes Later...
...and so, will we crush the dreams of that little boy? The boy who lies on his back, staring at the stars, dreaming of a better life for all of us? Shall we clip his wings? I say no cost is too great...
...for such a beautiful dream.
Thank you.
W-well said, Mr. Parker. Well said, indeed.
Mr. Thompson, your rebuttal?
Um...space. The final frontier. These are the voyages--no, wait...
Space. It's out there, you know...all the planets and stuff, just spinning around the Earth...

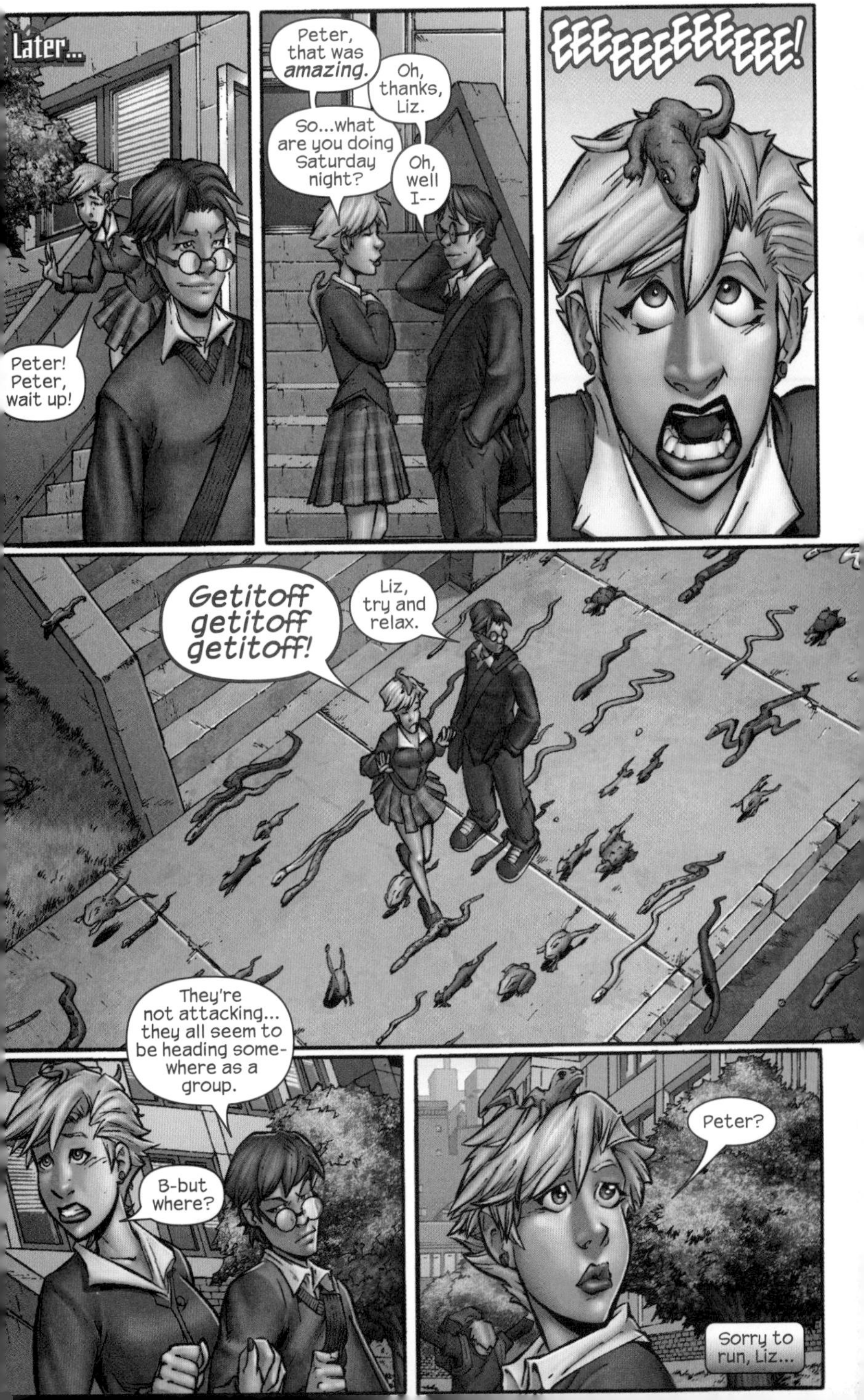

Later...
Peter! Peter, wait up!
Peter, that was amazing.
Oh, thanks, Liz.
So...what are you doing Saturday night?
Oh, well I--
EEEEEEEEEEEE!
Getitoff getitoff getitoff!
Liz, try and relax.
They're not attacking... they all seem to be heading some-where as a group.
B-but where?
Peter?
Sorry to run, Liz...

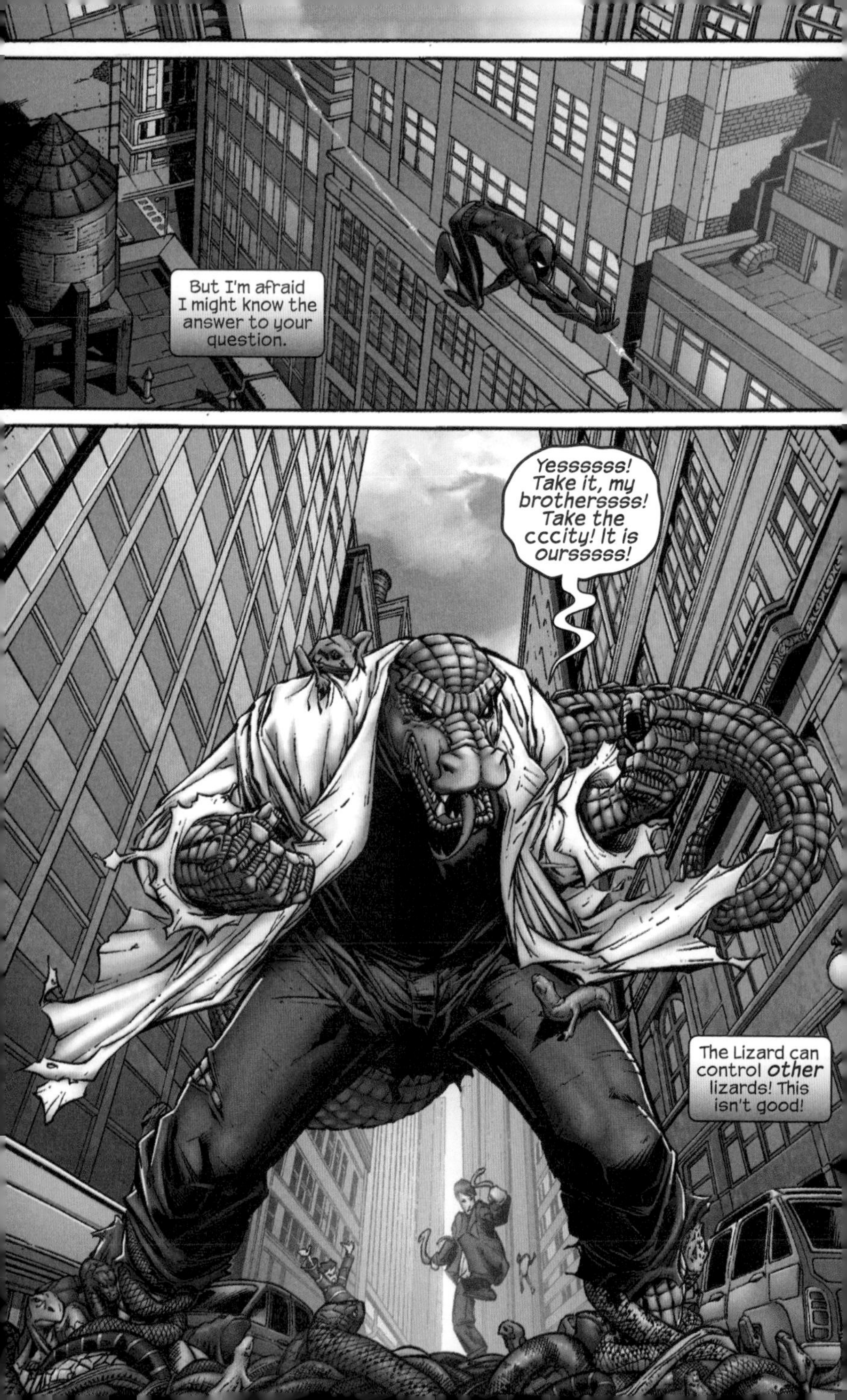
But I'm afraid I might know the answer to your question.
Yesssssss! Take it, my brotherssss! Take the cccity! It is oursssss!
The Lizard can control *other* lizards! This isn't good!

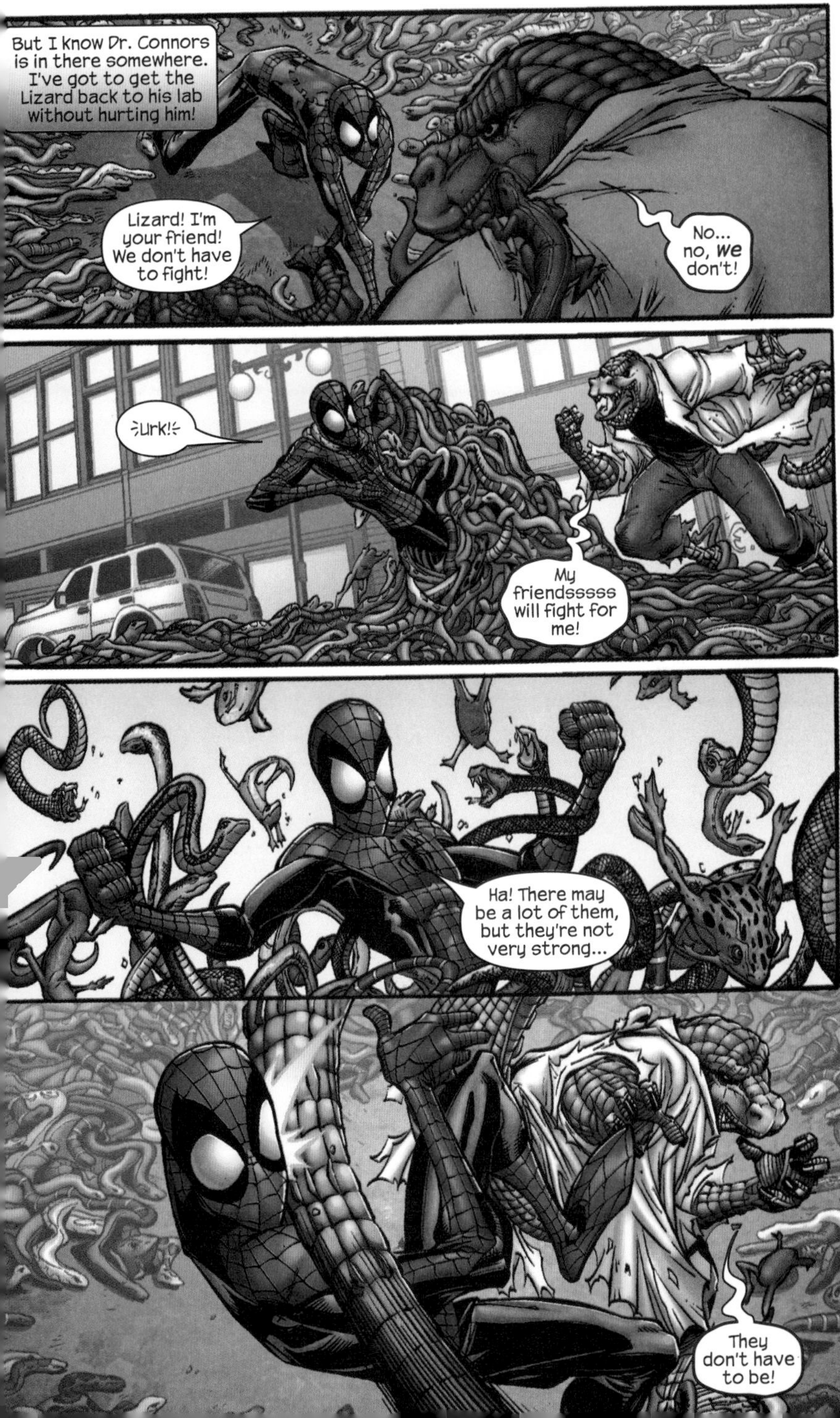

But I know Dr. Connors is in there somewhere. I've got to get the Lizard back to his lab without hurting him!
Lizard! I'm your friend! We don't have to fight!
No... no, **we** don't!
Urk!
My friendsssss will fight for me!
Ha! There may be a lot of them, but they're not very strong...
They don't have to be!

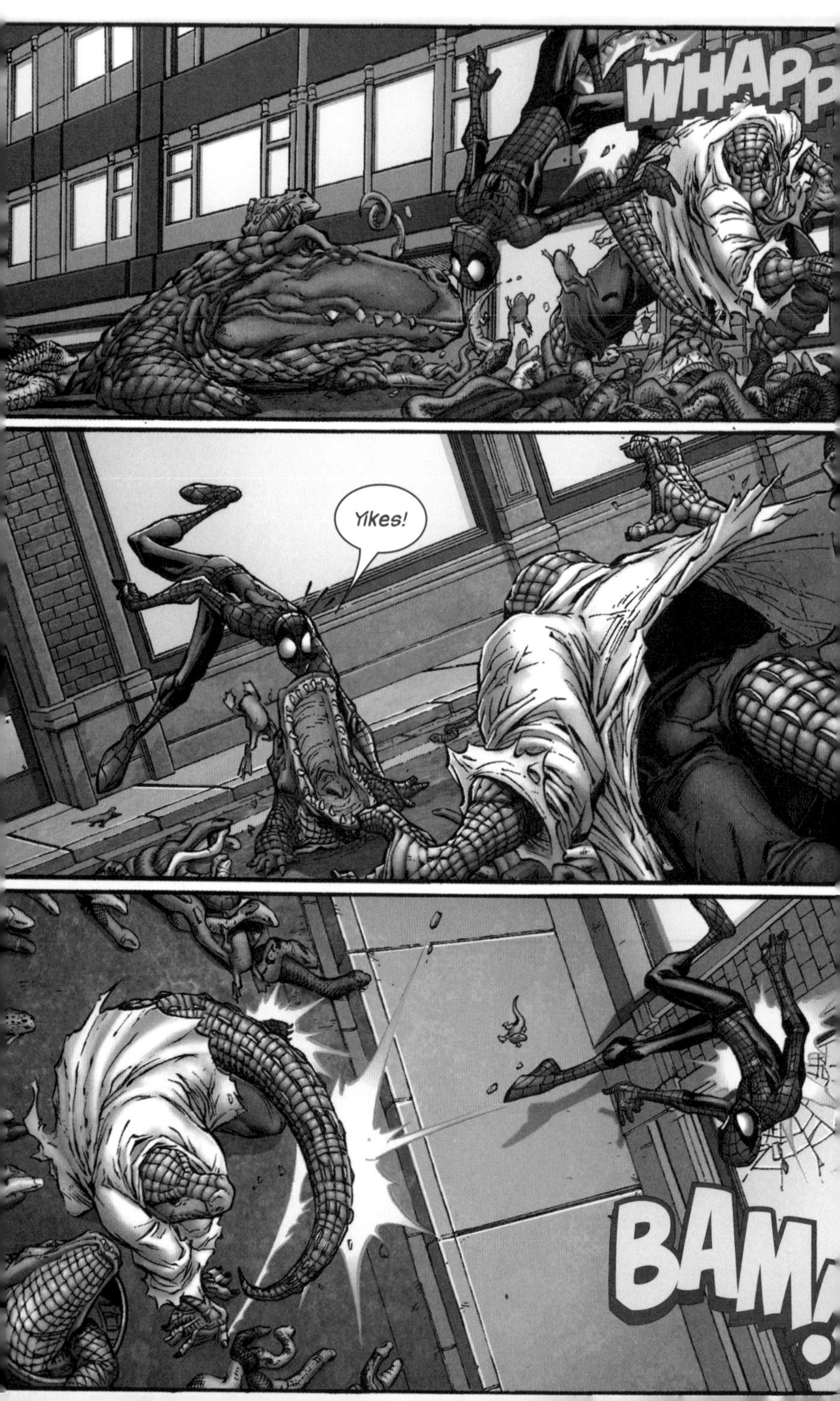
WHAPP
Yikes!
BAM

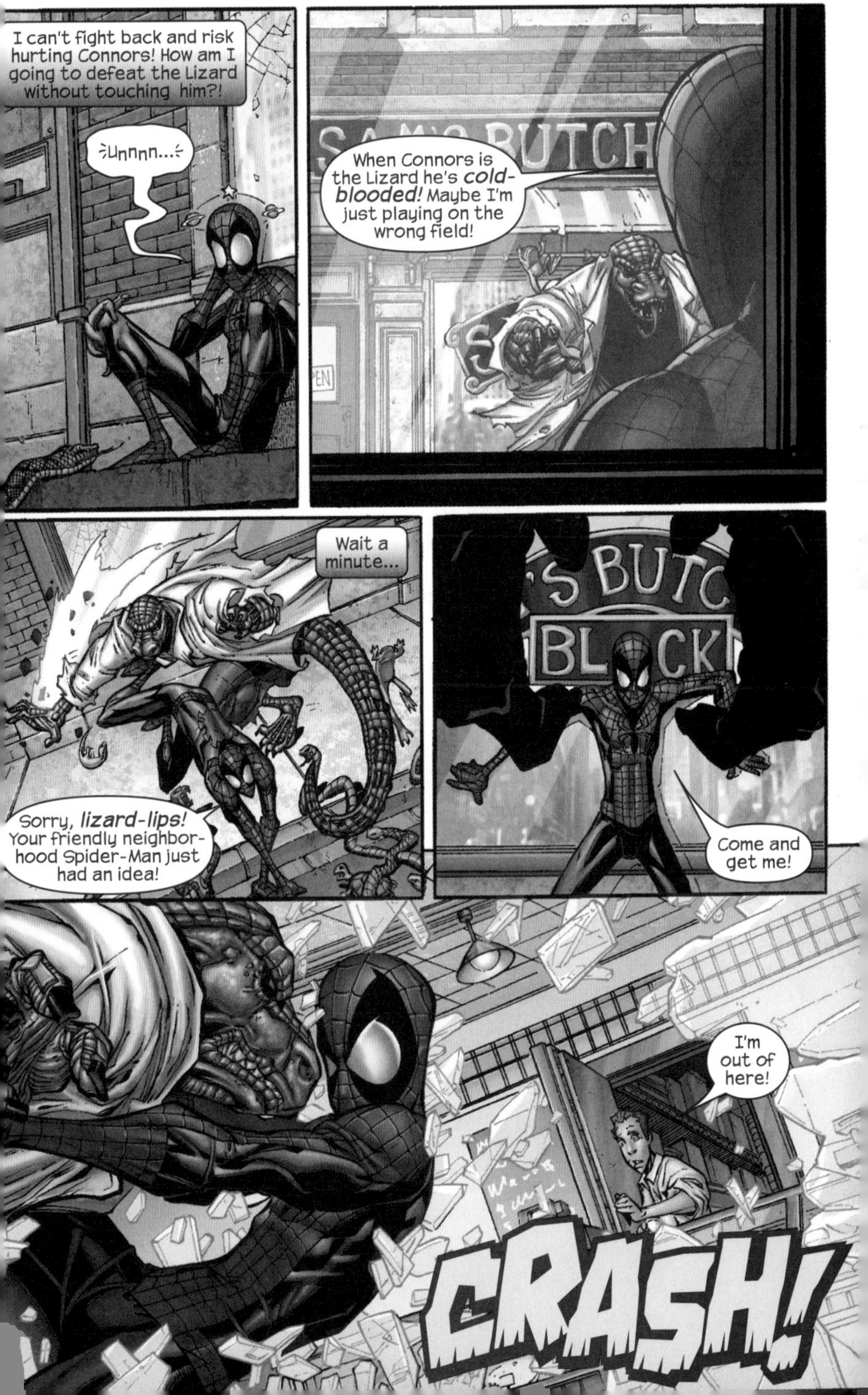
I can't fight back and risk hurting Connors! How am I going to defeat the Lizard without touching him?!
Unnnn...
When Connors is the Lizard he's *cold-blooded!* Maybe I'm just playing on the wrong field!
Wait a minute...
Sorry, *lizard-lips!* Your friendly neighbor-hood Spider-Man just had an idea!
Come and get me!
I'm out of here!
CRASH!

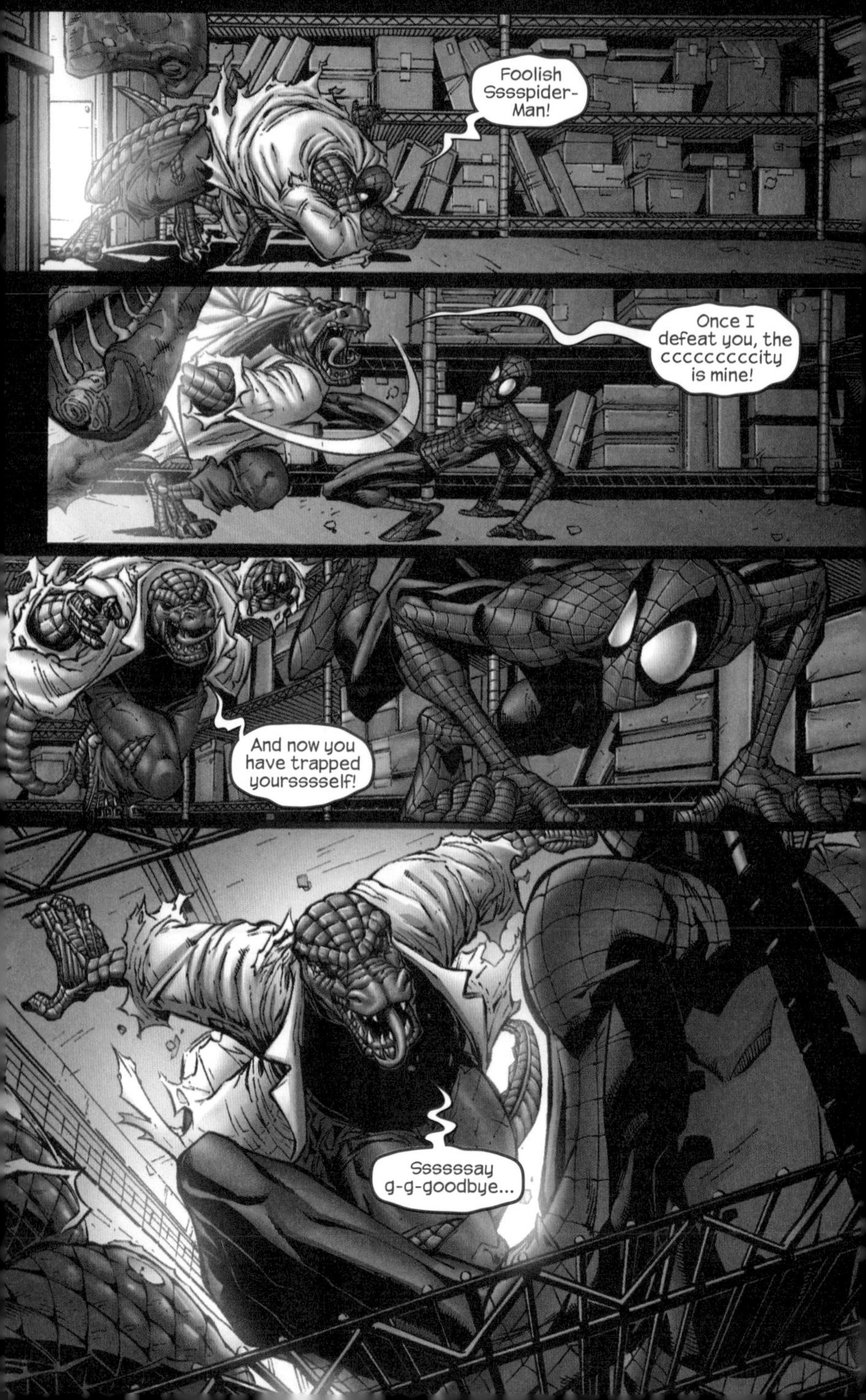
Foolish Sssspider-Man!
Once I defeat you, the ccccccccccity is mine!
And now you have trapped yourssssself!
Ssssssay g-g-goodbye...

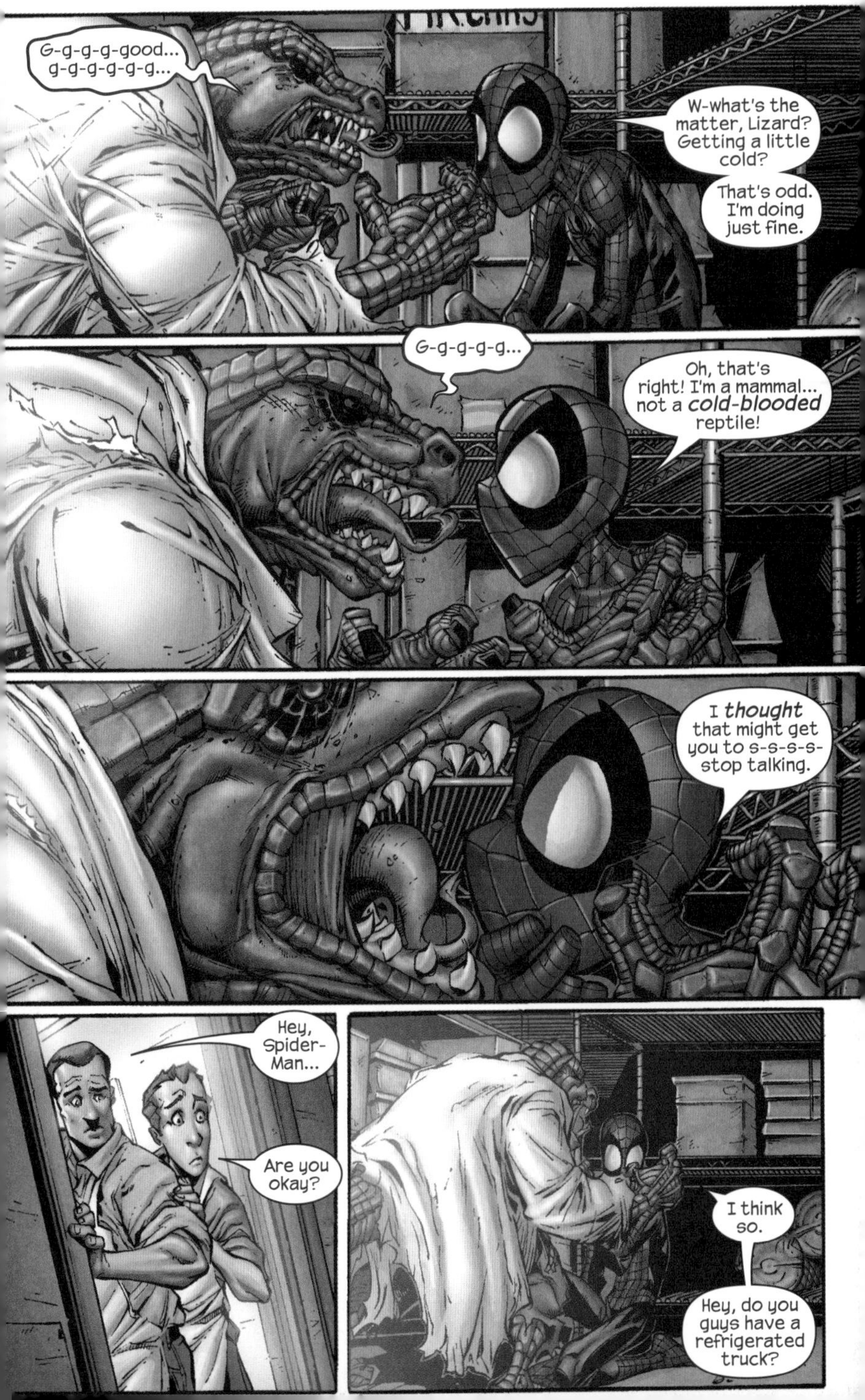
G-g-g-g-good...
g-g-g-g-g-g...
W-what's the matter, Lizard? Getting a little cold?
That's odd. I'm doing just fine.
G-g-g-g-g...
Oh, that's right! I'm a mammal... not a *cold-blooded* reptile!
I *thought* that might get you to s-s-s-s-stop talking.
Hey, Spider-Man...
Are you okay?
I think so.
Hey, do you guys have a refrigerated truck?

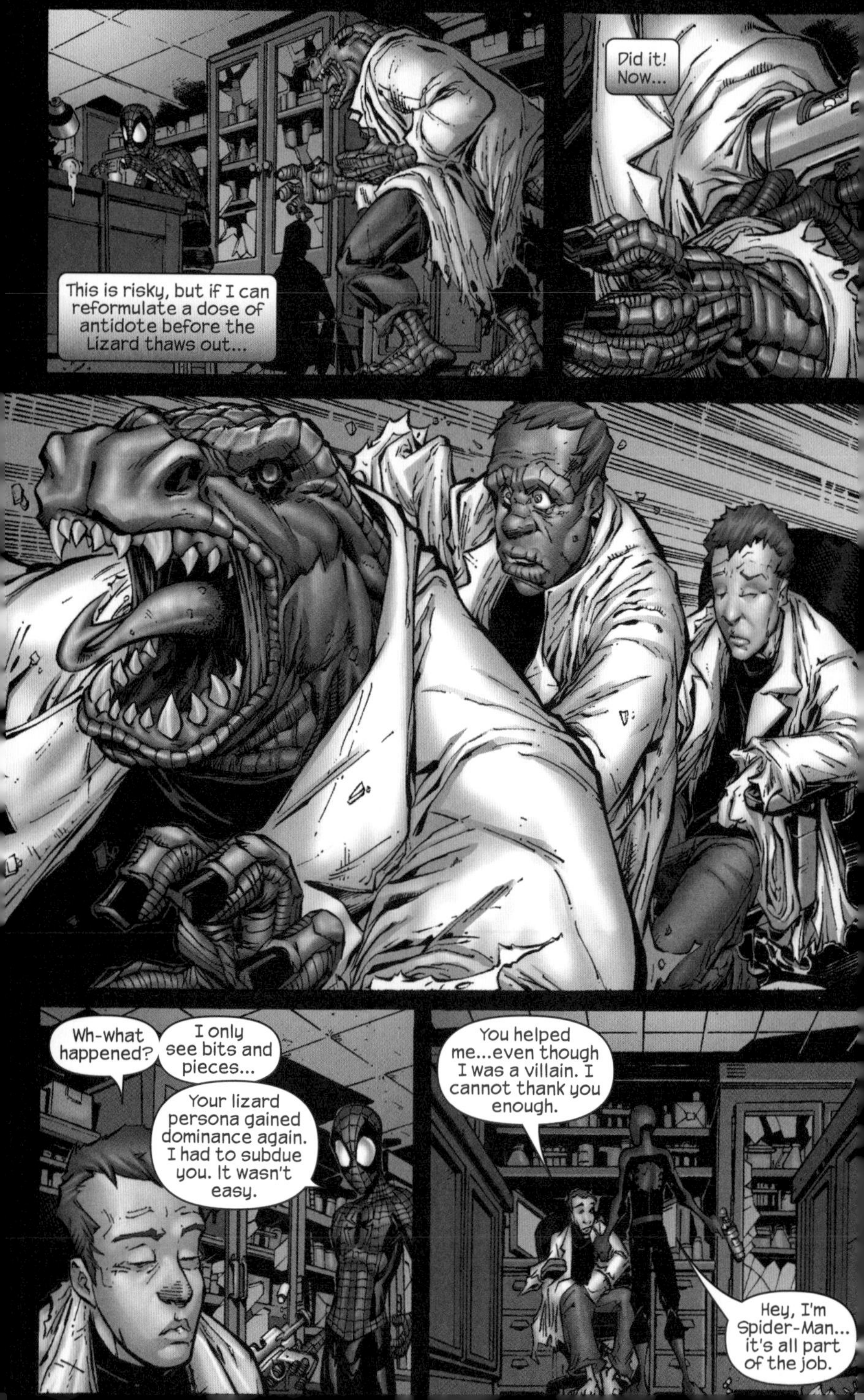
This is risky, but if I can reformulate a dose of antidote before the Lizard thaws out...
Did it! Now...
Wh-what happened?
I only see bits and pieces...
Your lizard persona gained dominance again. I had to subdue you. It wasn't easy.
You helped me...even though I was a villain. I cannot thank you enough.
Hey, I'm Spider-Man... it's all part of the job.

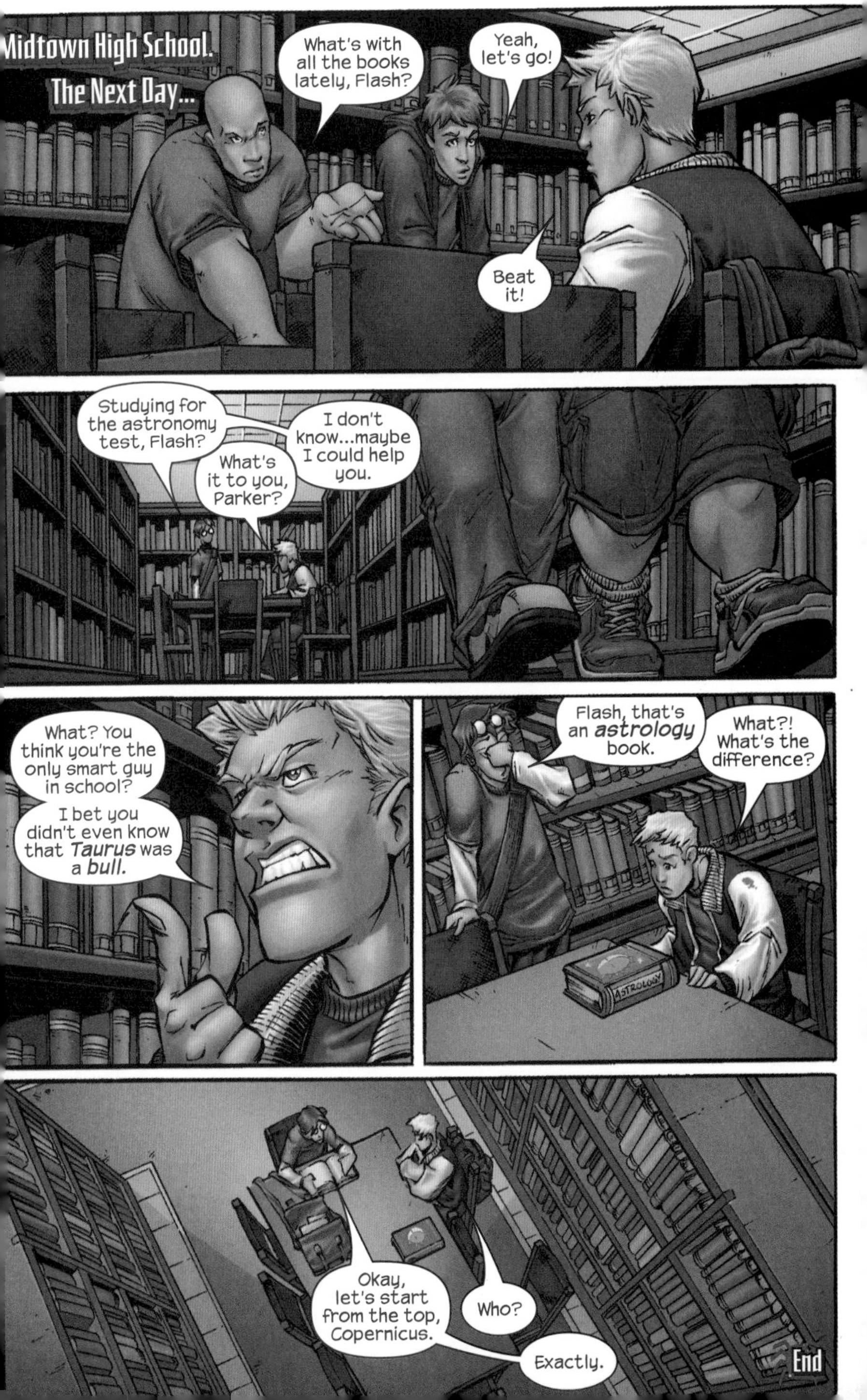
Midtown High School.
The Next Day...
What's with all the books lately, Flash?
Yeah, let's go!
Beat it!
Studying for the astronomy test, Flash?
What's it to you, Parker?
I don't know...maybe I could help you.
What? You think you're the only smart guy in school?
I bet you didn't even know that Taurus was a bull.
Flash, that's an astrology book.
What?! What's the difference?
ASTROLOGY
Okay, let's start from the top, Copernicus.
Who?
Exactly.
End

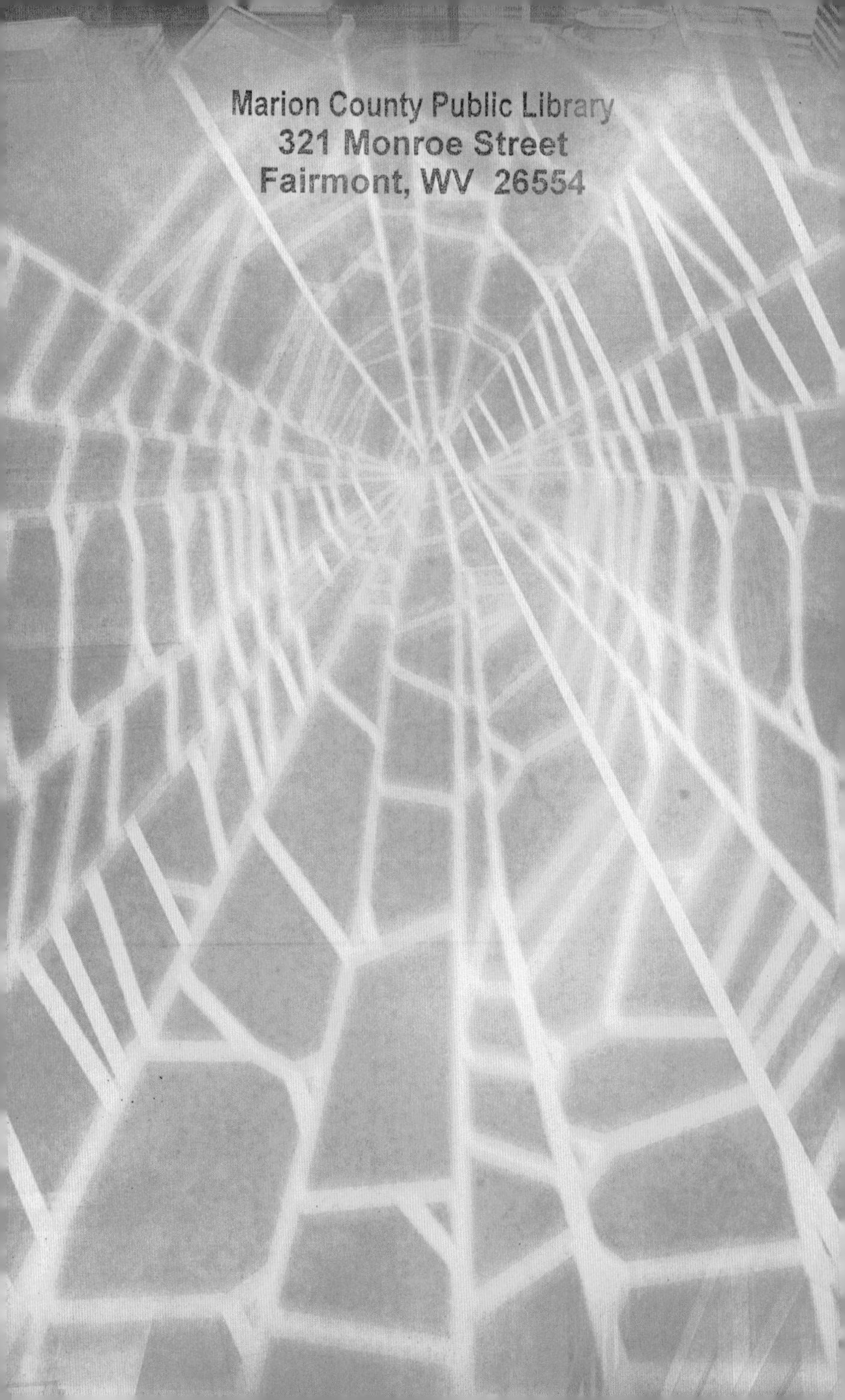